THE BALL

THE BALL

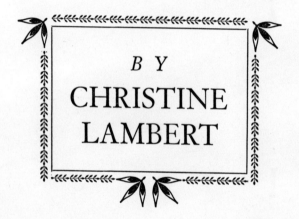

BY
CHRISTINE LAMBERT

ATHENEUM NEW YORK *1961*

FOR SILA

Library of Congress catalog card number 61–6744
Published simultaneously in Canada by Longmans, Green & Company
Manufactured in the United States of America by
Kingsport Press, Inc., Kingsport, Tennessee
Designed by Harry Ford
First Edition

CONTENTS

PART
ONE

PART
ONE

THERE she is," said Denise, but she did not turn from the window through which she had been watching for the arrival of the Countess de Fleury. Instead she remained standing there like something planted in the ground, a flagpole or a fence post, incapable of movement. Behind her desk, Jeanne, the receptionist, glanced at her wrist watch. "And, as usual, on the dot." She shrugged, and got up to join the nurse by the window.

They were about the same age, in their middle forties, oddly alike in the way each carried herself, as though the similarity of their lives gave them more resemblance than if they had been related by blood. Yet their intimacy was based merely on habit, humiliating and unsatisfactory, a final surrender to the fact that it was less exacting to share what there was to share in their enforced closeness than to fight for a privacy of thought and feeling. Since it was impossible not to see in the other—as in a mirror—the reflection of oneself, a woman no man had ever desired for a wife, Denise and Jeanne could never be friends. But now, standing side by side in their starched white uniforms, they were, for a moment, unaware of the contempt each felt for the other.

"He still loves her, doesn't he?"

Denise did not respond.

"Twenty years," Jeanne, who had not expected an answer, went on. "More. It must be more. I can still remember sitting opposite him, applying for the job, and seeing that picture of her on his desk. He moved it once, as if he wanted her to get a good look at me—as if it

3

were not a picture, I mean, but something alive, and he needed her approval."

"Thirty," said Denise suddenly, and she began to laugh. "Thirty years this summer. It's obscene. Mad. What insanity!"

"But you still have hopes, don't you, poor lamb? You still think he'll change or that she might die before you do, and then . . ."

"Why not?" said Denise. "Let me have my dreams. I haven't got very much else. Yes, I'm still hoping. Of course I am. Aren't you? The only difference is you're hoping for a man, any man, while I—" She broke off abruptly. "Did you arrange the flowers?"

"No, he did," said Jeanne. "But I put the champagne on ice. Don't worry, pet, don't worry. Flowers and champagne and caviar for the star patient who's never sick. Lord, he would have given up his Paris practice if she'd decided to live on the moon. As it is, we're lucky she settled on the Riviera. What has she got that we don't have? Rather . . . that you don't have? And at her age . . ."

"We can be had," said Denise. "Anybody could have had us, any time." She stared at Jeanne, her slightly protruding eyes narrowing with the effort to find an explanation for their rejection.

"Speak for yourself," said Jeanne, her lips trembling. "Don't think I don't know what you're doing when you stare at his photo and get those glassy eyes and your breathing almost stops."

The bell cut like a scream into her words. Almost at once the door opened and a gentle, melodious voice said, "Good morning. Good morning, Denise. Good morning, Mademoiselle Jeanne. I think the doctor is expecting me. Or will I have to wait?"

*   *   *

Seen from a distance, Emma Starr Fleury looked no older than thirty. Her body had retained the lines of well-proportioned youth—not an ounce of fat where it did not belong; the legs long and slender, with no thickening of knee or ankle; the arms still fragile; the stomach flat; the curve of the hips small, exciting. Her hair, though completely white, was alive with that quality of color that made it appear an almost natural silver blond. Most of all, though, it was the way she moved, with the assurance of breeding, like an Englishwoman, but without the angularity—rather, with the integrated softness and passion of a Russian dancer, which made people mistake her for a young woman. Close to, it came as a surprise to discover that her smooth, tanned skin was no longer taut, to find lines under her eyes, around her mouth, her throat. Still, nobody would have thought her older than fifty. But Emma Starr Fleury was sixty.

Sixty, Jacques Thiolat told himself. All morning long, all through the previous day, he had kept repeating her age, as if its reality could mitigate the tragedy. Of course it could not. And the attempt to think rationally only made his feelings for her seem more incomprehensible, showing him up as a fool. How could it have been enough for him to love without a chance of fulfillment? For thirty years. Masochism? No, no. It was not as simple as that. You didn't necessarily think of a monk who chose celibacy as a masochist. Or of a scientist, isolating himself from life, as insane. Or *was* all single-minded dedication to one goal not quite normal? Was it not, rather, this unquestioning devotion to one idea, one object, one person, that was missing in the world of today? Or which, if it existed, was looked upon as ridiculous or explained in Freudian terms? But was it enough to have achieved the unfaltering fidelity to a dream?

He had seen her twice before she had called him in

thirty years ago . . . more than that. . . . First, in the general store where she had been waiting for the owner's little boy, who had gone to pick wild strawberries for her. It was the kind of store in which one could buy any-thing—flour and *pots de chambre,* sugar and cinnamon, fishing boots, the skins of cats for rheumatism, pots and pans and cheap candy, and it was filled with the odor of dried herbs, of the dust that had gathered on the bales of material, of the stale bread the poor bought, of the soup cooking on a coal fire in the back room, and of strong antiseptic soap. Still, in all the variety of smells he had detected her scent, her body scent, and he had wiggled his nose as animals do to determine if danger threatens them. Her fragrance had tantalized and haunted him ever since.

The second time he had seen her she had been lying full length on her stomach, looking at herself in the water of the little pond behind the old mill, with its broken wing. Actually what he had seen, sitting propped up against a tree reading, when he had dropped his book sleepily, had been her face reflected in the water like an apparition. First her hair, then her forehead, the enormous eyes, the heart-shaped chin, and elongated neck. He had leaned forward and, startled to see another face so unex-pectedly close to hers in the water, she had given a little cry. He had introduced himself.

"A doctor," she had said, measuring him from head to foot. "Here? In this small village? How can you make a living? There are so few people."

"There's no vet."

He could still hear her laughter after she had disap-peared behind the mill.

Two months later a car from the castle had fetched him. He had sat next to the liveried chauffeur. The drive through the park had seemed endless, then the moat, with the carp jumping in the still air, an old man fishing from one of the small windows in the left tower, the wood of the drawbridge rumbling like faraway thunder under the weight of the Rolls-Royce, the courtyard, with its stone urns, the red and blue of geraniums and hydrangeas, a butler, a white hall, the proud curve of the staircase, and the fragrance of her body growing stronger and stronger with every step as he approached her room. At the door Count de Fleury, bowing politely, then telling him rapidly that his wife had been bitten by a snake. They had found her in the courtyard near collapse, her blood pressure low, her breathing exaggerated. Of course the swelling had been cauterized at once, but now she was in a state of shock. And Thiolat had recalled the afternoon he had seen her at the millpond stretched out full length on her stomach in the grass, looking at herself in the still water, her long bare feet amusingly dirty, her shoes and stockings lying beside her. There were snakes around.

In bed she had looked even younger than he remembered, like a young white swan shot from the sky. And he had stood there staring at her, unsure of himself, impressed by the millions she had inherited, by her marriage to one of the most brilliant men of his time, the magnificence that surrounded both of them, and her case, so surprisingly thrown at him. A young man, twenty-seven years old. He looked at his hands, weather-tanned and callused from menial jobs. He wished he had brought rubber gloves. He didn't dare touch her, reach into the waves of lace under which she seemed to be floating away from him. Suddenly she spoke. "I don't want to die. Not yet. Please." As if he were God, as if it were within his power to keep her alive. "Please," she had said again, as if she were asking a favor he could deny.

Had she become a source of strength he could not do

without from that point on? Was he a weakling, then, a man who had never learned to rely on his own power, afraid that without her he would forever flounder helplessly, no longer whole? Was he, deep down, a coward?

Why question at all? What utter nonsense to attempt to explain or justify anything. It was because there was no justification or satisfactory explanation that gods had been invented. Besides, it was too late. He had to accept what might be considered a wasted life. He turned to where she sat, watching him guardedly, her eyes almost closed, her teeth pulling at her lower lip as if she were biting back the urge to laugh. "What is it?" he asked, and then, for the pure pleasure of speaking her name, added, "Emma. What is it, Emma?"

"I'm trying to see you as others do. Meg looked a little tired last week but when I told her I'd call you, she wouldn't hear of it. She thinks you're too much of a *grosse légume* for you to be willing to give her the time."

Her eyes widened, and now, as always, he saw their dilation as the sudden bursting open of a bud. What made them so extraordinary was that the sclerotic coat showed nearly no white but was almost the same color as the iris—a pale blue.

"In spite of all this," she said, glancing at the Toulouse-Lautrec drawings, the low bookcases, the Japanese matting on the floor, the ultramodern sculpture of a horse, the profusion of flowers, the champagne in its white napkin—with only the neck of the bottle showing like a green snake with a gold head—and finally at the tall man dressed so casually that he seemed ready for a round of golf rather than a medical consultation, "I can still see you the way you were—the seat of your pants shiny and your hair cut all wrong." And she laughed gaily as she recalled more and more of the details that had amused and touched her during the first few weeks of their acquaintance: the hobnailed boots he had worn, so practical for the cobblestoned streets of the village, which had caused her butler to grimace painfully as he watched the damage they did to the highly waxed parquet flooring of the dining room; the way he had always forgotten to take off the clips that prevented his pants from getting caught in the bicycle he rode; his clumsiness in handling his long, gangling body as he sat on the edge of the *fauteuils,* as though he didn't dare dent the tautly puffed cushions, and later, more familiar, sitting back too far, so that he had to brace himself on their frail arms to push himself up.

"What a difference. You've come a long way."

"Yes," he said, not thinking of her for a moment but of the young man who had enjoyed reading Aristotle sitting up against a tree in the woods. "Thanks to you I became a success—in the international smart set."

The tone of his voice startled her. "You sound bitter," she said, frowning with surprise. "Wasn't that what you wanted?"

"Possibly."

"Possibly?" repeated Emma, in growing astonishment. "What do you mean? Don't tell me you wanted to become another Dr. Schweitzer?" And back into her memory came the evening when Fleury and she had decided to help the unassuming young doctor. "I thought you were ambitious, that you wanted to make a name for yourself—at least that was the impression you gave. And there you were, so alone, no money, no connections. Was I wrong?"

She was and she wasn't. What did it matter now? He sighed without knowing that he did.

"I was wrong, then," she said. "But you never gave any indication that you might have preferred to go to a country where people die like flies because they can't even get hold of an aspirin, or among lepers, or something like that. It would never have occurred to me that you might want something different from an office in the best quarter of Paris and the patronage of our friends. Why didn't you speak up at the time?"

"Probably because I always knew that though my mind was willing my flesh was weak."

She looked up at him then and knew that this was not a glib answer, that he had spoken the truth. But could she have persuaded him to move into a different field of medicine?

"How stupid of me not to have guessed what you really wanted."

That she should be so distressed about the past touched and embarrassed him at the same time. "For God's sake, Emma, of course it was my choice."

But to have committed such an error in judgment hurt her pride. How could she have been so unobservant? "And I thought you were happy."

The temptation to tell her the true reason for his betrayal of his boyhood dreams surged through him. He fought it back. Too late. Too late now. But he had often wondered if she was really naïve enough not to know why he had chosen the easiest way to make a career, or so arrogant that she took it for granted that men loved and wanted to serve her, or too wise to allow or acknowledge anything that could have no future. He had never been able to find out. Through all the years in which he had seen her regularly, she had never given him a chance to speak about his love for her. Yet she must know. She must have known from the moment they had met at the millpond. Fleury, he thought. She had loved her husband and remained faithful to him. To seduce a woman who was virtuous as well as content was impossible. But was it? Had he perhaps come to this conclusion only because it allowed him to save his pride and continue to love her? Or could he not love or desire any woman who was within his reach because he was afraid of being put to the test? For Fleury had died over two years ago, and still he had not spoken. Out of respect for her grief or—?

He looked at her and all at once was struck by the realization that he could not foresee her reaction if he were to tell her. Thirty years . . . But suddenly he had the feeling that he knew very little more of her than he had that day when, standing at her bedside, he had felt so insecure as a doctor and as a man. But of course this was not true. The many years of their friendship, with all its ups and downs, had given him an intimate knowledge of her fears and needs.

She was still obviously upset about what he had said. What had made him disturb her peace of mind? Oh, God, he knew, knew only too well. His desperation had made him stupidly frank.

"Here," he said, pouring the champagne and handing her a glass. "Drink this and forget what I said, Emma. I didn't mean anything by it. It was just a mood. I guess when one gets to be my age and realizes that the time for a change has slipped by, one can't help pondering what life might have been like if, at certain moments, one had made different decisions."

As if he would ever have chosen otherwise. What a hypocrite he was. Because he knew very well that even if he had never met her, he would never have had the stamina to fight disease in a jungle. How pitiful to cling to such a romantic conception of oneself, like an adolescent boy, dreaming of heroic deeds to impress himself and others.

"Emma."

She didn't seem to hear him. She was staring at the glass in her hand in which the wine hummed softly, as if a bee were caught in its golden liquid. "Funny," she said. "I never thought of myself as selfish. Whenever I found myself acting egotistically, I tried to do something about it. But I failed you, Jacques. I see only now why it never occurred to me that it would bore you to treat only the rich. I wanted you around."

The echo of her own words stunned her. She looked about the room as if someone else had spoken them. But she went on doggedly. "You saved my life. Remember?"

Saved her life, thought Jacques Thiolat. She must be referring to the snake bite, for on another occasion she had implored him to let her die. Well, if she was thinking of the day the copperhead had bitten her, then she was exaggerating wildly. Any good doctor could have pulled her through that. But this was obviously the way she had decided to remember it, and it made him glad.

"Oh, how frightened I was that day! It must have been a hangover from my childhood. Most children don't know what death means, but I did. I had a dog when I was five. One moment he was running around, then he was still. Terribly still. I tickled his stomach and he didn't move. I hit him and he didn't growl. I fetched a bone and dangled it in front of his nose, and when he didn't take it I pushed it between his teeth. It fell out. Then I walked away and told nobody about it. But hours later I went back and touched him and he was cold and stiff. We buried him in the garden behind the house. In a carton. In a hole. The governness said he was dead and I must forget about him. But I couldn't. A few months later I dug up the hole. I simply wanted to see him again." She paused for a moment. "I didn't know anything about decomposition. I had no idea what happened to the body after death."

She drank rapidly from her glass, then held it out for more. "Maybe that's why I've always wanted you around, available. You always make me feel that nothing can happen to me as long as you're there. Can you forgive me?"

He could hardly speak. "Forgive?" he repeated. "I want to thank you, Emma." Thank you, he would have liked to add, for not letting me be wasted.

"You are very generous," she said. Then the thought that what she had told him about her dependence on him might make him less honest, more guarded in the wording of his opinion about her health—and she had had some strange discomforts last month—made her lean forward.

"You know, Jacques," she said, her voice growing clearer, stronger with every word, "I've really been very lucky. In all these years you've never had to prescribe anything but vitamins or a few tranquilizers or an antibiotic now and then. But if the time comes when there is something seriously wrong with me, I want your word of honor that you won't withhold it, that you will tell me, Jacques, no matter what it is. I don't want to be caught by surprise."

"Yes, of course," he said.

She held out her hand like a child. "Promise?"

"I promise."

But unknown to him, beads of perspiration had formed on his forehead. Emma Starr Fleury noticed them. She glanced at the open window across the room. It was early in the season and a particularly cool day.

"What's wrong?"

"Wrong?"

"You took some tests last week," she reminded him. "You were going to let me know the results today."

"They're fine. Fine."

But she knew he was lying. "Tell me the truth," she said.

He had not intended to tell her, not until the very end, not even then if it could be helped. What did I say to make her suspicious, he asked himself. Am I so weak that I am unable to stand this knowledge by myself? He tried to command the muscles around his mouth to produce a smile, the superior, gay smile that had become his trademark. All he could manage was a distorted grin.

"It is serious, then?"

He nodded.

"Well?"

"Leukemia."

Her blue eyes widened in an expression of utter disbelief, her lips parted to laugh away such an impossibility. Then she swayed a little, as if under a blow that had hit her full force and without the slightest warning. He reached out to steady her, but she had closed her eyes and did not see his hand. Her voice was a whisper. "Leukemia. That's cancer of the blood."

He could merely nod.

She had opened her eyes again and was looking straight at him. "How much time do you give me?"

"Four to six months."

"And there's nothing you can do about it?"

He shook his head.

She was silent then, sitting very straight, locked in the monstrous self-control she always exercised. He wished desperately that he could say something to alleviate the shock, but only trite phrases came to his mind. He could not speak them.

"Will I have to suffer?"

"No," he said violently.

"No," she repeated. "You'll do something about it?"

"Yes."

Emma Starr Fleury rose. He put his hand on her arm. "Don't go yet. Or, if you want to, let me see you home."

She hesitated, then shook her head. "Meg and Titus are waiting for me at the Ruhl. I won't tell them," she added, as if she had just come to a decision. "Did you tell anyone? Do they know?" She pointed with her chin toward the waiting room.

"No."

"I don't want anyone to know. No one."

"I understand."

She crossed quickly to the door, and for a moment he thought she was going to walk out without looking back. But she stopped, her hand already on the door handle. "Thank you, Jacques," she said, "for never telling me that you were in love with me."

Outside Thiolat's house her car was waiting for her, but the chauffeur was asleep behind the wheel. He looked appallingly young and vulnerable. A strand of hair had escaped from under his visored cap and moved across his forehead with the rhythm of his breathing, like a tiny cloud of black dust. There was something sad and wild about his face, and Emma Starr Fleury hesitated to wake him. Then, not to embarrass him, she walked back a few steps in the direction she had come from and called his name. "Gino." She could see him straighten up, open the door, take off his cap and slick back his hair, all in one movement, and felt strangely sorry to have torn him out of his dreams.

"The Ruhl?"

"Yes, please."

The car pulled away down the Corniche and onto the Quai des Etats-Unis. To her left, undisturbed by motion, lay the sea, like a piece of blue fallen from the sky, and in the strong light of early afternoon the houses to her right seemed to be dipped in dazzling white, as though the sun's rays had sucked up all their color. Yet the pass-

ing cars, bicycles, people appeared painted a flat, lusterless
black, like giant roaches scurrying between secret goals
under the merciless radiance of a full moon over a vast
desert. Suddenly, from somewhere, Emma could hear the
broken sound of music.

They were already on the Promenade des Anglais, close
to the Ruhl, when she said, "Drop me here." Without
waiting for Gino to open the door for her, she got out of
the car. Only his astonished expression made her aware
that she was doing something unusual. "I quite forgot,"
she said, "that I have an appointment with the dress-
maker. Will you please tell Miss Meg and Mr. Vandendam that I am at Berthe's, and not to wait for me? I will
see them later, at home."

"And when does Madame want me to pick her up?"

"Don't bother. I'll take a cab."

She walked very quickly away from the curb. As soon
as she had reached the triangle of the small park, her
surroundings assumed their natural colors again. She
could see the deep green of the trees, the pink of summer
dresses, the purple and yellow stripes of huge umbrellas.
An infant came toddling along the path, looking crazily
drunk as he tried to keep his balance, which was made
doubly difficult because his pants had slipped down below
his still prominent navel, obstructing the free movement
of his fat little legs. Hands outstretched, he almost fell,
then found support by clutching Emma's skirt. She bent
and picked him up. Oh, if only I had had a child, she
thought, pressing the little body to her. But the boy
realized suddenly that he was being held by a stranger
and began to fight her, howling in fear of the unknown
face smiling at him from above. Emma put him down
quickly, looking over her shoulder to see if anybody had
noticed her defeat. A little farther on, an old man was

cranking a hurdy-gurdy on which a monkey, dressed in the red uniform of a bellboy, sat waving a minute French flag. She stopped and opened her purse. "How long do they live?"

The man stared at her, pretended not to have understood her question, and pinched the capuchin deftly with his mean, arthritic fingers to make him take off his hat. A moment later, the noise of the Place Masséna engulfed her. Emma took a deep breath, quite unconsciously pulling in her stomach and letting out the air noisily. She walked in the shade of the arcades until she found herself opposite the Galeries Lafayette. It had been years since she had entered a department store.

For a few minutes she stood quite still, overwhelmed by the babble of voices, the sound of the big fans humming like mammoth insects at strategic points. Unexpectedly content, she let herself drift along the aisles, a part of the stream of people, then stopped where a crowd had formed at a counter with handbags on sale. Their reduced prices were printed in enormous letters on white cardboard posters. Like the dozens of women around her, Emma picked up one bag after another mechanically, glanced inside at the lining, checked whether the mirror was whole, a change purse included in the bargain. "Can I help you, Madame?" The experienced eyes of an elderly salesgirl had spotted her. The angry shouts of those who had been ahead of her, protesting the salesgirl's disregard of them, made Emma feel singled out, isolated. "No, thank you. I just wanted to look." Clutching a bag, she walked away, only to be held back by a strong, restraining hand while someone close to her sneered, "You can never tell, can you? And dressed so fine."

The words failed to have any meaning. Emma looked blankly into the store detective's bespectacled eyes, then at the bag in her hand. Why was she carrying such an ugly thing? Never mind. "Have it sent to the Villa du Cygne," she told the woman.

Around the corner from the Galeries, in a narrow side street, Emma entered a small café. A table, well back against the wall and sheltered by the faded red canopy, had just been vacated. She sat down in the wicker chair, and presently a waiter, yawning loudly, came to wipe the marble top of her table and take her order. His heels were worn down and the cracked leather of his shoes betrayed his bunions. He wore glasses and his hands shook slightly. Gradually the café emptied and the street, now that luncheon was over, grew strangely quiet. A big white cat left its place on a low window sill and began to walk stealthily along a row of tables in search of food. It stopped when it reached Emma, meowed, its yellow eyes fixed, then jumped onto the free chair next to hers, lay down and began to purr. In a newspaper kiosk, the man who had just been yelling the names of his papers at the top of his lungs shoved the brim of his hat deeper into his face, as if he were lowering a curtain, and leaned back against the wall to rest. A sparrow flew from his perch on a pole to pick at the droppings of a horse. Across the street, a woman carried a dilapidated rocking chair into the shade of a house entrance and sat down to study a colored sheet of lottery numbers. For a while the scraping of her chair against the cement of the street was all that could be heard. Then a nun, bristling with authority, herded a group of children, all dressed alike in black aprons with little white collars, past the café to a bus stop farther down the street. After a while an Arab came, strings of colored beads dangling from his right arm, a number of cheap carpets from his left. He took one look out of the corners of his eyes at the clients of the café and went on, walking softly and whistling to himself. The sadness of the tune caught between the walls like something lost forever. Finally Scott came. And only when she saw him did Emma remember that she had been in this café before. And always with him. He often ate in this neighborhood, in some *brasserie* or other, then stopped here for a brandy. She had had no intention of meeting him today. Until a moment ago she had not even thought of him. For that matter, she had not been thinking at all. Now she realized why she had come to this place.

He was a couple of years older than she, maybe more. But he looked younger, the way some men do who are fated to live to a very old age, seemingly getting more vigorous with every new year, reaching their full bloom, like retarded children, when others have already begun to deteriorate. He was of average height, yet so powerfully built that he gave the impression of a tall man. He wore his hair old-fashionedly long and one always thought, on seeing him, that it must be a windy day, for it was forever flying about his face, set in motion by the abrupt movements of his head and shoulders. His face was broad, without any refinement—a short, stubby nose, a mouth that was large, with heavy, loose, extraordinarily red lips, strong, small teeth and a square chin. His skin had that leathery quality of fresh air and careless living and was at all times, winter and summer, a deep mahogany brown. His eyes were small, two brilliant black points, like the eyes of a bird. Only their glance had depth and beauty. Though his clothes were of the best material, he somehow managed to look disheveled. Judged from his appearance, he could have been a laborer who has decided to blow his savings on idleness, a sailor who has settled down in a city, a peasant grown tired of working the land. But he was a writer.

"Hi, Em," he said, not in the least surprised to find her there. "Scram, Butterfly!" He pushed the white cat out of the chair and sat down, spreading his legs.

"Butterfly?" said Emma. "Why in the world do you call her Butterfly?"

"I call all cats Butterfly," he said, "because they love to chase them. Haven't you ever watched a cat chasing a butterfly?"

"I can remember a time when you tried to trap them and called them Heavenly Meatballs."

"But you weren't hungry enough to eat them." He leaned back on the frail chair, which creaked under his weight, and roared with laughter. Then he turned to her and put his great paw over her hand. And immediately its fine bones, the smallness of her wrist, which could slide through the circle of his forefinger and thumb as through a ring, the muscular coolness of her skin, cold yet pulsating, startled him as if he had touched a live wire. It brought back a memory of the First World War. "Christ, Em! I can still see you standing in that hole."

1918. She had been visiting hospitals to report on the morale of the wounded American soldiers when she had heard that someone called Warren, Scott Warren, a young reporter, was going up to the front. The Red Cross driver who had been delivering newspapers to the fighting men had been killed a few nights before, and Scott had volunteered to take his place. He was driving a white-topped camion, and he had driven through the fresh morning air at breakneck speed until they had turned onto a road marked by a signboard, NIGHT ROAD ONLY, and he had slowed down to avoid the deep holes.

"The sign doesn't mean much, does it?"

Bent over the wheel, he had shaken with laughter, not looking at her, hardly able to stop laughing. "Fritz got the range on it because of our troop transports. Shelled it to make it impassable. That's why there's no daylight traffic on it. And our camion makes an extra-fine target.

See that hole there? That shell nearly got me yesterday. I can still taste the sand in my mouth."

Thin, fine columns of smoke on the horizon—one, two, three—a group of American soldiers mending blasted places in the road so that the trucks could roll at night, and Scott blowing a little horn that looked like a toy, making the men drop their tools and run to get their papers, grinning at her as if the sight of a girl eliminated the threat of danger. Farther ahead a broken truck by the roadside, a big French tank smashed flat, a wooden cross over which a helmet hung lopsidedly, dead horses, little graveyards everywhere. Then a hillside, with pup tents and the small openings of dugouts springing to life at the sound of the horn, hundreds of brown figures running, stopping only to grab the papers before dashing back to shelter. A village where crumbled walls exposed cooking utensils still on the stove; a mangled ambulance, a torn German uniform and, pervading everything, the stench of dead things, and Scott blowing his horn, the Pied Piper, and a wave of men rushing at them, and an officer's angry voice ordering them not to form clusters.

Driving on again, on and on, and the sudden stop at a crossroads, and an open hillside. The awful significance of men scanning the sky while they reached for papers and talked to her and Scott, and one of them, forgetting about his own safety, saying, "If that German balloon is up, believe me, we're out of luck. Shelling ahead. Shrapnel and gas." But Scott driving on in spite of the warning, getting her to help sort the papers as they bounced mercilessly, stopping now and then where nobody seemed to be around but where, at the sound of his horn, heads popped out of the ground, nodded and sank back to become one once more with the soil, and Scott and she, under no orders not to move, crawling as close as possible to the molehills of earth, pushing piles of papers in front of them.

Later, a landscape black with destruction. All by it-self—a garbage pail filled to the brim with severed limbs, legs, arms, hands, the only sign that an emergency hospital must have been there. A large area of yellowed ground, deathlike in its complete abandonment of human life, be-yond it hole-scarred fields stretching to a treed horizon that marked the last trench from which the men had to leap over the top at night to attack the enemy in hand-to-hand combat. Scott racing past a church now, with half its belfry torn off, past trees miraculously still alive, throwing the camion like a horse around the craters, singing loudly, wildly, blowing his horn, hurling the last bunch of papers to the ground without stopping, swing-ing the car about, heading back to headquarters, scream-ing above the roar of the violated motor, "You sure were a help. Best thing for the morale is a good-looking doll!"

And all at once the bursting of shells—in back of them, at their sides, ahead. Scott leaping out of the driver's seat, eyes aglow, voice elated as if with a personal victory. "They've spotted us!" Pulling her free from the camion, away from the road, to the ground, making her get up, making her run until finally they reached the mouth of a dugout.

They had to bend almost double to get into the narrow tunnel and crawl over the carcasses of rats, bits of bloody bandage, sharp-edged pieces of tin. And then a cisternlike chamber, high enough to straighten up in. Scott's flash-light lighting up several straw pallets where soldiers too sick to stand could rest. But nobody was there. And the sudden darkness as he turned off the light, his arms around her, pressing her to him as if she were the reward for his successful mission, clinging to her even as he threw her onto a pile of straw, shaking all over with the terror from which they had escaped, with suddenly re-leased desire.

"What's your name?" And when she had not answered, yelling like a madman, "Your name! Your name!" as if it were of the utmost importance to be able to speak a girl's name; his hands tearing at her blouse, his red, hot lips burning her flesh. It was then that she had screamed in fear.

It had sobered him. He had let go of her, tossing her against the wall like a piece of rubbish. "You stupid goddam little bitch."

No, he had not been a gentleman, thought Scott Warren, watching her frown with the memories he had so suddenly awakened. "As a matter of fact," he said, "you were very brave. I've always admired you for the way you behaved on that trip. But then you always were courageous."

Help me to be courageous now, Emma wanted to say. I've just been told I have only four to six months more to live. But before she could make herself say the words that would deliver her to his pity, she heard him laugh.

"That day," he said. "That blasted no-good day. You know why I've never forgotten it? Why I remember all of it as if it were a painting from which I could pick out a detail any time? Because, of all days, it was the birthday of my success."

He reached for the brandy the waiter had set down in front of him without being told, took a gulp, swished it around his mouth, swallowed and said, "Yep. It made me famous."

He emptied the glass and pushed away the plate that showed the price of the drink, burned into the rim. Emma had been brought up too strictly as a good listener to interrupt the silence that followed. Besides, she was just remembering something Thiolat had said, something about pondering over one's past, of what might have happened if at certain moments in one's life one had behaved differently. What would her life have been like if on that day she had not fought Scott but let him violate her?

"There you were," he said, "sobbing your heart out in that stinking cave. All of a sudden it was too much for me. I think claustrophobia got the better of me. I knew I'd go crazy if I stayed one more minute in that sealed-up hole. Even shells or gas seemed better. Lord, the relief of open sky. And air."

Yes, it had been like being buried alive. It had made her remember the dog that had died. She must tell Jacques that she wanted to be cremated. She must write it down.

"It was very quiet outside," Scott said. "They had stopped shelling. I lit a cigarette and just sat there smoking, so goddam happy to be alive I began to bawl. And then I saw the dead soldier. He was lying only a couple of feet away. On his stomach. I turned him over. He was covered with freshly dried blood. Shrapnel had got him. He was middle-aged, and I remember being furious suddenly and talking to him as if he could still hear. 'Pop,' I told him, 'this is none of your business. Act your age. Get the hell out of here. Go home, sit behind a desk instead of trying to play the hero. Your grandchildren will love you even if you don't fight the kraut.' Then I buried him. I took his papers and shoved him into one of the holes. It didn't take long to cover him. The blastings had left plenty of loose soil. But there was no wood to make a cross or anything to mark his grave. Then I took a look at his papers. It seemed ridiculous that he should have kept a diary, a grown man like him, in all that hell—written in such small print, the kind you usually find only on parchment. Quite a few words were misspelled. But it was all there, the whole business and what it meant to him—a search for identity. Well, I never turned it in. I found out who he was—just an ordinary guy who had felt it his patriotic duty to show the Kaiser he couldn't bully the world. He wasn't even married and his parents were dead. He'd been a draftsman in San Francisco."

The Search—Scott's first book, which had made him famous overnight, the diary of a very ordinary little man's search for identity in the hell of warfare. It had been dedicated to "the Unknown Soldier."

"I've never told anyone," he said. "Not Louise, not Helen, not any of my wives or mistresses, or any friend. Waiter, another brandy."

There would be many secrets she would take with her. Take where? Suddenly she wanted to ask Scott if he believed in a life after death. Then she saw his eyes, their savage, tortured glance. She couldn't let his confession pass as if it were not important.

"What made you do it?"

He shrugged. "People steal all the time—some because they're starving, others because they're envious, some for the sake of stealing, for the thrill. And they steal under false pretenses—somebody else's interest, his appreciation, a little warmth, even love. What people won't do to escape loneliness! But at that time I stole because I was starved for recognition. I had been trying to write ever since I could remember. Nobody thought I was any good. Sure, I was an able reporter, but to me reporting was always something vulgar, even when it was first-rate. After all, you were merely copying from life. I wanted to create. But I couldn't find a style. And then, there it was—simple, direct, universal. It went straight to the heart . . . as they said. I've copied it ever since—my famous style. And been copied in turn . . ."

He pulled a tobacco pouch and a pipe from his pocket. She watched him smell the tobacco before he tamped the pipe, watched his huge fingers manipulating it deftly, watched him shove the pipe between his small white animal teeth, strike a match, set fire to it, inhale.

"The obligation," he said, and because of a cloud of blue smoke she could not see his face, "the terrible obligation. I, who always wanted to be free, without obligations. I trapped myself, trapped myself without a chance of escape. That was what he did to me, that dead man. Why did he have to get killed just at that spot? I've had to live up to him. I've had to develop as he would have developed, think like him, see things as he would have seen them. I owed it to him to be better than I was, for if he had lived, he would have been a very good writer. First-class. I've paid the price a thousandfold. Ever since that day I've never been myself. Naturally I have," he said, as though she had contradicted him, "of course I have, but I also always had to be him, and I never succeeded in integrating the two."

"You could have made it on your own."

"I knew that only years later. Of course I could have made it on my own. And been free. But I was too impatient. Why did just that soldier have to have a diary? Why?"

"Fate," she said, having arrived at a conclusion that had nothing to do with what he was asking in his despair.

"Fate? I could have turned that blasted diary in. Since there was nobody to send it to, it would have ended on the garbage heap. All gone to waste. Was I destined to save it? To make it a classic? Or was I born a thief? A fake? *Do* we make our own fate? If I had . . . if . . . if . . . if . . ."

She rose to go to the washroom. It was in the back of the restaurant, opposite the kitchen, and a key had to be fetched to unlock it. In spite of its cleanliness, it smelled strongly of urine and it made her nearly sick. She had never been in quite so primitive a place—there were only two footrests above the ground to stand on—yet as she looked around her in disgust, she grew aware that in a short while, days she could count, nothing would matter to her any more.

A woman, obviously an employee of the café, knocked on the door. "There's a basin at the end of the corridor, in case you want to wash your hands, Madame." She held out a towel.

Emma looked at the woman without taking the towel. She was quite large, dark-haired, heavily made up, with the rouge distributed badly on her high cheekbones. A big wart in the middle of her forehead made her look as if she had three eyes—one normal one on each side of her nose and a third, right in the middle of her forehead. A three-eyed Cyclops.

"I have an incurable cancer," Emma told her. "I'm going to die in a very short time." And she began to cry.

The woman drew back, then tried to smile reassuringly. "One mustn't give up hope," she said. "I have a friend— oh, she was . . . Well, her doctor . . ."

When Emma came back to her seat, Scott Warren was gone.

Two life-sized swans flanked the gate at the entrance of the driveway leading up to the Villa du Cygne. Hewn in black marble, the spread of their wings still seemed to be cushioned by air, their feet hardly touched the platform of the pillars and their necks were stretched to achieve perfect balance for the precarious moment of landing. An artist had once made a cartoon of Emma Starr Fleury riding one of the wild black birds. Fleury had been indignant about the sketch, but Emma had been secretly delighted with the conception of herself as a witch sailing through the air, not on a broomstick, but on the back of a savage *Cygnus atratus*.

She had bought the villa in 1950 because she had fallen in love with it, and the thought that it might be sold to people who would take less pleasure in it had been somehow unbearable. At that time she had not intended to spend more than a couple of weeks of the season on the Riviera. Then Fleury's failing health had necessitated a gentler climate than the Loire or Paris could offer, and the villa had become home.

The house had been built in a time that still respected the laws of harmony between landscape and style. Instead of being put up on the most practical spot, permitting the vandalism of machinery to alter the grounds according to the requirements of owner and architect, its site had been carefully integrated with that of trees, rocks and sea, their color and formation. The road, once you left the highway, was rather narrow, curving past a variety of trees—palm and prickly pear, pomegranate and fir. Then suddenly, where the wind from the sea had stunted their growth, the road widened, and there the house stood, quite unexpectedly on high ground; the dark-green sheen of camellias, the feathery leaves of mimosa and the spiked green of laurel to the right, a formal flower garden to the left. Erected in a century that took security for granted rather than pursuing it as a goal, the house had been built to last, and with glorious waste. The softest pink tinted its stones so that all through the day it seemed to be caressed by the light of a rising or setting sun. Against the backdrop of the blue sea and the gold beach with its reddish-brown rocks, the villa's plain lines rose with dignity, yet with the unobtrusive surrender that the scenery demanded. It was the only home, of the many she had inhabited, that Emma had ever loved. Soon somebody else, unless she made provisions in her will, would live in it. She remembered an old Italian who, when she had asked him what would happen after his death to his treasured castle above Lake Como, had smiled benignly. "I shall burn it to the ground." It had seemed a wanton jest. Now she knew that he had said it not as a joke or to shock her but had meant it sincerely.

She paid the taxi and went quickly inside. "I'd like a tray upstairs," she told the butler. "By myself."

By living in many different countries, by learning from Fleury's scholarly discrimination, through tireless observation and comparison in the choice of furniture and its arrangement, she had acquired exquisite taste. Nothing was obvious, everything was so casual, so unobtrusive that a sense of well-being was established in the visitor before he grew aware of the value of the paintings, the antique chairs and tables and *objets d'art,* which might otherwise have distracted him from his comfort. Even the oval of the hall, with its twelve niches in which the allegorical figures of each month of the year gleamed in white marble, seemed merely appropriate as the entry to such a house. Emma walked through a hidden door between May and June, which opened out onto a staircase. Halfway up, a landing broadened sufficiently to offer space for a small moss-green sofa with a round table in front of it. Above it an enormous, curtainless window, reaching the entire length from ground floor to roof, let in the light —light that seemed almost tangible, a substance you could touch, wrap around you like gossamer veiling. At the same time it disclosed a view so wide one could see not only the flowering shrubs and the beach below but the town of Beaulieu, the chain of mountains that sheltered the coast from the winds beyond, and a great part of the serpentine shore line winding toward Monte Carlo. At night it became a huge web in which the stars and the white manes of waves were caught, and the lights of resorts and cars. Emma often wondered which of the former owners had been so much in need of letting in the beauty that lay outside as to conceive this window. She wanted to sit down, but her maid had heard her steps and appeared dutifully on the landing above her.

"Professor Thiolat phoned. He wants Madame to ring back the moment Madame comes in. And Mr. Warren rang. No message. Just to let Madame know he rang. Miss Meg is dressing and Mr. Titus is taking a swim before dinner."

Emma turned slightly, took off her sunglasses, which looked incongruously big and American on her little face, and squinting against the onslaught of light, discovered something floating on the water, like an inert object. There was nothing she loved better than to hurl her body from some height into the sea. Even now, at the mere thought her skin tingled in anticipation of the rush of resistant air, the cold embrace of the water. Nobody could force her to live out the time given her. They said that if you kept on swimming until exhaustion set in, death would pull you gently into the deep. According to her religion, suicide was a mortal sin, her education had taught her to regard it as an act of cowardice, and Thiolat had said there would be no pain. She put her glasses on again before facing the stout, elderly woman. Hannah was Swiss. Somehow, like the Vatican, Emma believed in the unfailing loyalty of that small nation's citizens, and most of her help was and always had been Swiss. She could picture Hannah dressed in the costume of a guard, swinging a halberd the moment she discovered a trace of tears in her mistress's eyes.

"Tell them they're on their own tonight. I don't want to be disturbed."

There was one ugly room in the house, a monstrosity. When the house had grown quiet, Emma found herself drawn toward it. In itself small, it was made even smaller by the arrangement of the photographs that hung so closely together; one could easily mistake them for hideous wallpaper. For in spite of his perspicacity, Count de Fleury had been a sentimental man. He had taken little from the castle, when they had moved to the Côte d'Azur, except hundreds of photographs of his family, and what a European of his bloodline considered family could not be described in a few sentences. It took into its clannish circle third and fourth cousins and their children and grandchildren, almost anyone who had ever drawn a breath in the illustrious presence of a Fleury. She had disliked most of them except for old Countess Marie-Clothilde, whom she had almost loved because she had been so marvelously mad, insisting on keeping the elephant some maharaja had presented her with, instead of giving him to a zoo, as anybody in his right mind would have done. Dressed up as an Indian princess, she had ridden the elephant through the formal park, declaiming aloud the poems of Hafiz while nipping at a bottle to settle her stomach, which rebelled at the swaying of the ornate seat. Marie-Clothilde. She had had enough lucid moments to know very well what she was doing. "What do you want, Henri? I don't do any harm, which is more than can be said of you."

Emma had added very few pictures to the collection. Some of herself, a beloved teacher, a friend—none of Adam, of course—and a picture of her parents, Jack and Amy Starr. Measured by the inelastic standards of society, Jack Starr had been a nobody, worse than that—an upstart with no respect for social frontiers. According to the objective rules of success, he had risen to the very top. Born in a small town in upstate New York, he had struck out for himself before he was quite fourteen years old. He had roamed the states from East to West like a gypsy, toting hardware. Exactly when and how he had established a business relationship with the men who were dreaming of an intercontinental railroad had always been unclear to Emma. She had been told so many versions—about a cousin who had introduced her father to the railroad people; about a friend in the national government who was responsible for land grants; about a hardware store owner in California who had lent him money—that she had resigned herself to whatever version of his youth he chose to give. She was equally resigned to the vicious rumors charging Jack Starr with corruption and maintaining that he had killed a man in the Utah desert and then claimed his land, that he had enriched himself at the cost of the immigrants solicited by one of the land departments he influenced secretly, that he had ruined his partner in the Wall Street panic of 1873. Vile lies—according to her father—invented to make him the scapegoat for sins others had committed. Besides, lived there a man who would not kill in self-defense? Or who would be stupid enough not to grasp at riches when the opportunity offered itself? By the time Emma was born, Jack Starr was sixty, the head of twenty corporations—with more than five thousand miles of railroad track, three thousand miles of steamship lines—and one of the largest landholders in America, and he had been married for only three years, as though he had never had time to take a wife before.

Emma could still see him in the big house he had built on Washington Square, sitting in the high-backed chair to the left of the fireplace that evening after the party. He usually sat there every evening, all by himself, tired of the men he saw all day in his office, yet with no friends he could call on in his hours of leisure—a little man with fine, silky hair, a smooth face, Milkface Starr, who gave the impression that he would have difficulty lifting one of the great logs from the wood basket and tossing it on the fire. But the small bones, the satiny skin, the round blue eyes with their innocent glance were like camouflage for the iron muscle, the unyielding will power and a shrewdness that had been victorious over most men. An ornate silver tray had been placed on the table before him with a choice of brandy and after-dinner liqueurs, a box of cigars, a lighted candle. They were carried in every evening and carried away again with the bottles still filled to the brim, the glasses clean, the neat rows of Havanas undisturbed. For Jack Starr neither drank nor smoked, and those whom he might have been expecting never came.

Emma had come in to say good night. She always had to say good night to him three times, in a never-changing ritual. The first time after finishing her dinner, the second time when he had finished his, the third time when she was ready for bed. Maybe this procedure enabled Jack Starr to pretend that he had fathered not just one child (and a girl, at that) but several children of different ages, because he would address her each time in a different fashion. First as the little girl she was, picking her up, swinging her through the air and slapping her behind playfully on his way out of the nursery. The second time, in the dining room, she would have to eat a bite of his dessert and, maybe, sit on his lap while he peeled an apple. The third time, in the library, she was allowed to pull up a footstool close to his chair and they would talk. Mostly it was Jack Starr who talked, pointing out on the maps he was always studying the places he had been to or the cities where branch offices of his firms were located.

For some reason or other, on that particular evening he had not been at home at his usual hour, and when she entered he had tapped the arm of his chair, indicating that he wanted her to sit there. Even before she had settled herself he had asked, "How was the party at the Hills'?"

Emma had described it all—the lawns that had been watered the night before to make a smooth, safe skating rink, the many-colored Japanese lanterns glowing like exotic fruit in the barren trees, the little booths from which the children had been served hot chocolate topped with mounds of sweet whipped cream, the different cookies, the teeny-weeny hot dogs, the chestnuts roasting over a brazier, the lighted-up Ferris wheel, the marvelous presents each child has received.

"What did you get?"

"A doll."

"Well, show it to me."

"I—I—" she had stammered, and burst into tears, tears he could not stop because they were her only refuge, because if she had stopped crying, she wouldn't have known what to do, and she worked herself into a fine fit of hysterics, throwing herself on the floor and hammering with her fists against it. It had all come out, the lies of the last three years, the horrible fact she had tried so hard to hide—that she had never been invited to any of the parties her governess had brought her to and fetched her from again, not suspecting how cleverly she was being deceived by a little girl who knew exactly, from all the excited talk at school, where a party was going to be held, when it would begin and end, and what was going to be served, what games and entertainment could be looked forward to. Why had she lied?

Emma could have given a variety of reasons: fear that her father might think she had misbehaved and therefore been punished with rejection; pride, which made it impossible to admit that apparently nobody wanted her; instinctive comprehension of how deeply her exclusion would hurt her father. She preferred to remain stubbornly silent.

The governess had been called in. "Emily always wanted me to stay in the car when I dropped her and wait in the car when I called for her."

Jack Starr had looked at his daughter, impressed by her cunning, amused by the authority she obviously exerted over her governess, and burning with rage. And where had she been while everybody had assumed she was having a good time at a party? Walking. Walking until the time had come to rush down the front steps of wherever the party had taken place, always a little ahead of the time it ended. And who were the children who came to play with her? The milkman's, the butcher's, the policeman's from around the corner. That his daughter had done much to give him a reputation of amiability did nothing to appease Jack Starr's mounting fury. Though his anger did not show in his face, Emma knew he was outraged, knew what it meant when his voice grew gentler and gentler, became a mere whisper, when his eyes lost all expression until they looked like round blue circles someone had painted on each side of his nose, and she began to tremble.

She had not been allowed to leave when the door closed on her governess, but was told to sit down on the high-backed chair on the other side of the fireplace, and she had realized that she was in for a whipping. For Jack Starr had rolled one of the large maps into a tight roll and kept hitting the air with it, as if to test its power. He had said nothing, just sat there looking about the room, surprised—as he might have looked if he had found himself suddenly in alien surroundings—looking at the walls hung with the masterpieces he had had agents buy for him when it became fashionable at the end of the nineteenth century for the new millionaires to prove to themselves what they had achieved by collecting "art"; looking at the priceless porcelain, the rare first editions of books, the regal quality of the furniture. And when he had taken it all in, he spat in a high, perfect arc into the fireplace. As the blob of saliva landed on the burning logs, it made a small hissing noise, and Jack Starr had started to laugh, loudly, uproariously, and spat again, in a climax of self-mockery and defiance. Then he had slapped the roll sharply across his knees and turned to Emma.

"I'm proud of you, Emily," he had said. "Other people will tell you it's a sin to lie and that you ought to get the licking of your life. But I say more power to you, daughter. If you let the world know it can hurt you, you get plowed under. That's the way the world is. Keep your tears to yourself and your chin high, and people won't use you as a target. In the long run it'll make you independent. If you don't protect yourself, nobody will. I'm going to whip you now, but only because you let yourself be caught. You should have provided a doll to show me."

Nevertheless the governess had been fired the next morning, and a few days later Emma was told she would no longer go to Brearley; a private tutor had been engaged to take over her education. She was ten years old at the time. Two years later she was sent to a boarding school in Switzerland. During her holidays she traveled with her father. At sixteen he brought her back to New York, at seventeen she was married to Henri, Count de Fleury.

You, thought Emma, looking at the photograph of her mother. If you had lived, would it have made a difference?

Though Amy Starr had died six years after she had presented her husband with a daughter, Emma remembered her vividly. Even as a child it had bothered her sense of harmony to see her parents side by side—the small, fine-boned man dwarfed by the tall woman, an amazon without any visible battle equipment. Jack Starr had chosen his wife as a breeder might choose the animal most suited to his purpose—a strong, fine, healthy girl to bear his offspring. Apparently it had occurred to him that he wanted an heir only at an age when other men were already enjoying their grandchildren. Amy Burlington, of English descent and good family, had seemed the right answer. Nobody could foresee that she would bear him only one child in six years, and a girl. Her failure had made her more deeply religious than was to his liking. But if she thought she could produce more little Starrs by praying endlessly, lighting candles and working for the poor, it was all right with him as long as she didn't take too much time kneeling on her *prie-dieu* at night.

Emma used to think of her mother as "the woman in black" because she usually saw her on the way to or from church. It had always surprised her that her mother was light of skin—the little you saw of it in the long-sleeved, fishbone-collared dresses she wore—not black like Hattie the laundress. Often, though, Emma would picture Amy Starr not as human but as a gigantic bat, for she moved so noiselessly you hardly ever heard her enter or leave a room, and she was fond of a black woolen shawl she wore across her shoulders. Within it, her arms would stir like wings and would gather Emma into their blackness in a perfunctory gesture of tenderness. Emma sensed the impatience, the resentment and pity with which her mother regarded her, a daughter, long before Amy Starr asked her to include the request for a little brother in her nightly prayer. "Lord, who art in Heaven, give me a little brother. . . ." And then her mother had died. And everybody had said she had caught pneumonia kneeling for so many hours on the cold stone floor of the unheated chapel.

No, Emma decided. It would have made no difference if her mother had lived. She did not know if Amy Starr had loved her husband, but she would certainly have considered it her duty to side with him, even if it had meant sacrificing the happiness of her only child.

The telephone rang. Jacques Thiolat's voice. "Emma? Thank God! You left so abruptly. I just wondered—where have you been all afternoon? I called several times. Why didn't you phone me when you got home? I worried about you. I'd like very much to come around for a nightcap . . . if . . ." And for an instant she longed for his presence, as a child who has suffered a nightmare doesn't want to be alone. Then, just as suddenly, she was annoyed. She shook her head. She would not allow fear to break down the barriers of reserve. "No. Not tonight, Jacques. And don't worry. I'll take a sleeping pill," and she laughed a little, quickly, assuredly, haughtily. "Really —I'm perfectly all right. Good night."

Yet the moment she heard the click of the receiver in the cradle, doubt about her behavior assailed her. Had she sounded so unconcerned, so much above the little matter of dying that he would recognize her pretense? And hadn't she been unkind? After all, he had loved her all his life. And to know herself loved and admired had been like an extra carpet on which to walk over the hardness of reality. She reached for the telephone, then withdrew her hand. By now Denise would have entered his study. Having eavesdropped in the corridor, she could now bring him a drink, and very possibly they would go to bed, and Jacques would betray Denise, as he had betrayed every woman with whom he had slept, by imagining he held Emma in his arms. Poor Denise. Poor Denise? Emma searched in the pocket of her blue dressing gown for the pack of cigarettes. Slowly she struck a match. Poor Denise? Why poor? After all, Denise had spent most of her adult life close to the man she loved. No, Denise didn't deserve pity. She was not fatally ill.

The cigarette trembled on Emma's lips, stuck, and came away with a flake of her skin as she pulled at it sharply. She rose from the chair behind her desk, where she had settled down when she had first entered the room, and walked over to the window. The night air came in with the scent of roses, wet sand, and the sharp smell of fish rotting somewhere on the beach. Vaguely she grew aware of two figures running hand in hand along the edge of the water, swinging their arms to the rhythm of their hearts. As she had run along a deserted beach once in the secrecy of night, feeling the heartbeat of the boy she loved, steady and strong in the grip of her hand. Suddenly she could see herself as she had been then, not quite seventeen, all the happiness in the world contained in the admiring look Adam had given her curls, cascading absurdly from under her floppy hat; in his voice humming *Sweetheart* —of course—and in their conviction that soon the yards and yards of voile her dress was made of would change into the lace of a wedding dress. Adam . . . Falling in love with him had been like discovering why she had been born, why there were trees and flowers and birds, a sun and a moon, why stars existed, and music, street corners and wide meadows. The world was theirs—or, rather, they were the world, and all things innate and alive were created for them. She had never met anyone afterward with whom she could compare him. There had been a sense of strength about him that had seemed to her far more powerful than her father's. And though, when she had looked at him in a certain way, she had known he was moved by the same passionate desire she felt, she had never been able to make him do anything he didn't want to do. And this had thrilled her. His attitude that there was nothing on earth that could restrict him unless he voluntarily chose to obey had filled her with boundless admiration. She felt a wholly new confidence in herself.

How happily she had told her father about the young man she had been meeting secretly, and Jack Starr had listened without interrupting her before he asked, "And what does he do, your nice young man?"

Well, Adam was some sort of mechanic. During the day he worked in a garage—that's where they had met, when something had gone wrong with the car—and in the evening he went to night school. He was studying for an engineering degree. No, he had no money, just like her father had started out in life. And Jack Starr had smiled, and never said a word that might have warned her— merely, "Of course I'd like to see this young man of yours." And then, two weeks later, he had a talk with Adam in his office and came home to tell her that before seeing Adam he had had him investigated, and found out that he had already promised to marry a girl of his own class. Confronted with the information, Adam had not been able to deny it.

She couldn't believe it. She had gone to the garage where he worked, but he had given up his job. And then, when she didn't hear from him again, she believed her father. Three months later, she had married Henri, Count de Fleury, First Secretary at the French Embassy in Washington, and slated for an ambassadorship in South America.

Jack Starr had made it an occasion no one would forget. Never had the people of New York seen so many orchids as had been delivered—truck after truck—to decorate St. Patrick's Cathedral. At the moment when the young couple left the church, a swarm of several hundred white pigeons had been released, clouding the air above the bridal coach. Ostentatious, yes—vulgar, perhaps—but oh, what showmanship! Traffic had been stopped at Washington Square, where the trees were lit with long white candles, making them look like chestnuts in bloom.

Flowers had been planted among them and little fountains splashed champagne into the air for the refreshment of the guests the house could not hold. The Mayor of New York had made a speech, and senators and congressmen had mingled with leaders of society, Army men, Navy men, and members of the diplomatic corps of foreign countries. Then she and Henri had sailed for Europe.

Fleury had been more than twenty years older than Emma, and he had married her for her money. Only she had not known it, not until after their wedding. They had still been on their honeymoon in Italy when she had come into the little salon that separated their bedrooms and heard him talking on the phone about the preceding night. She had believed it was a political gathering. Now it was unmistakably clear to her, from the way he spoke, that he was talking to a woman, intimately. To her utter confusion, he had not even made an attempt to deny it but nodded, shaking his head at her sobbing, and had said, "Let's be civilized about it, Emma. And let's leave personalities out of it for a moment. You bear a famous name, which I expect you to honor. I have provided you with a social position that includes certain obligations you will have to fulfill. In return, I have the chance, through your dowry, to reach the goals I have set for myself. Divorce is out of the question because it would be harmful to my career. But this bargain in no way precludes our learning to respect each other and, I hope, become friends. You will see that I will be a very good husband."

The room—all pseudo-Florentine furniture, pretentious like all pseudo things—had suddenly seemed like a room she had never entered before, and it had taken her some time to realize that night had fallen outside. She had not gone blind with sudden shock. Then she had snapped on the light and drawn the curtains before she turned to him again.

"A bargain? What bargain? I was not aware that a bargain was made."

It seemed to her that he whistled softly, but she could have been mistaken. He had put his hand on her shoulder —gently, almost as if in pity—but his voice was casual. "My dear, marriages are rarely made in Heaven, and if they are, they seldom work out. Knowing this, parents feel it is their duty to choose the companion who offers their son or daughter the best chance for mutual satisfaction. Remember the old sagas in which even the daughters of gods had to marry whomever their fathers selected, and if they refused, they were punished, exiled or changed into an animal until they obeyed?"

A week later, they returned to Washington. On entering Fleury's apartment, which they had decided to keep until his appointment to Peru in the autumn, Emma had seen Adam's handwriting on a small white envelope on a tray in the hall. His letter had been written on the day of their wedding, more than four weeks before.

"This morning I saw your picture in the paper. I couldn't believe it was you. Because I never gave up the hope that one day you would marry me. Why didn't you come that evening? I waited for you for hours, with everything ready for us to get away, just as I had explained in my letter. I was so sure you were strong enough to defy your father. I thought you loved me enough to leave him and the life you led with him. I didn't think it meant so much to you. And I would never have promised him not to see you again until I had my degree if it had ever entered my head you would marry someone else. Emily, why didn't you come? Why didn't you answer? Why didn't you wait for me? Why wouldn't you take the chance? I'm being shipped off to Europe any day now.

I'll never forget you, my darling. And in spite of everything, I wish you happiness. For me, I know there will be none."

And it was clear to her then that she had been deceived, that there had never been another girl, that Adam must have written to her after he had gone to Jack Starr's office. Oh, the terrible scene when she had confronted her father with Adam's letter and demanded to know the truth! And her father sitting there, admitting quite unashamedly that he had lied about Adam and had intercepted his first letter. "Of course I didn't want my daughter to marry a grease-monkey!" For nights she had lain awake condemning him for his unpardonable interference in her life. Only then had she fully realized his stubborn pride and the revenge he had taken on society by denying her Adam and buying her a title. And she had grasped the full depths of his mortification, how carefully he had planned every step of her education, from the day he discovered that his daughter was not being accepted—his merciless insistence that she learn to speak and write four languages fluently; the riding lessons, the tennis lessons, the dancing lessons, the endless walks through museums, the tiring sightseeing tours, the poems and maxims she had to be able to quote by heart, the petit-point embroidery with which he liked to see her busy herself on the evenings he read to her, haltingly, because he was not used to reading and many words were unfamiliar to him; the lists of wines and liqueurs they had studied together, the menus he would collect from famous restaurants for reference. . . . And she had misunderstood it all for fatherly interest, and been amused and touched that in his old age he should acquire an education after doing without it all his life.

"The art of living," Fleury told her one evening when she had found it particularly difficult to smile, "consists of one's ability to make the best of given circumstances. You must learn to develop it."

"It is a talent I do not possess."

"A talent? Not at all—a point of view. Bungle its practical application and you have bungled your life."

When she had insisted on leaving for France with a Red Cross outfit, he guessed that she was not just being patriotic; still he had pretended admiration and respect for her decision. Only on the morning of her departure, on deck of the troopship, he had said suddenly, "May I ask what became of the boy you were in love with before we met?"

He was referring to Adam; as she found out from Henri, her father had talked quite frankly, as if Adam had been an item that had to be mentioned in a business transaction.

She had stared down at the railing, at the thousands of brown-clad soldiers coming aboard, in the hot, silent, foggy morning, under the direction of men in British Navy uniforms. "Yes. He's over there. And he doesn't know that my father lied to me."

"It is possible that you may run into him. You are very young, Emma, and you're hurt and disappointed. But I like to think I can trust you to respect the name you bear. Only, above everything else, make it a law unto yourself —never forget to be discreet."

She didn't need to turn around and gaze at the row of photographs showing Henri, Count de Fleury, swathed in lace for his christening, the fat baby that could have been anybody's baby on a bearskin rug. Did every family really own a rug like that, or did the photographer furnish it? Henri on a horse, at school, at confirmation, in uniform, in hunting dress, at the wheel of a car, in tails.

For her, somehow, he had always been in tails—possibly because he had to dress formally so often, but most likely because he was always so meticulously groomed that he gave the impression of having just bathed, been massaged, showered, discreetly perfumed and helped into his fitted underwear. Not once during her marriage had she seen him in rumpled clothes, or unshaved or without a buttonhole. He had been tall for a Frenchman, very slim, with a narrow, august face laced with decadence—like the canvas of a fine old picture, delicately cracked with age—with strangely elongated hands and very soft and softly brown hair. Dignity had oozed from him like the aroma of noble wine from a cork. He carried himself with the easy arrogance of breeding, so assured that he could afford to be humble. And humble he was, in all the fields of which he did not possess sufficient knowledge, according to his standards. But there were few branches in which he was not superior. By education he was a lawyer and historian, by intellect a scholar, a mathematician, a student of art and philosophy, with literature, music, ballistics and astronomy as hobbies, completely self-sufficient.

Miraculously, once she had conquered her shame at having been bartered, her humiliation at being made love to by Henri for the sake of eroticism alone—after she had learned to live with the knowledge of his clandestine affairs and to accept his rights as a European male, for whom marriage was a contract a wife had no right to violate—his company began to seem much more worth while than that of any other man. He taught her to find pleasure in learning, provided her with books he wanted her to read, and drew her patiently and generously into discussions. Soon, more and more self-assured by mere association, she took pride in being hostess to the most illustrious men and women of her time. Henri's appointments had taken him to many parts of the world, back to Europe after the First World War—and it had been fas-

cinating to restore the ruined castle where he was born
and which France now claimed as a national monument
—to the Far East, the Balkans, Central Europe and,
finally, to London. And everywhere Emma had been a
success. Jack Starr's daughter, who had not been accepta-
ble as a child, was now besieged with requests to receive
her former schoolmates. As always, Jack Starr had succeeded in what he had undertaken.

Emma must have been about thirty when one night, in
Berlin, after a long and strenuous dinner at the Chan-
cellery, she and Henri were walking the dogs along the
edge of the Tiergarten, and he said, "The successful
ones have always been the life buoys of the average man."
She had not listened to the end of his sentence because
her glance, following the dogs running free, had fallen
suddenly on a park bench where a boy and girl sat kissing
in the light of a street lantern, oblivious to the gnats
dancing about them.

"You know, Henri, I have never had a lover."

And for a moment he had digressed from his pessimistic
calculations about the threat of Hitler's rise to power, and
looked at her. "I didn't think you would."

They had walked on silently and she took it for
granted that he had dismissed her statement, but then he
had added, "I could not let you commit yourself while
you were still a child, with no sense of values. But now
you are grown up. The choice is yours."

A few years later, he retired. He had always opposed
France's policy of maintaining peace at any price, and had
warned the government again and again to stop Hitler
while there was still time. But France had been backed up
by Great Britain, and in the end he resigned in protest.
They had stayed in London, and later Fleury put himself
at the disposal of General de Gaulle. At the height of the
blitz, he had been badly hurt when he was buried in

the cellar of a bombed house, and had never quite regained his old vigor or his immense capacity for work. For a time, he acted as an adviser to the heads of his country, and then he had withdrawn to his castle on the Loire. He had died an easy death, without fear, without struggle, without pain. "Don't cry, Emma. I've been very lucky. I regret very little, least of all the bargain I made with your father. I was ambitious then and needed money desperately. You have made me more comfortable than I had any right to expect. You have been a superb wife, and I want to thank you from the bottom of my heart for everything you did—and didn't do. No, don't tell me you loved me. There is no greater self-deception than to imagine oneself loved. But you have appreciated me, and for over forty years have given me proof that you did. What more could I have asked for?"

And that, thought Emma, is the story of my childhood, of my marriage . . . my father, my husband . . . the two men who molded me. That was quite normal, wasn't it? She had let herself be molded, like most young girls of her time. She had never rebelled. Would she have rebelled if her father had not lied to her about Adam? If her father had not intercepted his letter, would she have run away with Adam? And become a different person? Had she always been so passive? Had that first devastating disappointment, the thought that Adam had deceived her, killed all her initiative?

She stood in front of the open window shivering. A slight wind had sprung up and it played with the waves which, topped as if by spun sugar, licked at the beach. It blew the scent of dewy flowers and gently stirring trees into the house. My childhood, my marriage . . . my life, she thought. And now it is over. In a few months it will be over.

She fled from the room, forgetting to close the window,

and the door fell shut behind her with a great hollow bang. She ran down the staircase, past the huge, uncurtained window where otherwise she never failed to linger, if only for a fleeting second. "And it has been a good life," she said aloud. "A good life." On every stair, louder and louder, "A good life." All the wonderful places she had been to, all the people she had met, all the beautiful things they had been able to surround themselves with. No real worries. No sickness. Anyway, never anything serious. One great disappointment—no child.

The oval entrance hall was brilliantly lit, but now the niches with their twelve figures reminded her of the Escorial, the burial place of the Spanish kings. The last time she had seen it, gone down the narrow, slippery marble stairs into the rotunda, there had been a coffin missing. . . . She could call Jacques. How late was it? As if that mattered. He would come at once. Why hadn't he come anyhow, even though she had said no? After all, he was a doctor and should know how she felt. Scott. She could call Scott. But Scott would be drunk by now. And at last she knew why he drank so much. To steal . . . to rob a dead soldier . . . She opened the door to the living room. "Meg?" But of course Meg was not there. Hadn't she asked Hannah to tell Meg and Titus they were on their own? Titus, though, might be around. He and Meg did not like each other particularly. What was it the girl called him? An intellectual gigolo. And Titus called Meg a puppy in heat. She saw the floodlight still burning outside. So both of them were out. She opened the front door. To her left she could see the garage with its door up, like a huge jaw with the teeth missing. For the little Citroën and the Mercedes were gone. But her Cadillac had not been touched. She could take it, drive up to Monte Carlo and back over the Corniche. As she hurried toward the open garage she almost stumbled over the hem of her dressing gown. She had forgotten completely that she was not dressed.

She turned back, walking slowly now, listening to the pebbles scraping against each other under her feet, tiny bits of white gravel being shifted at will by her steps. High above her, under the floodlight, night bugs tumbled drunkenly. Panic . . . Did I panic, she asked herself, as they are panicking in their fight against the light they know must kill them? Watching their desperate efforts to escape death made her feel one with them and heightened her terror. She rushed toward the path that led across a piece of lawn to the beach. But the grass, lit by the brilliant light of the big lamp, had lost its soothing quality and glittered, an evil green, like the eyes of animals whose shape one cannot see. Beyond it the rocks rose, throwing their shadows against the lighter dark of the night, tearing it to shreds with their sharp edges. Below them the sand looked like black lava that the sea had suddenly spat up while its waters flowed, an even deeper black, toward the horizon, as if to swallow it up again. No . . . not yet, not yet. She still had six months to look forward to, six months of being alive. The woman in the washroom—perhaps she was right. Never give up hope. Doctors didn't know everything. Science might invent . . . But it was hopeless. There had been tears in Jacques' eyes.

Back inside the house, Emma went into the library, poured herself a drink from the tray set out on the round red-leather-topped table, tossed it down, then filled her glass again and went upstairs, slowly now, and as she took stair by stair, careful not to trip over the hem of her long gown or to spill her drink, walking erectly, she could hear the wood expand and contract under her feet, and she said, "It has been a good life." But has it? the wood seemed to answer back. Has it? Has it really?

In front of her bedroom, she stopped, hesitating to enter

the loneliness of the room. Here she would be alone not only with herself but with her body. How humiliating that fear should be permitted to influence so small a decision as the turning of a doorknob.

She sat down in front of her dressing table, a large mirror with two broad shelves like wings on either side, which, just like a bird's, could be folded back. She let her gown slip from her shoulders, hesitated, then took off her nightgown and stared at her body, naked now, in the mirror. How healthy it looked, how young, how attractive still. She had always been proud of it. And she had felt so secure within it, in its perfection and muscularity, its almost tireless capacities. Yet it had betrayed her. It had let in a monster that was creeping up on her like an enemy stalking its prey. And she hated it for having given her no warning. Leukemia. A normal cold, a little wound on her gums that would not heal, a nosebleed—who would ever have paid attention to such symptoms? But Jacques had. A routine check-up, her throat . . . "Say 'ah' again," and the spatula pressing down her tongue until she coughed. "I'd like to check that again." And when it had not healed, a blood test. And a pathologist in some laboratory . . .

The woman in the mirror was crying. Tears of anger, of helplessness and self-pity. Emma reached for her nightgown, pulled it over her head, buttoned her robe up to her neck, button by button. Had she learned nothing from Henri? Did she still not know how to accept facts? "Try to make the best of circumstances as they are, try to master the art of living." But she had not understood that what he really meant was living as a preparation for dying gracefully and at peace with oneself.

But she was at peace with herself. There was nothing for which she had to reproach herself. She had been a good daughter and a good wife. She had done her duty always, and she had done it gracefully. She had never given in to temptation. She had never hurt anyone consciously. All of us have to face death, she told herself. Why, when I have had so much, am I suddenly so greedy for life? Dignity, she thought. God, give me dignity.

When Emma woke up the next morning, she awoke to one of those incredible and precious moments in which only the body comes to life but the mind is still suspended, without past or future, in a present innocent of memory. She opened her eyes and saw the day waiting outside the draperies. A deep, silky blue at night, they were changed now by the light into a transparent aquamarine. She saw the sun filtering through them, throwing odd designs on ceiling and walls, and watched them change their form as the wind from the sea tugged at the curtains. She reached out a hand to press the bell before she remembered. And the sudden impact of reality made her slide between the covers, instinctively looking for shelter.

For a few minutes she clung to the little jade pear in which the bell was set. Then, regaining courage, she decided that none of the time that was still hers must be wasted. How she would act in four or six months was to be no concern of hers now. That would come later. Now she had to learn to look upon her surroundings, the people and the landscape—as she had looked upon the foreign countries Fleury's assignments had taken her to—as something transient; deeply conscious but not frightened at the prospect that the day would come when she would leave the men and women who had become her friends, the houses she had made her own, imbued with her personality, the flower beds she had watered, the animals she had cared for, the cities she had explored, the food to which she had adjusted her palate, the whole atmosphere of a foreign land. But parting, even when she had known from the beginning that it was inevitable, had never been easy. Always during the last weeks of her stay she had been haunted by the feeling that she had overlooked one thing or another that would make recall more easy, more precious and poignant. Then she had pretended to herself that she had just arrived, so that everything familiar might once more be strangely beautiful and impressive, and she had set out on trips that, up to then, she had never found the opportunity to take. Perhaps this was the way to face the final departure. She pressed the bell.

Almost at once—or so the few minutes it took to boil water seemed to Emma—Hannah came in with a tray on which a teapot stood in a little lined basket next to a cup. She was holding the morning paper folded under her arm and let it drop into Emma's lap with impressive precision before putting the tray down on the bed table.

"Madame slept well, I hope? It's a fine day. Eighty-five in the shade, with a tiny breeze. The water is just a bit over seventy." She poured the tea, adjusted the pillows behind Emma's head and, despite her heavy weight, went nearly noiselessly to draw open the curtains. Emma, watching her every move, thought, Nothing has changed. Nothing will. Half a year from now Hannah, with the same loyalty, will be carrying a breakfast tray in another house, to some other woman, will straighten her bed, open the windows and I will be just a cipher. Madame No. 11 or No. 23 . . . God knows how many positions Hannah has held. Unless I leave her a sum she can retire on. Which I may do . . . She closed her eyes. Why not, if it was that easy to insure herself remembrance? But did she particularly care to be remembered by Hannah?

"The masseuse will be here at five o'clock sharp, and Cook would like to see Madame. I put out the white slacks and the white top and the linen jacket, or would Madame rather—"

"No, that's fine. Thank you." Emma was lifting the cup to her lips when she heard the crunch of a car on the graveled driveway below. "Is that Mrs. Webster?"

"Mrs. Webster? Madame, it is only seven o'clock. Your usual time."

Somehow it pleased Emma that she should have awakened just as on every other morning, at her accustomed hour, as if there had not been a night of fear. What a comforting thing habit was, the discipline of habit. Something one could rely on. But who, at this hour, would dare disturb the peace of the morning by driving a car up to the house? Thiolat? If he should take it into his head to visit her without being called, and at such an unusual hour, just because he thought she might be in need of him, he would set everybody in the Villa du Cygne wondering. And this could not be allowed. Emma frowned. "Who is it, Hannah?"

Hannah, she could see, merely pretended to glance out the window. She knew who it was, yet she was hesitating to answer.

"Well?"

Hannah turned. She had obviously come to a decision. Her face was set and she folded her hands tensely in front of her, the way she always did when she had something she wanted to get off her chest, as if gripping her fingers gave her more assurance.

"Miss Meg," she said. "I would have spoken to Madame about it anyhow. I've warned her. But the young people of today—they simply won't listen. For over a week now, Miss Meg has come home when the sun was already up. But never as late as this." She fell silent, listening to the cautious footsteps in the corridor.

"Do you know where's she's been and with whom?" Emma found herself wanting to ask, and stopped. She had always avoided saying or asking anything that might establish intimacy with a servant, nor did she want more knowledge of her guests than they might expect her to have. Meg, though, could not exactly be called a guest to whom Emma owed this kind of courtesy. She was a grandniece, and a child at that.

"Please ask her to come in."

"Now? Madame has not even—"

"Now," said Emma. Yes, now. Anything that would take her mind off herself, that would keep her thoughts busy with other people's affairs, tiresome as they might be, should happen now. Besides, at this point even Meg was part of the foreign land in which Emma might have missed something worth experiencing.

The young girl who entered was dressed according to the mode currently favored by young people—black stockings reaching just to the knee, black shorts, a heavy knit sweater of coarse wool, a purple scarf tying back her hair, but somehow she looked wrong in this costume. Anyhow, Emma had expected her in an evening gown. Meg's face in no way showed that she had not slept all night. Perhaps the tiny shadows around her eyes were an indication, but then all girls her age used eyeshadow. Otherwise she looked radiant, even prettier than usual without powder and lipstick. Oh, to be eighteen again, to have been up all night and think nothing of going to bed now and sleeping as long as one wanted, late into the afternoon, all day, as if time were nothing that had to be measured.

"So Hannah spilled the beans."

"Good morning, Meg," said Emma, smiling at the defiant tone, smiling at the girl leaning against the door (still holding in her left hand the shoes she had taken off to steal by unnoticed), but smiling, too, because she had learned a long time ago that no reprimand was more successful than pretending that none was needed.

"Good morning," said Meg, but she didn't move.

She looks like an apple, thought Emma, a Golden Delicious bred to perfection, to uniformity, like all American girls her age, tempting to a taste that cherishes conformity for its security. They all seem to be the same size, to have the same color hair, the same cut of clothes, the same makeup, the same way of speaking, of moving, of laughing. Did we? Of course we did. Perhaps they're different when their anger is roused. They don't take authority for granted as we did.

"Won't you sit down?"

"Oh, don't make such a thing of it, Aunt Emily. So I've been out every night. So I didn't ask your permission. I know what you're going to say, and if you want to tell my parents there's nothing I can do about it. And if you want to send me home—"

She stopped suddenly, her lips parted as if she wanted to add something, then she compressed them into a thin, sullen line.

"But you don't want me to send you home, do you?" said Emma. Then she added, "You wouldn't like to miss the ball, would you?"

"What ball?"

When had she planned the ball? During the night. At some moment or other in her desperation she had considered possibilities that would give her a chance to live on in the memory of all those who had known her— flawlessly, the epitome of the picture she had been at great pains to paint for them all her life. Now, in broad daylight, the ball did seem to be the answer, a truly grand affair about which everybody would talk for years to come. Remember that August on the Riviera? The ball on

Cap Ferrat, at the Villa du Cygne? She died shortly after that. Yes, who would have imagined it? The way she looked and laughed and danced . . . so young . . . What happened? She went away, didn't she? On a trip and, suddenly, she died. Heart? Yes. Of a heart attack. And that's the way it's going to be, Emma decided. Nobody but Thiolat would know the truth. A heart attack. Leukemia was something that aroused pity and terror. She wanted neither. She would give the ball, and shortly after that she would go away. On a trip or a cruise, or maybe just to some small town where nobody knew her.

"Yes, a ball," said Emma. "End of August." That would leave nine weeks for the preparations, sending out the invitations and arranging everything. Everybody would accept save those, perhaps, who were not in Europe and the few who couldn't afford the trip for such a celebration. For them she would enclose a ticket with the stiff white embossed invitation. And by the end of August those terrible people would be gone who nowadays descended like a plague of locusts everywhere during the summer, traveling in old jalopies, on motor bikes and on foot, carrying tents and canoes on top of their cars, and radios that blared all the time, bringing their families, babies and grandparents, and cooking utensils, respecting neither peace nor beauty, not even private property if a place suited them for a camping site.

"Everybody will be there," said Emma. "Everybody who is somebody, although each one may cherish a different god. Some diplomats—I might even ask a few Russians from the embassies in Paris and London. And a few scientists. I think I shall ask some actors and actresses, to give the society clique something new to look at. They're so bored with each other. A sprinkling of royalty for old times' sake and some new millionaires to give the present its due. The usual crowd of writers, directors, and painters, the black sheep of families who have made good or have simply had to learn to make money. And a few of the real artists of our time. Business people? I think so. It's all become so interlinked in the last years. The tribes have been forced to meet and forget the differences of class and profession, at least while they watch the various war dances. And my friends, of course. You wouldn't like to miss it, Meg," said Emma, and pointed to a chair.

But Meg chose to plunk herself down on the foot of Emma's large bed. She still looked sullen, but with the sullenness of fear now. "Haven't you ever been young, Aunt Emily?"

"It's because I've been young that I want to talk to you."

Emma watched Meg throw a glance of resignation and boredom ceilingward, and she stretched out her hand to this child whom she had invited to spend the summer with her, for no other reason, really—though the Browns had tried to suggest that it was her duty to her mother's family—than that it didn't make any difference whether Margaret Brown was in the house or not. "My daughter is spending the summer with the Countess de Fleury—yes, her aunt—on Cap Ferrat." It would have seemed so small not to give them the chance to brag about it. But how could she expect Meg to see her clearly when neither had made the slightest effort to get to know the other? To Meg she must be just an old aunt to whom she had been boarded out because it would be not only socially advantageous but cheap as well.

"You know," she said, "you should have taken along a bathing suit on your nightly excursions. Then you could have changed in the car and nobody would have been absolutely certain if you hadn't just come home from an early swim." (The doll. "You should have provided a doll," her father had said.) Emma shook her head. Suddenly it was she who knew how to be devious, and she saw Meg's lips break into a smile.

The smile made Emma feel as if all of a sudden there wasn't much difference in their ages—only a couple of years, which allowed her to give advice to a younger girl. She had never really had a girl for a friend. She had been sent to so many different schools and the time had always been too short to establish intimacy between herself and her classmates. "Also," she said, "your timing is stupid. What does an hour more or less matter as long as you don't have to put in an appearance at breakfast? If I'd been you, I'd have slept on the beach rolled up in a blanket, and then, around eight or nine, I'd have strolled into the house quite openly, possibly singing at the top of my lungs—anyhow, loud enough so that nobody would suspect I had anything to hide."

"But I bet you never did anything on the sly."

Oh yes, I did, Emma almost said. Oh, yes. There was a time when I knew all the tricks. And I never relied on servants for help or secrecy. I never trusted people who had less than I not to betray me for a gratuity. I taught myself to climb down from the first floor and, believe me, in the beginning that wall seemed like the peak of the Matterhorn. I would have made a fine mountain climber by the time it was all over. And I learned to get through the garden without anyone hearing me—noiselessly, like a soldier on reconnaissance. The iron fence was easy because Adam rushed from the shadows the moment he heard me whistle, and would reach his hands through the bars to make steps for me. He was so strong he could hold me on one hand, like a trapeze artist, while he moved the other a little higher. So I hurdled the fence, and on the other side he would lift me down and hold me in his arms.

"I'm sure you never did anything on the sly," Meg repeated, looking at her narrowly and helping herself, without asking, to a cigarette.

"No, I never did," said Emma, "because when I was your age I was already married." And she took the little gold container, which Meg was still holding, and lighted a cigarette, too. "I was married before I was eighteen."

"And you married him because you loved him?"

Because I believed he loved me, thought Emma. Strange that after all these years that winter she had met Fleury could be recalled suddenly with every variation of its emotions, as if no lifetime spent as his wife lay between the girl she had been then and the woman she had become. She could feel again the fury with which she had sworn to hide her defeat after the first stupor of her disappointment over Adam. "I'll show you . . . I'll show you that I can live without you . . . I won't die of a broken heart." And off she had gone to parties, to dances, to the theater, reacting outwardly exactly as her father had foreseen. Actually she had been lost and hopelessly insecure. There was nothing with which she could identify herself except the fool she thought Adam had made of her. Doubting her reactions to the people she met, her judgment and her own worth, she had been surprised and pleased by Fleury's attentions. It was reassuring to be singled out by a man of his stature, a man older and wiser than Adam. His position, his title, his manners of a man of the world had impressed her. His courtship had given her back her self-respect. Here was not only somebody who loved her but a man who was held in esteem by everybody. And she had begun to love him in return, until that night . . . that night in Florence when she found out that he had married her for her money.

"You loved him, didn't you?" asked Meg. "Didn't you?"

"Yes, I loved my husband," said Emma, and she looked

at Meg's black-stockinged legs, long, slender and muscular, like two twin snakes curled on her white blanket. Love? There were so many kinds of love, and what she had felt for Adam she had never been able to feel for Henri or for anyone else.

"You were lucky," Meg told her, and she moved so abruptly, shifting her body into a more comfortable position, that Emma could feel the mattress bounce. "I don't love him."

"Love whom?"

"The boy my parents have picked out for me."

"I didn't know you were engaged."

"I'm not. Not really. But it's taken for granted that I'll marry Harold."

"I thought you were all set to go to college—Radcliffe, isn't it?"

Now Emma was interested. She smiled at the girl lying full length across the lower end of the bed, but there was no answering smile, just a resigned shrug. "Not Radcliffe. Simmons. My marks aren't very good. I don't care. I'm not really interested in anything particular, I mean, like those girls who want a career or have a vocation. I guess Dad figures he might as well save the expense since Harold is so hipped on an early wedding."

"But that's nonsense. Your father is a rich man."

"Oh, Aunt Emily," cried Meg in mock despair. "Don't you know greedy people when you see them? Money, money, money. Sure he has enough but that's no reason not to want more. Well, I guess the real reason is that he's afraid Harold will slip through his fingers if he has to wait for me to finish a college education. Harold has all the chances in the world—politically, I mean. And how handy that's going to come in. You know—they play golf together, sit around, slap each other on the back. . . . And what little odds and ends of information can't be dropped sinking a putt or over a drink. And Harold wouldn't even be committing an indiscretion. After all, it'd all be in the family."

Little Meg. Little Golden Delicious. She certainly wasn't a daughter who trusted her father implicitly. Emma tried to remember Meg's parents, Helen and William Brown. Such good, solid names. But she had forgotten what they looked like—handsome, no doubt, judging by their daughter, well groomed and undistinguished. And they would have to be invited to the ball.

"And your mother? Why does she . . ."

"Mom? Oh, she's worse than Dad. She thinks Harold's Presidential timber." Meg snorted and shook her head like a Shetland pony impatient with the cruel hands of its young rider. "But let me tell you, he's a bore. He wears his hair in a long mane. . . ."

"I'd say that's in his favor," said Emma. "I'd hate to be young right now and have to stroke a crew cut."

"I don't know," said Meg, "as you'd have much chance to be tender. You don't start at the head nowadays, you know." She blushed, but only because she had suddenly grown aware of whom she was talking to. Then she shrugged again. "Actually," she said, "I haven't gone the whole way with any of the boys, like most of my friends. Necking, sure, but I'm what you call romantic, or a sissy, sappy, or just plain old-fashioned. I want to love and be loved in return."

And I thought you were living for sensation, thought Emma, watching Meg bounce on the bed in her excitement. Graduation, college, engagement, wedding, the first child, maybe even the first divorce—all the milestones on the road of an ordinary American woman's life, lived for the highlights, not for the subtler things that mattered, the in-between things that got you from station to station and, in the end, made you. The tears you suppressed, the fears you conquered or gave in to, the smile you forced for someone else's sake, the letter you never sent, the lonely walks through wind-swept streets, the lies you told against your better judgment and the truths you withheld.

"You're not very modest," she said. "Don't you know you're asking for heaven on earth?"

"And why not? I don't think it's such a big order," said Meg. "You had it. Others have. If a hydrogen bomb falls tomorrow I want at least to know what it feels like to have loved with all my heart. I want to love. I—I—" and she hammered her fists together for greater emphasis. It sounded as if she were applauding her own determination. "And I simply can't love Harold. I can't love him just because his family has been something or other in Washington for generations, or because he's regular. Ugh! How I hate that expression. He's a bore, a bore, a bore! He always says the right thing and he's a good boy who loves his mother and remembers all the names he should remember and can recite *Who's Who* backward in less time than it would take you to look up a name and I always know what he's going to say. I sit there like the man in the hotel room, waiting for the other shoe to drop. And my hands get clammy and my skin starts itching all over."

She looked at her palms as if she expected to find them sweaty, yet she didn't give Emma a chance to say anything. Apparently she had never before told anyone in such strong terms how she felt, and was unconsciously aware of the fact that if she didn't make a clean breast of it now, she never would. "Once, to test him, I said, 'Let's elope, H.' Everybody calls him H. 'Let's elope,' I said. 'Today. This afternoon. Now.' And do you know what he said? 'Darling,' he said, 'there's nothing I'd like better, but we mustn't be selfish. We must think of what it would do to those who love us, your parents, my mother. Don't you see how cruel . . . ?' "

In spite of herself, Emma could not help smiling. The child gave such a perfect imitation of the scene that she could see the stodgy young man's horror over the proposed act of impulse, but Meg was almost in tears. "See what I mean? He's a stick. But then, he isn't exactly young."

"How old is he?"

"Same age as Bill. Twenty-eight. That's how we met. I mean, my brother brought him home one night. They roomed together at Harvard."

Twenty-eight. What an idol this generation made of youth.

"And why does he love you?"

"Because his mother told him I was the girl to love." Meg took another cigarette, but this time she offered Emma one and held a match for her before she went on. "Daddy's money is nothing to be sneered at. It would come in handy for campaigning. And Dad's being a banker would sort of guarantee that his son-in-law isn't subversive or in favor of giving good American money to foreign countries."

Emma watched the young mouth speaking the words with such surprising ease, surprising because it lacked all trace of bitterness or criticism. But then perhaps each generation had its own mysterious way of accepting certain conceptions and protesting others.

"And are you going to marry this Harold?"

"No," said Meg. "Not if I can help it. Oh, don't send me home, Aunt Emily. You don't know how difficult it was to get here in the first place. I was the one who dreamed up this idea of your inviting me. One evening we were cleaning out a desk and there was a picture of you and

this beautiful house, and it came to me, just like that
. . . ." Meg snapped her fingers. "Everybody was going
to Europe, all my friends, but me. I was supposed to
spend the summer on the Cape with Harold and his people. As mother pointed out, I was lucky to have somebody who loved me true. . . . Well, I simply had to get
away. Please don't send me back."

"And with whom have you been out these nights?"

It was highly unfair to ask that question at this point.
Emma was well aware of it. Of course she could justify
her curiosity by telling herself that, after all, Meg was in
her charge, her responsibility, but she wasn't looking for
vindication. She wasn't hypocritical enough for that and
she had never been self-righteous. She knew this was the
psychological moment, and she used it. But though she
had taken trouble to keep her voice casual and soft, Meg
was immediately alerted to danger. For a minute or so she
looked confused, as if she couldn't believe that she had let
herself be trapped. Then she blew one perfect ring of
smoke after another, following each of them with her
eyes, as if her life depended on their perfection. Emma
watched the smoke float from the girl's pale lips, solidify
miraculously, rise into the air, gradually lose its shape,
lengthen into an almost straight line and dissolve without
leaving a trace. Earth to earth, thought Emma, dust to
dust, nothing to nothing. She was almost startled to hear
Meg speak.

"He's nobody, Aunt Emily. Just a young man who
wants to make good. No background, no money. But he's
different from anybody I've ever known. And he makes
the whole world seem somehow different. Brighter. As if
the sun were shining all the time. With him I feel—well
—alive."

All her worldliness, her objectivity and intelligence fell
from Emma, as a dress, stored too long, falls apart when

you lift it from what you thought was a safe place. She was seventeen again, younger than Meg, not practical, not critical, and therefore a thousand times more vulnerable. There was a contraption standing in front of the garage Jack Starr's chauffeur frequented, four wheels with a sled bench fastened on them, with a motor in front that wasn't covered, like one of those watches in which you can see the little wheels turning time forward tirelessly, and a tall boy in overalls was tinkering with it.

Emma had got out of her father's car. "Does it work?"

"You bet," he said. "Want to go for a ride?"

She had shaken her head and he had shrugged, as though shrugging off an insult. "Well, of course it isn't a Pierce-Arrow." He had almost turned away, but then he caught her glance at the chauffeur and grinned. Two days later she had found an opportunity to leave the house unobserved.

His name was Adam Forbes. He came from a small farm, but no farmwork for him. Ever since he had first been taken for a ride in old Dr. Bell's car, the Brush runabout the country doctor had had the courage to buy, he had known what he wanted to do. He had run away from home after a big scene with his parents, who had wanted him to stay because they needed his help.

This was what interested her. What he had to say about motors she had smiled at politely, pretending an interest she did not feel, a little cross that he should talk on and on about spare parts, their price, and where he could get them cheapest. And off they had gone on trips that seemed to hold more adventure than all the journeys to Europe, to places she had never known existed. Junkyards—together they had climbed across the sharp-edged hills of scrap iron, looking for a carburetor, a discarded muffler, a generator. "If it's bust, I can fix it." On one of these treasure hunts he had asked her to marry him. Sit-

ting in what was left of a car, on a leather seat with the
stuffing coming out of it and half a rusty hard-top shel-
tering them, he had asked her to be his wife. "You
mustn't be afraid, Emily. Of course I can't offer you a
house like the one you live in, nor any of the things you're
used to. Not right now, that is." As if she had cared for
the luxuries with which she had grown up, as if she were
afraid of missing them. "No yachts, no servants, but one
day you'll be proud of my name, too. I'll be one of the
great inventors. There won't be a car that won't have a
four-wheel power brake. I'll make good, you'll see, I
promise you. I'll go on going to night school. . . ."

"You won't have to. My father will see to that."

"I don't want your father's money or his help. You'll
have to do it my way or not at all. No, I'm not stupid and
I'm not foolishly proud. I just want to run my own life.
And yours. That's the way I am. You'd better think it
over."

"Did you hear what I said, Aunt Emily?"

"Yes, I heard you," said Emma. "I heard every word of
what you said." She wanted to open her arms and draw
Meg to her heart, the same Meg who a little while ago
had meant nothing to her. From one minute to the other,
a kinship the girl was completely unaware of had been
established between them. A kinship of romanticism?
Yes, one could call it that. "You met him over here, didn't
you? You've only known him for a week?"

Meg nodded. "And I'm not sure that I love him. I think
I do. Of course my family would never accept him, but
why think of that now? All I want is a chance to find out
if he's really the guy I want. Give me that chance, Aunt
Emily. Don't send me away."

That Emma remained silent had nothing to do with
her decision. It was a silence that was completely removed
from the moment, a silence in which memory unfolds,

but Meg did not know this. "And don't worry for a moment, please," she said. "I was taught what it was all about in the sixth grade. They had models in plastic, life-sized. We had to draw them for better understanding. And my school wasn't even considered progressive. I know how to take care of myself."

"I'll give you the chance you want."

But Emma heard neither the girl's whispered thanks nor her leaving the room—only an echo of Meg's bravura, her toughness and childishness, lingered for a moment, then was drowned in Adam's laughter. They were standing in a subway station. Emma had never been in the subway, and every time a train thundered by she clung to Adam, as if afraid it would blow her from the narrow platform. It had amused Adam. "Never got to hold your hand that often before. If only I'd known, I'd have met you nowhere else." But then he had let her hand go and asked, "Now, do I look all right?" For he was on his way to his appointment with her father. And he had turned around for a last inspection, dressed in his best, the shirt he had ironed himself meticulous, the shoes as shiny as glazed chocolate, even wearing a hat, a brand-new fancy one, and his handkerchief folded in his breast pocket like the wing of a dove. Emma tried to regard him critically. He certainly looked different from the way she was used to seeing him look. She preferred him with his hair ruffled, with his shirt open at the front and in a suit that allowed his body more freedom of motion. But for her father that would never have done. For her father he looked just right, conventional, serious, a young man who had a solid future. "Perfect," she said. "And now don't forget that he's a very old man even if he doesn't like it. He's seventy-seven. And he's used to having his own way. So don't be touchy and get offended if he gets very personal."

"I know. I know. You told me all that before. Don't worry, my darling. I will be very polite."

"Tell him you'll have your engineering degree in no time, that you might work with the railroad, even if it's his. Don't tell him right away that cars are all you care about. And don't be so terribly proud."

"But what do I have to offer but my pride? My pride and my love for you."

"And if he tells you he'll keep you out of the war, don't flare up—"

He didn't let her finish. "But that's the whole point," he said. "That's why I'm asking him for your hand before I have my degree and a decent job. Because if we don't marry now, what time are we going to have together?" And then he had looked at her in a way that had made her feel almost faint with desire. "Let me handle it my way, Emily. Everything will turn out all right. Trust me. You must learn to trust me." And he had laughed again, gay, carefree laughter. She had never heard anyone else laugh like that. "After all, the only difference between Jack Starr and me is that he's made his millions, I haven't yet."

He had jumped on the train and she had never seen him again.

Lying in bed on the morning when she had to face the fact that she would die within a few months, it seemed suddenly extraordinary that in more than forty years she should have made no attempt to find out what had become of Adam. But of course that was not true. She had tried to reach Adam; she had written him a letter the moment she had found out what her father had done to them. But her letter had been returned with "Address Unknown" stamped across it twice. She had joined the Red Cross with the expectation that she would be sent overseas, not only to get away from Henri for a time until she could adjust herself to a kind of marriage she had not wanted, but also hoping vaguely that somehow, somewhere, she would come across Adam. It seemed too unjust to let him believe that she would not have met him that night and gone away with him if she had known the truth. And later? Later, thought Emma, and sighed. What good could possibly have come of trying to see him again? She was the wife of another man. But now?

Emma lay motionless. Adam. To see him again now. If he was still alive, if he could be found, her lawyer in America would find him, even if he had to engage the services of detective bureaus all over the world. Adam Forbes. Six feet two inches tall, with hair the color of ripened wheat and eyes as blue as violets, with a dimple in his right cheek. Tiny ears for a man his size, but perfectly shaped, like the ears of an animal, of a fox. A scar on his forehead, directly above his nose. When he was not tanned it didn't show, but in the summer it stood out, a long, thin white line from the root of his nose all the way up to his hairline. How had he got it? She couldn't remember. She would invite him to the ball. There was no doubt in her mind but that he would come. But she was held as in a vise by the many years in which she had not allowed herself to indulge in sentiment, when her need to love, her longing to give had been permitted to manifest itself only in the care of her flowers or the patting of a dog or the caressing of a horse, and during the inconspicuous hours spent in hospitals and orphanages. He'll be bald, she told herself, frail with age; perhaps he may have lost his laughter. And what could we possibly have to say to each other? This is sheer sentimentality, childish and silly. Don't spoil the picture you have of him. Let him live on as you see him now, young, handsome and strong. But what had he been beside that? Who had he been, he, the only man she had ever loved? Or had she perhaps never loved him, only been in love with love?

Her hand trembled as she reached for the telephone on her bedside table, but her voice was clear and steady, the voice of a young girl. "I'd like to put in a call to New York," she told the operator, and gave her the lawyer's number. "Try to get through as quickly as possible. And please be good enough to ring back and let me know when I can expect it."

PART
TWO

GEE, thought Meg, walking along the wide corridor toward her room, that sure was something! And she shuddered in retrospect over the danger of being sent home that she had just escaped. But then instead of entering her room she turned sharply and retraced her steps, past Emma's bedroom, to the top of the stairs. There she paused and listened. But the house was still quiet. Mrs. Webster had apparently not yet come, for Meg could hear no sound in the library and Titus seemed still to be asleep. Under her hand the wood of the railing felt like satin. She couldn't resist it. In an abundance of relief she straddled it, *shush-h-h,* and hopped off on the floor of the hall downstairs.

She went straight to the dining room and opened the door to the pantry. She could hear muted voices coming from the kitchen and nodded, satisfied. They were having coffee. All the rooms facing the sea had French windows that opened onto the terrace. Meg slipped through one that stood ajar. Hydrangeas formed a low, solid blue wall the whole length of the flagstones. Meg jumped it, scraping her leg against the balustrade. A big hole showed in the middle of her stocking over the knee, but the skin was hardly torn. She ran around the corner of the house. The graveled courtyard lay empty; still she did not dare cross it. Instead she made for the path leading between the rocks, down to the beach.

After a couple of yards, where she knew there were some rocks that were easy to climb, she doubled back and came out between the shelter of some fir trees that had been planted here as a windbreak. From there she scram-

bled down to the driveway and followed it until she
reached the point from which a path led to the back of
the garage. Thick dark-green ivy, so green that it looked
almost black, covered the entire wall, trailing along strong
wires up and around the dormer windows of the living
quarters. Meg bent and picked up some pebbles. Her aim
was perfect. They pelted against the glass like hail. But no
window opened. Meg tried again. Still no response. And
yet she was sure she had not heard Gino's voice among
those of the servants in the kitchen. She whistled, softly
at first, then louder. A window opened gently, almost
noiselessly, and Gino's horrified face appeared in the
frame.

"It's me," said Meg. "Give me a hand."

"Not here," whispered Gino. "Not here."

"Help me up."

"Sh!" He put a warning finger over his mouth. "Sh!"
and shook his head.

"Idiot!" said Meg. She grabbed a wire with each hand
and set a foot tentatively on a crosspiece.

"Not here, Margareta!" said Gino, again folding his
hands in a gesture of prayer. But Meg only laughed. "It's
easy. Like a ladder. Bless the gardener or whoever
thought this one up."

"Prego, Margareta!"

But she had almost made it. Her head was just below
his. "Don't you love me any more?"

Meg took tighter hold of the ivy-spun wires. She
could feel the vine break against the palms of her hands
and the bitter, acrid smell excited her as no smell had
ever excited her before. She leaned back as if she were
holding the ropes of a swing and swung back and forth.
"If they don't hold, I'll fall and break my neck and it'll
be your fault. Do you want me to fall? Do you, Gino?"

She swung again and a wire snapped with the sharp

noise of a report. The ivy shuddered and Gino grabbed her by the shoulders and pulled her up and across the window sill into his room. "But this is wrong, wrong," he kept saying. "This is very wrong."

Meg put her hand across his mouth to silence him, and now, instead of the sap of the ivy, she could feel his lips against her palm, alive and moist, and she began to tremble with delight. "Don't tell me you've never done anything wrong in your life."

"But *la contessa* . . ."

"She's quite something, the old girl. Listen—she knows that I've been out every night for a week and she calls me in and what does she do? Bawl me out? No. She tells me how to get away with it. I can't figure her out."

She laughed at Gino's surprised face, but was not quite sure if he had understood everything she had said or was merely astonished that *la contessa,* as he called Emma Starr Fleury, should have behaved in this most unexpected way.

"Did you tell her about us?" he asked, pointing first at her, then at himself, in an effort to make himself quite clear. "You and me?"

Meg giggled. "That would be asking too much. No, of course not. Just that I was in love with a young man who had no money."

"Then you must go," said Gino. "I don't want to cause scandal." Whenever he was excited his English got worse and his voice, so gentle and soft by nature, became loud and shrill. "And I do not want to lose job. I need job to save money. In a year I will have saved enough to be chauffeur no longer. Then you can come see me in my room. This not my room, this her room. You must go."

"I don't get you," said Meg. "You make love to me on the beach, on the rocks, in the woods, everywhere—why not here?"

"This different," Gino insisted, and he shook his head so violently that his black curls tumbled into his forehead, making him look even younger than he was. "Very different. Beach, rocks, wood belong to everybody, but room here, bed, kitchen, all hers."

But Meg had no understanding of this distinction. She sat down on the bed and looked about her with curiosity. In itself it was a quite ordinary room, square, with space enough to move around, a closet built into the wall, a small desk, two straight chairs and one more comfortable one with a chintz slipcover, a bed with a good lamp beside it, and a dresser with a mirror. To the left of the bed, behind a heavy curtain, she could hear a shower dripping, and to the right there was a little niche with a tiny stove and cooking utensils. Right next to the door a house telephone was fastened to the wall. What made it different from other simple rooms she knew was that a bowl of fruit, neatly arranged, stood on a table, and a stone crock filled with wild flowers on the floor. The wall alongside the bed was plastered with postcards and photographs.

"Please go," said Gino, looking at her beseechingly, his eyes filled with embarrassment.

"Listen," Meg told him, "you are not very wise. I thought you'd like a short cut on your road to fame. I'll have quite a bit of a dowry. Someday I'm going to inherit from the old girl. If I decide to marry you, I can make life a lot easier for you."

"I like money," said Gino, "I like short cuts, but I do not like *la contessa* to be mad at me. She has been very good to me. She engage me, take trouble with my papers, everything. I want her to be proud of me someday, come to my concerts and clap her hands and say that is my Gino, not have her cross, think I take advantage of her. Three years you stay, she say, three years you stay, then we see. She knows I play beautifully. She gets teacher for me, gives me time." He pointed to the violin case on one of the chairs. "She give it to me after my first year. Not really great but lots better than I can afford."

"Play for me," said Meg, leaning back against the wall and crossing her arms behind her head. Gino shook his head. "Not time now. Not when telephone can ring any moment."

"She hasn't even had breakfast yet," said Meg, counting the items of Emma's meal on her fingers as if to assure herself that it would take quite some time to eat them. "One glass of orange juice, two cups of coffee, one piece of toast and a hard-boiled egg. It never varies. Then she has Cook come up and talk over the week's menu with her. And then she goes into the library to work for an hour with Mrs. Webster on some papers my uncle left, which she thinks should be published, and after that she walks with her dogs and maybe Titus, for an hour. She won't bother us for two and a half hours at least."

"Please let me do my work, Margareta. I love you very much but I must do my work."

To Meg it was almost sensational that he should stand there, as far away as possible, determined not to touch her, when every other boy she knew would long since have kissed her, wouldn't have wasted even one of the many minutes Gino already had lost. And though she didn't understand his point of honor, she sensed an integrity that was challenging.

"That's your mother over there," she said, dropping her pursuit of his passion for a moment and pointing to one of the photographs. Gino smiled for the first time since she had fought her way into his room. "Yes. That big fat woman is my mother. All women big and strong in my family, all men like me."

Small and muscular and graceful as young jaguars, thought Meg, and she trembled again with pleasure. "And the priest?"

"My brother. He was raised in a seminary. But he is a good one. He doesn't drink his parishioners' wine or eat their bread."

"And this one?"

"Carlo. He is a bricklayer."

"And the one on skis?"

"Paolo. He is a guide. A mountain man."

"And the little girl?"

"My baby sister. The *bambina*. Sweet, oh, so sweet. *Bionda,* like you. A good girl. A very good girl."

"And these four here?"

"Dead. Not enough food during the war."

"And the house? The little one over there?"

"My home. I told you about. On top of a mountain, high over the Lago di Garda. All stone. And the chickens. See the chickens? They all have names. Brown little chickens, they come like birds when you whistle. And see the little boy? Riccardo, my oldest brother's first son. *Un angelo.*"

Leaning over her he took the photo from the wall, carefully loosening the thumbtacks so as not to spoil the snapshot. Meg took the picture from his hand gently, but instead of looking at it she let it slip to the floor, and as Gino bent to pick it up she lifted her hands and caught his head to her. "Gino."

He smelled like no boy she knew—of unripe olives, and the sea, and linen dried in the sun, and the saddle soap he used on the leather upholstery of Emma Starr Fleury's sports car, the white Mercedes. Once their lips met, neither of them knew any restraint. For a minute or so their only physical contact was their locked mouths. Except for this closeness they kept apart, in silent knowledge that they needed space to undress each other. Meg undid the buckle of his belt, which held up his white linen pants, while he unbuttoned the coarse wool of her sweater. Then, for a searing moment of separateness, each had to leave the other to strip off the last garments that prevented skin from touching skin, and their coming together, naked now, was like two flames that had been devouring the same log from opposite ends until they met and were united. "Be gentle," Meg whispered, falling back onto the bed. "Be gentle."

"Mine," the boy said. "You are mine. Say that you are mine. Mine alone. Forever and ever. *Amore mio . . .*"

She cried out once when his teeth pulled at her hair to make her move her head, then she knew no more pain and lay in deep silence, all of her surrendering to feeling, feeling him take possession of her.

Titus, of course, was too handsome. The quality of his beauty was almost embarrassing because it made other people aware of their own shortcomings. Everything about him was so perfect he never seemed quite real but, rather, like a sculpture of Phidias. His body: the shoulders broad, the torso proud, the hips narrow, the straight, strong long legs, the small wrists and ankles with the elongated fingers and toes—the shape of his face: square about the forehead, then tapering down from the cheekbones and ending in a marvelously proportioned chin—his nose: the bridge barely noticeable, then the nostrils flaring out over a beautifully drawn mouth—his hair: golden, as if cut from sunshine, like a helmet above his small, round head, of a quality that was not soft, not coarse, just ablaze with vitality. One looked at him as one would look at a statue; then realizing that he was human, one began to search for flaws with almost sadistic exigency and, finding none, fell victim to a feeling of

inferiority. Even the timbre of his voice was like music—
not loud but clear, soothing and exciting at the same time
—and his smile seemed to contain the kind of power that
could make an apple fall from a tree, should he have desired it, right into his hand. His beauty had always been
against him. People, much as they admire masterpieces,
prefer them dead.

Against him, thought Emma, and against her. She had
little doubt that everyone thought she let him escort her
so frequently only to prove that a thirty-year-old man of
such princely appearance preferred the company of an
elderly lady to that of a young girl, and that naturally,
therefore, he knew what side his bread was buttered on,
or he was homosexual, or both. Even if it had been true,
it wouldn't have bothered her. If necessary, she would
have paid him as she paid for any aesthetic pleasure. If
beauty was the only thing he had to sell to make a living,
it was worth just as much to her as what others had to
offer. And homosexuality as such had never disturbed her.

She had known him on and off for four or five years.
Sometimes she had had him as a weekend guest or for
longer, for Henri had enjoyed playing chess with Titus
and been amused by the nonchalance with which Titus
regarded life—always the observer, never taking part.
Then, after Henri's death, Titus had somehow understood how to make himself indispensable by calling her
every night to chat for twenty minutes or so—amusingly,
refreshingly, about whom he had seen, what he had done
and particularly what he had not done, what he had
heard or read—and by calling her every morning to find
out how she had slept, if there was anything he could do
for her, run an errand, drive her to her lawyer's, get tickets
for a play or a concert. It had seemed only natural to invite
him to spend the season at the Villa du Cygne. Once,
though, she had thought it necessary to mention in passing

that she would leave the art treasures she had inherited from her father to museums, and the bulk of her fortune to medical research and only small sums to distant relatives, and Titus had smiled his broken, arrogant smile.

"I have always considered it a terrible bore to have to take care of more money than I need, and what I need I have," he had said. "Also I would find it rather strenuous to have to comply with the duties of a legacy hunter. I didn't even accept the proposals of several young heiresses because I cannot see any reason why I should put myself out in any way. And since when, if I may be so impertinent as to ask, do you place so little value on your company?"

That had settled it. Emma knew that he could have married almost anyone he wanted. He was of good Pennsylvania family, way back of Dutch origin. His manners were enchanting, and he could do many things with style—sail a boat, play golf and tennis, ride and shoot and fish, even fix an electric wire or an aerial, and he enjoyed odd jobs like chopping wood or repairing furniture. But what he called having "enough money" would always remain a secret, for his income, left him by a stepfather, was so small, her guess would have been that he spent it all on his tailor. And on his car. Otherwise there certainly was no need for him to spend it, like ordinary human beings, on food or rent. He was constantly turning down the most incredible invitations. The people he knew seemed only too glad to pay his traveling expenses, or lend him a villa or an apartment complete with servants and a well-stocked wine cellar. Once in a while, though, he would settle down to work—illustrating a book that was being privately printed or being done in a limited edition, strange, decadent illustrations—or he would paint a portrait for an absurdly high fee. "To tip the servants." He was a first-class draftsman and could imitate almost any style, sometimes mixing the techniques, the old with the new, so that the result achieved was always attractive and at times quite original.

"Would you do me a favor?" he said now, as Emma came out of the library where she had been working on Henri de Fleury's memoirs for almost two hours. "Invite her to come for a swim with us and stay for lunch." And he pointed with his chin toward the library.

"Mrs. Webster? Why, of course," said Emma. "Didn't I ever ask her to join us on the beach?"

"She's only been working for you for the last ten days," said Titus, "and you usually like a three-week trial period before social amenities."

Only ten days? It seemed much longer since she had begun the final editing of Henri's notes, but then, since yesterday, time had become irrelevant, the faraway past had moved unexpectedly close, become more vital, more real than what had happened only a little while ago, and the future loomed ahead like an impenetrable jungle in which she would have to cut her way through dense forests, cross rivers, conquer sudden rapids, with only the ball as a main base to be reached nine weeks from now. "Do tell her she is very welcome."

"If I tell her, she won't accept. She's too well brought up, unfortunately, not to take advantage of manners. You see, she's trying to avoid me."

Emma took this as a joke, but she stuck her head into the library once more and extended the invitation. Then she whistled for the dogs, two large brown poodles that came rushing from the hall, where they liked to lie on the cool marble floor watching the hidden doors between the niches.

"May I walk with you?" asked Titus, following her onto the terrace with the wide-brimmed straw hat she had forgotten.

"Why not?"

"Because you look absent-minded. Also I noticed that your light was burning on and off all night."

For just one moment then, walking beside Titus along the beach, she debated if she should not make him her confidant. He was discreet—if not by nature, then by necessity. No one could have been borne through life so successfully if he couldn't be trusted. And he was not personally concerned. If she should feel the need to talk about herself, Titus, unlike Thiolat, would not choose his words cautiously, nor could she hurt him. She could almost hear him saying, "How charming to think of you as a ghost, teasing the Philistines. For, you know, I do believe in ghosts. I can't quite see you as a white lady frightening tourists in your castle on the Loire. I'd rather imagine you upsetting teacups and blowing out matches and spilling red wine on particularly valuable lace, opening zippers that should be closed and closing doors that should be open." Emma smiled. Yes, Titus would make fun of death as he made fun of everything that was unavoidable, but she decided against taking him into her confidence, and said simply, "No. I didn't have a good night."

"Nor did I. We went to the casino and, believe it or not, she'd never set foot in a gambling place before. She thinks they're highly immoral and would have all such places outlawed, and she made me stop just when I was in a lucky run." He dug his hand into his pocket and produced a number of large chips.

"That's silly," said Emma, who liked to try her luck at baccarat or roulette. Then, thinking of Titus's finances, she added, "Well, maybe it was wise. But who—if I am not being indiscreet—has the power to stop you from doing anything you like?"

"Mrs. Webster," said Titus, and threw a large red chip into the air as if it were a ball.

Emma slowed her steps. "Mrs. Webster?"

"The young lady you engaged to help you with your husband's papers," said Titus. "Why do you look so surprised?"

Because I've never really looked at her, thought Emma. And there she has been, working right along with me every day. All she could remember was that Mrs. Webster was an agreeable, clean-smelling young woman who had seemed the most efficient and sympathetic of all the applicants answering her advertisement for a part-time secretary with a fluent knowledge of English and French. She was equally surprised that this young person, who was an anonymity to her, should have been able to assert her will on Titus.

"You guessed it," said Titus, still playing with the red chip, but gently now, tossing it only a few inches from his palm, tossing and catching it as they talked. "She is the most desirable, lovely creature I have ever laid eyes on, which is, of course, entirely my point of view. And as you know, I am not easily what is generally called 'in love.' " He frowned because he could not find a less trite expression to describe his feelings.

"I can't recall—at least not since I've known you—that you ever were."

"And you are quite right," said Titus. "But if you remember, I confessed to you one night when the moon was high and the nightingales were singing that the only woman I ever really loved was my mother. And when she died, for years I measured every girl I met against her, knowing quite well that none of them could be so wonderful. And when I got over doing that, I started to see all girls the way my mother would have seen them, through her eyes, which made them even more impossible. And when I outgrew that phase, I just didn't seem to care what they were like. Suddenly they were just girls to have fun with, with no deeper meaning."

Yes, sitting next to her in the garden on the Loire, with the scent of lilacs and peonies wafting through the evening air, he had told her that his father had committed suicide after the Stock Exchange crash in 1929, leaving his wife and infant son without means, at the mercy of the luckier branch of the Vandendam family, who hadn't felt like doing a thing for their less fortunate relatives. And his mother had slaved to bring up her son until her strength had given out and she married one of her wealthy suitors. She had died of an overdose of barbiturates; anyway, that had been the official cause given. Titus had always been convinced that she had tired of living with a man she didn't love and had chosen this form of escape the moment her son finished college. But Emma had forgotten or, rather, pushed all this into some deep recess of her mind because it had disturbed her to think that Titus might be replacing his dead mother with her.

She looked at Titus, at the sun in his hair, which made it seem yellow like Adam's, and wondered how many days it would be until she heard from her lawyer. "But are you capable of love?"

"I feel like a well that someone sealed up because he thought it had run dry, and all the time it's been filling up and filling up. . . . If Susie hadn't appeared, the waters might have oozed out in all directions, trickled onto the ground, here, there, everywhere, until nothing was left. And the spring might have gone underground and never broken through again."

Emma walked very quickly, as if she could not bear the sound of his young, passionate voice talking of love. A spring can dry up. What happened to you, Adam? When there was no one you could love, what happened to you?

She stopped abruptly, remembering now quite clearly the data Susan Webster had given her. "But Mrs. Webster has a husband."

"Precisely," said Titus. "A man called Jim. She mentions him every five minutes. You could almost tell time by it. And she has a very strict moral code. She won't even let me kiss her. Also she is convinced that she loves him. And she keeps telling me how happy she is. But I know she isn't."

He bent sideways and flipped the large red chip like a flat stone into the sea. It skimmed the water seven times, disturbing the smooth surface at first in large circles, then, as it lost force, in smaller ones. Emma, watching it, thought, And this is how love is tossed into your heart. The first touch is powerful, its circle wide; you think it is a whole world. Then, as love flies on, it hits not quite so hard, not quite so painfully, and the circle grows smaller until it peters out altogether, and love is drowned and falls to the bottom—of what? And it is also like being tossed into life—you are allowed to skim along the surface, and with each rebound, each small distance you cover, your strength diminishes. . . .

"How do you know she isn't happy?"

"Look at her eyes," said Titus. "She has the saddest eyes I've ever seen. Animals have that look when they are fatally hurt. Like a horse that has broken its leg and knows it is going to be shot. My mother sometimes looked like that."

When they came back to the point where the path between the rocks led to the beach, from which a line of boards covered with canvas had been laid to the edge of the water, Susan Webster rose from under one of the gay umbrellas that Gino and the butler put up every morning. She was wearing Meg's bikini and was quite obviously uneasy because it revealed so much of her body, for she

bent hastily to throw a towel around herself, draping it
with quick, deft fingers into a sari before Titus, who was
retrieving his sandal from one of the poodles, had a chance
to see her nudity. And that is what she should always
wear, thought Emma, not those ordinary, everyday cot-
tons that make her look like everybody else, but a sari. It's
right for her. She could almost be mistaken for an Indian,
small as she is, and with her coloring—a symphony in
brown and black, hazelnut-brown skin and black, shiny
hair, and with those enormous eyes, like black cherries.
She was like a flower Emma had overlooked in her garden, one of those strange pink lilies that, when you open
them, surprise you with a white, shiny, iridescent drop,
a huge tear, at the bottom of the calyx. And Titus was
right—her eyes were sad. Had she been born with this
melancholy glance or had life put it there? And then
Emma saw Thiolat.

There was nothing unusual about finding him sunning
himself on the beach. He came often, sometimes even
bringing friends for a swim, but somehow Emma had
not expected him this morning. Of course he would come
this morning, had to come to see for himself what kind
of night she had had after what he had told her yesterday.
But as he rose from his deck chair, Emma did not see in
him the young man she had helped to a career, nor the
trusted friend he had been for almost a lifetime, nor the
doctor she had depended upon for nearly thirty years, but
Death personified. And she wanted to lift her hands
palms out to push him away, across some indistinguish-
able line of demarcation. She wanted to scream, Not yet,
not yet!—as if he had gone back on his word that she still
had at least four months to live, and had come to tell her
that the time was now. The next moment she was angry
with herself and reflected coldly that it was wrong to have
such an intimate relationship with one's doctor that his

presence had of necessity to bring reality with it and the temptation to make use of his knowledge and ask questions out of turn.

"Has Meg told you yet?" she asked. "About the ball? That I'm giving a ball? End of August. A truly grand affair."

Titus and Susan looked at Meg, who seemed to be fast asleep, lying on her stomach with arms and legs spread like a frog too tired to jump, but Thiolat looked only at Emma. What indomitable spirit, he thought. "Will I be invited?"

"I don't know," said Emma, and didn't know if she was joking or not.

He took her gently by the arm and panic gripped her again. She cut loose from him and walked quickly toward the dock, out of earshot of the others. But he followed her.

"I will have time . . . there will be time for it?"

"Of course," he said, keeping any doubt out of his voice. "Of course. But I do want you to take these." He pulled a small bottle from his bathrobe. "As directed. And I want you to come to my office regularly to—"

"I know. I know," said Emma. "What do you think I did last night? On my way home I got myself a medical textbook and read up all about leukemia and its treatment. There's little I don't know now. I even know you were generous to give me six months, that it might be less, depending on how it goes. But I prefer not to talk about it. You take your tests. They should tell you all you need to know. What they don't, I won't. I don't want to talk about it."

She peeled off her slacks and jacket and dived into the water. Like a fish, he thought, like a small, silvery fish who, with the hook securely anchored in its gills, still fights. He unbelted his bathrobe and swam after her. And

now it became a race between them, and she swam faster
and faster until she grew short of breath and the blood
hammered in her temples and she turned on her back,
floating with her eyes closed, unable to stop him from
coming nearer and nearer.

"No woman your age should exert herself so much."
She didn't answer and kept her eyes shut.

"Emma, you shouldn't read medical books. No book, no
doctor can foretell the course of a sickness. Every case is
different."

"I won't die or become bedridden before I've given the
ball?" And he knew she would be well enough, even if
the odds were against her, because she would will it.

"I shall give the ball," said Emma, "and directly afterward go away. Somewhere. I don't know where." And
suddenly it occurred to her that she might want to include him in her plans, and she smiled at him for the
first time.

"Of course I will come with you wherever you decide
to go."

Now it was Emma who said nothing, because his tone
irritated her, his taking for granted that she would let him
accompany her. "Let's not talk about it now," she said.
"Do what you have to do, whatever you consider your
medical duty, but don't remind me that I'm dying. Don't
treat me as if I were."

Perhaps this was all he could do for her, he thought,
listening to the echo of her imploring voice—behave as
if he had forgotten that she was fatally ill, administer the
medicines and blood transfusions as he would administer
pills and injections for any ordinary ailment, showing no
concern when he saw traces of exhaustion in her face; behave, in short, in a way that would enable her to pretend
her life was not running out.

"Emma—" He turned on his side to look at her but she had swum away.

Susan Webster phoned the next morning to say she was sorry but she had a splitting headache and could not come. Emma told her not to worry about it and sat at her desk in the library all morning, completing the list of guests that were to be invited to the ball and writing the invitations. Titus offered to get them to the post office, but Emma said she wanted to go to Nice anyhow, and that it would be better to send them from there. But she drove only to Beaulieu, handed her mail to the desk clerk of the hotel where she and Fleury had stayed in former years, when the Villa du Cygne was being readied, then parked her car at a garage and walked to the little house Susan had rented for the season. It lay above the highway that curved along the shore, on a level a little higher than the railroad tracks, and for the last hundred yards the road leading to it was unpaved and ran between an embankment on one side and a wall covered with bougainvillaea on the other. Finally there was a wooden gate swinging in the wind, a few steps, and Emma found herself in the small square of a garden.

To her right ran a low stone wall across which one could see the sea; to her left, set back, stood a house, all white, with long green shutters from which the paint was peeling. Behind it, much to her surprise, she saw the terraces of a vineyard, a mist of blue-gray spray on the carefully trained vines, a few chickens scratching the soil for worms. The garden itself was planted with fig, orange and lemon trees. A goat was tethered to a pepper tree and several large straw baskets were filled with dark-red and white geraniums.

Emma knocked on one of the shutters, and when there was no answer went around to the side of the house and tried the door. It led directly into the living room, which was empty. "Susan," Emma called softly, and wondered suddenly what impulse had made her come, and almost turned to leave. Then from somewhere upstairs came the sound of wild sobs, and Emma climbed a rather primitive staircase to the upper floor. There the door to one of the rooms stood open, and after a second of hesitation Emma entered it.

On a wide double bed, which took up almost all the space, Susan lay crying into her pillow. For a moment Emma stood perfectly still, filled with such envy she had to swallow to control it. Not even during the night following her first visit to Thiolat's office had she permitted herself to indulge so uncontrollably in grief. The last time she had cried like this had been when her father had told her that Adam had promised to marry another girl. She had not been able to weep when she found out why Fleury had married her and that her father had lied to her. And she had been proud of this iron discipline. Or had it been an incapacity to give in to suffering?

"Susan," she said softly. "Susan." And when Susan did not react, Emma put a hand on the trembling shoulders. But Susan was not conscious of who was standing next to her, she felt only the presence of another person, knew that she was no longer alone and would not be talking into a vacuum if she spoke, and she lifted a tear-smeared face. "He isn't coming. He promised and now he isn't coming."

"Who isn't coming?"

Now Susan recognized the voice and sat up, staring at Emma horrified.

"Oh, Madame—I'm dreadfully sorry. If you'll just give me a minute," and she jumped from the bed and disappeared into the bathroom. Where she had buried her head in the pillow, the linen was wet through. Next to it lay a slightly crumpled photograph. Emma picked it up. It showed a man in his late thirties, a narrow, highly intelligent face that gave the impression of a very self-contained person. He was smiling, but his smile had a distant quality, as though he couldn't share what he was smiling about with anyone. She put the picture down when she heard Susan's voice.

"How very good of you to come."

"I was worried about you," said Emma. "You and Titus did quite a bit of swimming yesterday. I was afraid you might have caught cold."

"No," said Susan. "I'm very ashamed of myself. Maybe I had a little bit too much sun, but I could really have come to work. I simply—well, I had a disappointment, I guess." And Emma sensed that the girl was glad she had come and longed to talk, yet would never have dared approach her. "I was looking forward to the arrival of my husband—though I should have known that something would come up at the last moment. It always does. We've been planning this vacation together for the last five years. Four months. A real rest. And we rented this house. I came on ahead, he was to follow a week later. That was in May. And now it's almost July. And he says he'll be lucky if he can get away by the middle of August. But please, please do come downstairs and let me fix you something to drink. It's terribly hot and messy up here."

They sat in the garden, near the pepper tree, from which the goat had munched most of its bark, their glasses of lemonade untouched in front of them. "This house belongs to the man who owns the vineyard," said Susan. "I thought I was terribly lucky to find it." Her sad eyes looked even sadder and her mouth curved in bitterness.

"You love him very much, don't you?" said Emma.

"My husband? Jim? Oh yes, I do love him. It's only

this dreadful devotion to his profession. You see, he's an engineer. I've never seen anyone work so hard. First there's the idea, then it's being constructed, and then when it doesn't work. . . . He doesn't give up easily and he won't let anyone else finish what he has begun. I admire him so much for his courage, his stamina. But . . ."

"But?"

"But I guess I'll never get used to that kind of disappointment," said Susan. "In the beginning I sort of shrugged it off. I've been married ten years, you know. I married Jim when I was twenty. But I find it harder and harder to laugh it off and think, Oh, well, tomorrow . . . next week . . . next month . . . next year . . ."

An engineer, thought Emma. Like Adam. When he told me he was going to invent a car with a four-wheel drive that could travel over any terrain, I thought—I don't know what I thought, but certainly that it could be done without neglecting me. And she wished she could have another look at the photo of Jim Webster, who, like Adam, racked his brains, pored over plans, tried to realize a dream.

"You," said Susan, "you have so much more experience than I. I know that in spite of your glamorous life you must have been lonely, too, at times, and wished you could see more of your husband. Please don't misunderstand me, but I've been working with you on his papers long enough to know how much you were left alone. How long can one stand being lonely?"

Emma looked at the long-fingered brown hand mechanically caressing the little white goat. How long could one stand being lonely? How long could one stand being content with a dream? The same dream?

"Lonely or alone?"

She watched Susan stop stroking the head of the animal and gaze for a moment across the stone wall at the sea.

Then she turned her sad eyes to Emma and nodded. "Both. Lonely and alone. I knew that I would have to be alone a great deal and I never really minded it. I always found something to do—a job, like now, or I read, walked. . . . I even like to take care of a house. The irony of it is I thought he was lonely and needed someone to be there for him. But he doesn't."

She fell silent, then spoke in a small voice. "It frightens me sometimes that I'm jealous of his work. But I am. I'm certain many women feel that way about their husband's profession. But you see, not even the nights belong to me. He has a pad and pencil and every so often he switches on the light and makes a note or a drawing. At first I tried to become a part of it but I have no understanding for mathematics or mechanics. I can't even be a good sounding board because I ask the wrong questions, questions that just interrupt him. So I lie there feeling useless and wasted."

Fleury and she had separate bedrooms from the beginning. She had had no idea what his nightly habits were.

"I wanted a child desperately," said Susan. "But Jim didn't. He says he isn't vain enough to want to propagate himself, especially not with the shape the world is in. Of course that doesn't hold water, I know, and so does he. The truth of it is he'd just hate the obligations being a father imposes. And he is decent and honest enough to realize he wouldn't be a good one."

Silence fell again, and a man who had been spraying the vines above them came down the narrow steps between the terraces, his canister on his back, his face and hair and suit colored by the chemical. He raised a hand to his forehead and went on. When he had gone, Susan's voice grew even smaller. "After I'd been married three years, there was a young man who liked me very much. I used to go out with him on the nights Jim called to say he wouldn't be coming home but would sleep at the shop. But he didn't stay satisfied with—well, with just going out, and when I said no to anything more, he went away. And two years ago there was someone else. I had to say no again."

Now Emma took her eyes away from the small, grave face and stared out to sea. How many had she refused? To how many had she said no, knowing it would mean separation and that she would be robbed of even the pleasure of friendship? How much had she missed?

A train thundered by below the wall, and during the time it traveled past them its great noise was caught and held by the wall, then it whistled shrilly as it curved away, the whistle lying on the calm air long after it had gone, echoing back the word to her—missed, missed. . . . And suddenly she could see Scott standing in the library of the castle on the Loire—when had it been? Oh, so long ago, during the last war—no, just after it was over. She tried to push the memory away but it came back sharply, clearly, relentlessly. It was raining outside, a dismal, gray, cold rain, and Scott had just brought in whatever he could find that would burn in the big fireplace. And as he knelt in front of her, he looked up at the ceiling, which was two floors above them because the library was huge, with a gallery along its walls.

"It's hopeless, Em. It would be just enough to warm our hands for a few seconds. Doesn't this damn place have a small room with a fireplace anywhere?"

"Only my dressing room."

Not even Henri had ever entered it, but now they went upstairs, both of them lugging branches and crates and wet logs and paper. It was a round room with a ceiling that had been lowered and was inlaid with mirrors. It warmed up quickly and kept warm because, despite her protests, Scott loosened some inside shutters from windows in other rooms and burned them. "What the hell—

you'll have to fix up the whole place anyhow."

It was October, and they were alone in the house; except for an old caretaker somewhere on the grounds there was no one else about. She had left Henri in a hospital in London and gone to France to see what had become of their house in Paris and the castle, and to find out which of the people on the estate were still alive, and who among their friends needed help the most. The house in Paris had been looted, but here everything was almost as they had left it, in spite of the fact that the castle had been requisitioned by the Germans for a while. But there were no carp in the moat any longer, and many of the trees had been cut down for firewood.

"And see what I found in the library," she said, and held out a neat folder containing, on typewritten sheets, a list of every item in the castle, down to the number of rolls of toilet paper. "God damn them!" he yelled. "I've always been scared to death of efficient people. They apply it to everything they do. Well, that's how they could murder six million Jews." He had just come back from an official tour of concentration camps in Germany.

But though no spoon was missing, there was nothing to eat. The Germans had slaughtered the cattle, the fowl, taken the grain, and it was then that Scott tried to trap whatever cat he could spot. "They're serving them in Paris at the finest restaurants," he assured her, "only they call it rabbit stew. It tastes fine. You'll never know the difference." But she preferred to subsist on vitamin pills.

The night before they were going to leave, he took her in his arms and kissed her. "I tried that some twenty-five years ago, remember?" he said. "Only then you didn't mean anything to me. You were quite right to scream."

She didn't scream this time, only gently tried to break his hold. But he shook his head. "Why do you think I'm here, Em? I flew from Frankfurt to London for no other reason but to see you. And you weren't there. . . ."

He was in the Air Force, and they had seen each other quite frequently at the Park Lane Hotel whenever he got to London. "I called your apartment and they told me where you were." And he kissed her again, and his kiss sent the blood through her ice-cold limbs until she could feel herself burning with desire. "Let me go, Scott."

He didn't even answer.

"It's impossible."

"Oh, hush, hush, will you?" And childishly, desperately she said, "I love Henri."

He lifted her from the floor and held her pressed against him so that his face came to lie on her belly and she could feel the heat of his breath through the material of her dress.

"Scott. I have never slept with any other man but Henri."

In his surprise he put her down. She could see that he didn't believe her. "And how old are you?"

"Forty-five." And she began to cry.

He misunderstood her tears but they convinced him that she was speaking the truth, and he shook his head as if she had said something obscene.

"You've missed a lot. But why? Why? You're not frigid. Why? Wasn't there ever anyone who—"

"No."

"Poor Em," he said then. "Poor Em," and she tried to explain that she was truly devoted to Henri, that her upbringing, her social position, her moral code had all made it impossible for her to have an affair.

"That's a bunch of bull," he said, "and don't be so goddam proud of it. It wasn't your morals that were strong but your passions that were weak, or"—and he looked at her narrowly, almost squinting—"I'll tell you what I think. You're afraid of love."

For a moment then she pondered what he said. Could it be that Henri's superior, skillful technique of eroticism, to which she had been able to respond, had frightened her because it separated mind from body, had terrified her because she could imagine how it would feel, how she would be changed altogether if the two were ever integrated?

In that moment, when he saw her face soften, he pulled her to him again. "Come, Em. Let me take the fear away. It can be wonderful . . . wonderful. . . . I promise you." And his kisses were like an aphrodisiac until, at the last moment, when she already felt his weight, she slipped from under him, letting him lie on the floor face down, moaning softly.

"I'm sorry, I'm boring you," Susan was saying, and when Emma shook her head, the girl insisted. "Of course I am. Forgive me for talking so much about myself. I usually don't. I don't know what came over me. But it's done me a lot of good. Thank you for listening."

Thank you, Emma wanted to say, for giving me a moment of truth. "Tell me something honestly, if you can— do you really still love your husband or only what you hoped he would mean to you?"

Susan grew very pale. "I think I do," she said. "Both. Only—sometimes I'm not sure, not sure at all."

"Then don't be afraid to find out," said Emma. "Find out before habit becomes stronger than feeling, before you start pretending instead of living, before you've lost every chance of finding out whether life hasn't something more to offer."

Titus waited until it had grown quite dark, then he got into his car and drove at breakneck speed to Beaulieu. His Alfa Romeo was small enough to go up the dirt road so that, unlike Emma, he could leave it in front of the gate. Several times during the day he had tried to reach Susan, but though he had let the telephone ring endlessly, it had never been answered. He felt absolutely certain that she was at home. As far as he could judge, she was not a girl who would go out anywhere alone. But as he came up into the small garden now and saw the house in absolute blackness, with the ground-floor shutters closed against the night and only one window half open on the second floor, his heart contracted with the fear that she might, after all, have wanted to escape her loneliness and gone out. He waited until his eyes had grown accustomed to the darkness, and he could find his way by the light of the rising moon without making a sound. Then he moved quickly until he was standing directly under the half-open window, and began playing softly on his guitar.

At first he sang an Italian song, keeping his voice low, but when it failed to bring any response, he broke into German: *"Guten Abend, gut' Nacht . . . mit Rosen bedacht . . . mit Näglein besteckt . . ."* After he had gone through that, and waited awhile, straining his ears to detect the smallest noise and keeping his eyes on the window to catch any possible movement of the curtains, he began humming a hillbilly tune, the words of which he had forgotten, but its melody was sweet and gay. Then he sang to her in French. And it did not seem foolish at all to be standing there in a small garden on the French Riviera trying to court a girl with a serenade, though he would have shaken with laughter two weeks ago if anyone had told him that Titus Vandendam would resort to such shenanigans or that there existed a woman who could resist him.

But the house remained mute, growing whiter and more spectral as the moon climbed the sky, and the closed shutters grew darker and darker until they looked like squarely built men in black uniforms guarding Susan

Webster's determination to remain faithful. Titus dropped
the instrument, moved on tiptoe carefully away from under the window and sat down on one of the chairs where
Emma and Susan had talked in the afternoon. But he
didn't know that Emma had been there. He knew only
that he had to wait here, if it took an eternity, until he
saw Susan Webster. If she had gone out, she would return
at some time or other; he would hear her steps coming
along the dirt road, and before she could spot his car and
hide, he would have run to meet her. If she was upstairs in
her room, she would come down in the morning.

Twenty minutes passed before the sudden gold streak
of light from her window cut into the shadow of the pepper tree on the cement. Titus tensed but he didn't stir. He
could hear her moving in her room, then the opening of a
door, but no sound as she came down the stairs. Then all at
once she seemed to be right behind him, unlocking the
shutters of the small living room, and her step was so
light that he didn't see her until she had reached the low
wall and there she stood, gazing at the sea, which lay
silvery where the moon shone on it, with black spots
where the light had not yet reached it, like a huge mirror
from which the argentum is peeling. She stood very still,
and Titus sat in his chair, incapable suddenly of moving,
afraid of only one thing now—that she, thinking he had
gone, as he had wanted her to do, would be frightened if
he so much as breathed. And he did not know what to do,
and grew afraid that, rather than scare her, he would
indeed let her pass back into the house and lock the shutters, without revealing his presence.

If only you knew how unlike me all of this is, he
wanted to shout across the small distance that separated
them. And then he knew that this was precisely why he
loved her—because she made him feel like a quite different person from the one he had come to regard as himself.

He was no longer proud of his indifference or content to be merely an observer. She brought out in him a need to love and be loved that he had not felt since his mother's death. He almost regretted not having gone away when he had stopped singing, instead of hiding in the dark like a hunter stalking his prey. Then the night wind sprang up, rustling the leaves of trees and flowers, and he could see her shiver and how she lifted her arms to hug herself against the chill. A minute later she turned, and now, as she walked toward the light pouring from the living room, he could see, through the thin material of her nightgown, the outline of her body.

"It's me," he said. "Titus. Don't be afraid."

She stood as if nailed to the ground, her head bent slightly in the direction of his voice, her mouth opening in alarm, but she did not speak. He wanted to ask her if she was angry at finding him still here, and apologize for tricking her, but instead he said, "Have you eaten yet?"

And perhaps because she had expected anything but a question concerning so trite a matter as food, she responded, and shook her head gently.

"I thought so," he said. "Well, I've brought everything."

He jumped up to reach for the hamper he had put down near the chair next to his guitar, talking all the while, not giving her a chance to interrupt. "No. You don't do a thing. Just tell me if you'd rather eat inside or out. I think it would be very pleasant here, don't you? But wait, I'll get your coat."

He rushed inside, blinking when he came into the electric light, but at once saw the blanket lying on the dreadful little sofa near the false fireplace, and since the door to the staircase stood open, he could see a clothes rack and took her white raincoat from it. She didn't resist when he put it across her shoulders and led her to a chair and covered her with the blanket. And he knew suddenly that she was dead tired, too tired and dazed to fight his presence.

He had packed the hamper with great care, A red-and-white checked tablecloth, two wooden candlesticks complete with candles, cutlery, plates and wineglasses. There were fresh figs still packed in tissue paper, thin slices of *prosciutto* and an arm's-length of white bread, hard-boiled eggs, cheese and a basket lined with leaves on which tiny wild strawberries lay like deep, dark rubies. There was even a pot of thick cream to go with them and a bunch of hothouse violets that looked unreal, like artificial flowers cut from light-purple velvet. These he put on top of her napkin. Susan took the flowers and held them up to her face, then she made a little roof over them with her hands, as if the night wind might blow them away.

"Headaches get worse without food," said Titus, uncorking the bottle. "I hope you like Sancerre." Then he looked his masterpiece over. "You tell me if I've forgotten anything."

Susan spoke for the first time. "You have forgotten nothing," she said. "Nothing."

He lit the candles and poured the wine, tasting it before he filled her glass and lifted his to clink against hers. "Then let's fall to. *Bon appetit.*"

She ate very slowly, thinking, Why can't it be Jim sitting opposite me? Why doesn't Jim ever think of a picnic like this instead of opening the icebox and eating a piece of sausage or cheese right out of the paper? But you don't judge a man by whether he can set up a good picnic or not. Jim used to bring me flowers, too, when he was courting me ten years ago. Now he forgets my birthday and says I'm too old to be childish about it. But if he comes here, to a different country, perhaps he, too . . . And she looked at the guitar, its ribbons bereft by the night of their gay colors and witty inscriptions, and she grew afraid of her thoughts and of the silence between them.

"How did you know I spoke German?" she asked.

"You told me you had taken up languages because you thought you might like to apply for a job at the United Nations and wanted to find out which came easiest to you."

"Even in French my pronunciation is very bad," she said, and sighed. "You see, unlike you, I have never been anywhere. This is my first trip abroad. Which country do you like best?"

"Oh, I don't know," he said. "America? Well—the American picks his nose, the Frenchman digs in his ear, the German scratches his head, all of them seem to have dandruff, the Italian twirls a toothpick between his teeth, and the Englishman, if he has a mustache, combs it, and if he hasn't, he cleans his fingernails with the thumb of the other hand. The Indian—"

Susan laughed. "Really, Titus, why do you say such things?"

"When you are not happy or when you are alone, you notice only what you don't like, because you look for things that correspond to your mood. Most people are at greater pains to protect their bitterness than their moments of happiness. But if you and I were to travel together, I am sure I would see only what was beautiful."

She almost asked, "And where would you take me?" but it seemed too playful, too flirtatious, so she fell silent again, ashamed even to have thought it.

"Shall I make coffee?" he asked.

"Not for me, thank you. I don't want to be wide-awake again. But if you . . ."

He shook his head, stuffed everything back into the hamper, then threw the cushion of his chair to the ground and sat down so that his head was level with her knees. For a long while neither of them spoke, then he reached for her hand, kissed it and held it against his cheek. "Tell me about yourself, when you were a little girl. Were you happy?"

She hadn't thought of her childhood for a long time. Yes, she had been happy as a child, because her parents had been happy, outgoing people. They had loved and spoiled her and shared their happiness with her. They were convinced that she was happy now, because she wrote such glowing letters home, mentioning the presents Jim was always giving her, which existed only in her imagination, and the wonderful success he was having with his work, which, thank God, was true.

"Very happy. And you?"

He shook his head. "We were so desperately poor, we were too worried to be happy. There was always the rent we couldn't pay, the gas was shut off more often than it was on, so was the electricity. I sat in the dark often, alone and afraid, worrying about my mother, who was out working. I'd think something had happened to her. But she had forbidden me to leave the room after dark. Sometimes I thought she would never come back. I did so many jobs when I was a youngster—all of them horrible—that I promised myself never to do a lick of work when I grew up." He fell silent, and Susan thought, I made a mistake in my judgment of him. I thought he was just lazy and a sponger.

"Go on."

"When I was twelve, I had t.b. That was when my mother started to sleep with men. I had a series of uncles."

He could feel her hand against his cheek flutter like a bird trying to escape, and he took firmer hold of it. "But you see, she did it for me, to get me the care I needed— food, sunshine, doctors. It only made me love her more and hate myself worse than any of the men who took advantage of her."

"Jim was poor, too, and sick when he was a little boy. But it was his mother who was dead, and he was alone all day for weeks on end until his father came home in the evening to cook him a meal." And perhaps, thought Susan, it was this period that had formed Jim, had made him so self-contained, so unsentimental, unable to understand her yearning for everyday tenderness.

"You mustn't compare," said Titus. "You mustn't ever compare people with each other. Don't insult me by comparing me with another man you've known. I'm no better, nobody is, nor worse—just different. He is he and I am I. And now I am going to kiss you."

She moved her head away but Titus did not touch her mouth. He kissed the palm of her hand and the inside of her arm and the curve of her shoulder and her neck, her throat and the point of her chin, and then he sat back again and kissed the toes of her foot, which had moved aside the plaid and felt cold against his lips, and he kissed the soles of her feet, which had never been kissed, and when he felt her shiver he tucked the plaid around her feet again and lighted cigarettes for them both. But she flung hers away into the moonlight, a tiny shooting star that fell to the ground and died in the dew on the grass, and cried in despair, "Take me, Titus. Take me now. If you don't do it now, the moment will never come again."

"No, Susie, no," he said. "Not when you speak in that voice, when you don't want it with your heart, when you let me only because you're desperate, with an expression on your face as if you were going to throw yourself into an abyss."

"But I could never come to you otherwise," she cried, "because I love Jim—because I don't want to be like all those loathsome women who have affairs. And Jim trusts me. And—"

He put his hand gently over her mouth. "I know," he

said. "I know all that. You told me. And even if you hadn't, I can tell what you want and don't want. But you see, Susie, I have had many affairs and they have left me so empty. I don't want them, either."

"Then why did you kiss me?"

"Because I love you, and I wanted to kiss you. But you don't want anything from me except, perhaps, oblivion."

"And what do you want?"

"To love you," he said, "not to rape you. And, possibly, marry you."

"Marry?"

"I can work," he said. "It's only a question of making up my mind. I can get a job as an illustrator, or as a customer's man in a brokerage firm, with my connections. . . ."

"Marry?" she said again, as if it were a word she hadn't learned in any of the languages she had studied. "I've never thought of divorcing Jim."

"Then think of it now."

She made an odd little noise, a mixture of laughter and tears. "You are mad!"

"I don't think so," he said. "I don't like the woman I love to turn into a sneak, a thief, stealing a little time here, an hour there. Nor do I like to share her with another man."

Silence grew between them again while the moon traveled higher and higher and even Venus was extinguished by its light. "You'll go to bed now and sleep," he said, and he took her hand and led her through the living room and up the stairs that had no banister but were merely boards between two walls, and into her bedroom, and sat her down on the large, untidy bed. Then he straightened the linen, puffed the pillows and went into the bathroom to get an aspirin and a glass of water for her. "I'll be in the next room."

"You'll be *where?*"

"I'm going to stay here," he told her, leaning against the foot of her bed. "I'm going to wake up with you tomorrow morning and have coffee and *brioches* with you in the kitchen and then take you for a long walk before you go to work. In the afternoon we are going to drive somewhere, perhaps across the border to Menton, or the other way, to Cannes, or, if you prefer, up into the mountains into the Vallée de la Tinée. And in the evening we'll dine anywhere you like. Susie, I am going to see you all the time except for the hours you work for Mrs. Fleury. And I won't rape or seduce you. I won't even kiss you any more, but I'll be there because I want the chance. That is, I will if you don't tell me to go away and never come near you again. In that case I'll pack up and go to Kyoto."

"That's Japan."

"Correct," he said. "Thousands and thousands of miles away."

They faced each other gravely across the bedboard. George left me, thought Susan, and Richard married somebody else, and Jim is not coming until August, if he comes at all. And he doesn't want an affair, nothing messy or secretive and humiliating. He—he wants to marry me.

She looked at him again and saw how beautiful he was, with his golden hair and his classic features and build. And who would have thought that he was not just a playboy?

"I don't think the bed's made up."

"Don't worry," said Titus. "I'll find the linen. And I make beds very well. I learned it in the Army. You know, I spent two years in Korea. Well, I'll tell you all about that tomorrow. Good night, Susie. Sleep well."

The cable came four days after her call to her lawyer in New York. It came around noon, when Emma had just

gone down to the beach to join Titus and Susan and Meg
for a swim. With a sudden, sharp conviction, she knew
that it was the answer from her lawyer when she saw
Gino—dressed as usual, all in white—appear like a flag
of truce above the rocks. Still she did not move. She just
watched him come closer, rapidly, for Gino never moved
slowly. He seemed always to be running, like some young
animal that doesn't yet know its strength is limited. She
even enjoyed watching the perfect co-ordination with
which he jumped from the last rock down onto the white
sand that had been meticulously raked in the early morning hours; how, with one movement, he produced the
cable he had stuck in his breast pocket, waving it in explanation of his uncalled-for appearance, then placed it
neatly, before handing it to her, on the small silver platter
he had carried in his left hand.

None of the others paid any attention to it. Susan and
Titus went on with their conversation without even glancing at her, and Meg asked if Gino had time to explain the
Mercedes to her, which she was so anxious to drive. Still
Emma did not open the neatly folded paper. She pushed
it into one of the deep pockets of her beach coat, lighted a
cigarette and sat for a while with her legs pulled up,
smoking, feeling the cable burning her thigh as if Adam
had placed his hand on her. When she had finished her
cigarette, she rose. "I think I'll go for a walk."

Nobody said anything. Meg had followed Gino up to
the house and Susan and Titus had turned over on their
stomachs, lying very close together, as if the beach were a
wide, wonderfully comfortable double bed on which to
rest after making love.

Emma walked away, but even when she had gone quite
a distance it still didn't seem right to read the cable, and
she retraced her steps, looking for the footprints she had
made only a few moments ago, but they had already been

washed away by the water. She went up to the dock and
loosened the rope that held the dory. It rocked as heavily
as if not only she but another person, too, had got into
it, and Emma spread her feet, distributing her weight to
steady the boat, before she reached for the oars. And only
when she started to row did she realize why she had to
read the cable in a rowboat. For it had been in a rowboat
in Central Park that Adam had first told her that he
loved her. And suddenly she could feel his breath again,
like an unexpected warm breeze wafting across her face.
He had pulled in the oars, left his seat on the bench and
stretched out next to her in the wide-bottomed boat. Staring up into an immensely clear blue summer sky, she
hadn't noticed it until his cheek was close to hers. For a
moment neither of them had stirred or spoken. They
stared at each other as if each were seeing the other for the
first time. She wanted to close her eyes but forced herself
to keep them open—a child who enters a world of which
she has dreamed, and, blinded by impending reality, is
afraid of missing any of its strangeness. He had pushed
his right arm under her head, cushioning it, and the
touch of the bones of his shoulders against the nape of her
neck had made her shiver suddenly, uncontrollably. Then
his left hand had wandered up her leg and under her skirt,
gently, persistently, knowingly. Unable to form words, her
lips had broken apart, offering themselves to his, and
closed again in a violent spasm on teeth abruptly clenched.
When his mouth had finally met hers it was as if she had
thirsted all her life, ever since she had first met him, for
this moment. She had never been able to forget the magic
force of his tongue. Her first kiss.

With slow, even strokes she rowed past the sailboat and
the Chris-Craft, her eyes closed, hearing, in the water
slapping against the sides, Adam's voice saying "Emily,
Emily . . ." When she could no longer see Titus and

Susan, she pulled in the oars and tore open the cable. The text almost covered two pages: "Adam Forbes, born 1897 in Elmira, N.Y., died in Toledo, Ohio, 1950, of a heart attack. His position at the time engineering department Willys Overland, where he helped develop the jeep. Distinguished service record in World Wars I and II. His wife Ellen, whom he married in 1934, died in 1957. One daughter, Felicity Forbes, born in 1936, lab technician, working at present at Cornell Medical Center, New York. Address: 540 Fort Washington Ave. Do you want us to contact Miss Forbes? Awaiting further instructions."

Emma had to read it twice. It had never occurred to her that Adam could be dead, and she could not believe it. Emily . . . Emily . . . Hadn't she just heard his voice? Hadn't she just felt his hands? Then, all of a sudden, very coldly, she thought, What is the matter with me? I had to count on it. Two world wars. He might have been killed in the first. But he had not been killed in a war. He had died of a heart attack in 1950. Fifty-three years old —which was no age at all.

The boat drifted, carried by the tide; a cloud above her sailed across the sun and for a moment all color seemed gone from the world.

Adam dead.

Dead for ten whole years.

No.

He was still vitally alive. Because I love him, thought Emma. Because I love him, remember him, the way he looked, the way he moved, the way he talked. And who, she thought, will remember me and keep me alive? Whom have I allowed to love me so that ten years after my death he will feel it is incredible that I am dead? Scott? No. Thiolat? Perhaps. But since she had never reciprocated his love, never shared his dreams, they might die with her. But as long as she lived, Adam would live, and that, she told herself, could be six months more, at the most.

And he had married. A woman called Ellen. Ellen was
a Norwegian name but that didn't mean anything. Who
had this woman been whom he had married seventeen
years after they had lost each other? He had waited a long
time. Had he loved her? Had she loved him? But she,
too, was dead, unable to remember Adam and keep him
alive, unable to tell her what kind of man Adam Forbes
had become. They had had a child. Emma looked at the
cable again. Felicity. Felicity Forbes. Not Ellen, not
Emily, but Felicity.

A child, thought Emma, and she let her hand dangle
in the water as if the sea could cool the hot envy of her
blood. Adam's child. On how many had they planned,
Adam and she? Four. Three at least. Two boys and a girl.

Adam's daughter. But not hers.

No. No further instructions. She was not interested in
getting in touch with Felicity Forbes. 540 Fort Washington Avenue. What a dreary neighborhood, except that it
was near The Cloisters.

It would be no use anyhow. Children never had a clear
picture of their parents. Authority colored their relationship. They either loved their parents too much or hated
them or were indifferent. No child could ever judge truly
the relationship between its parents.

Emma pulled her hand from the water. It looked dead-
white with cold. As it would look . . . She began to
massage it automatically. A heart attack. What a beautiful death. No fear, no pain. From one moment to the next
it had all been over. Or had it?

Oh, Adam, Adam, who were you? And now she had to
die without knowing.

She reached for the oars and headed for the beach. Titus
and Susan had gone but the imprint of their bodies was
still clearly visible where they had lain, a man and a

woman who still had a whole lifetime ahead of them. In
her room, Emma stripped off her bathing suit, and when
she came back from the shower she saw the cable, which
had fallen to the floor. She tore it into tiny pieces and
threw them in the wastepaper basket. And that was that.
Death was final. Adam was dead. And she would never
know now. . . . Dead, dead, dead. And there was nothing left of him except her memory. But that wasn't true.
Fort Washington Avenue—she could not remember the
number.

She knelt down on the floor. Piece by piece she took
the torn shreds of paper from the wastepaper basket, and
still kneeling on the floor, fitted them together like the
pieces of a jigsaw puzzle—not thinking once that Fort
Washington Avenue, New York, might suffice to trace
Felicity Forbes, or that her lawyer had the exact address
anyhow—until she read the number herself. And then she
smiled. She got up and went into her dressing room and
sat down at her writing desk.

"Dear Felicity. You may or may not know who I am.
My name is Emma Starr Fleury. Strangely enough, I
heard only today that you were an orphan. I am a distant
relative of your father, Adam Forbes, and I would very
much like to meet you. My lawyer in New York will get
in touch with you within the next few days and I would
be so pleased if you could see your way to spending a few
weeks with me at my house on the Riviera. . . ."

How sweet it was to have something to look forward to,
and how unaccustomed. There had been few days in her
life when Emma had felt like this, almost like a child
filled with anticipation, deeply curious and excited. Yes,
excited. She could remember her mind being stirred at the
prospect of going to live in a foreign country, of experiencing for herself the impact of an alien people, of being

allowed to make the wonders of the world her own, of walking among yellow-clad monks in a mysterious temple, hunting with the Swahili in Kenya, and watching the sun set over Hong Kong's waterfront, but all these things had merely fascinated her mind, never touched her heart. Because none of the things Henri or anyone else had offered her had ever been passionately desired. And the rare moments in which she had yearned for one thing in particular, she had kept prudently to herself. Not since her secret meetings with Adam had she responded with such emotional vulnerability to any event as she did now to the arrival of Adam's daughter.

She looked at her watch again. Only six minutes had passed since she had been told the plane from Paris would be half an hour late. I should have taken Gino, thought Emma. I could have sent him in every few minutes to inquire if anything had changed, to look at the blackboard and see if any other time of arrival were chalked up. But long before this day had finally come, Emma had decided to fetch Felicity herself, to drive out to the airport alone, so that from the beginning she could establish an intimacy with the girl. Even the presence of a chauffeur might handicap her in showing her tenderness to an apparent stranger and might disconcert a girl not used to servants. Emma looked up into the sky, her entire being willing the machine from Paris to cut through the air, to paint its shadow on the apron, but only a few private planes, like oversized blue, red and yellow parrots, circled above her. "Get out of the way," Emma wanted to say, for the noise of their motors made it impossible for her to listen for the sound of the expected craft.

One day Adam had been late for lunch, and she had sat in the small, shabby restaurant where they used to meet in his hour off, unable to move her arms or feet or to speak. She was as tense now as she had been then, and it took great mental effort to make herself get out of the car, light a cigarette and walk up and down. Then her ears picked up a faint humming and suddenly she saw the plane, far away, no bigger than a large gray bird for a moment, then coming closer, its humming turning into a roar, then silence, and suddenly it was landing.

Now Emma had to rush, for she had not been aware of how far she had walked away from the parking lot. By the time she reached the barrier separating her from the apron, all the passengers had alighted and were already walking off to the baggage cart to pick out their luggage. Only one person still stood next to the steps, a tall, thin girl. Too tall, thought Emma, too thin, and plainly dressed, and she looked around and over her shoulder to make sure there was no other young girl all alone whom she might have overlooked. Then she waved.

The girl did not seem to see her. Emma waved again. A mechanic, fitting the black hose of his gasoline tank to the plane's, noticed her and called to the girl, and the girl lifted her arm halfway in an acknowledgment of Emma's greeting, then began to walk slowly toward the barrier. And it was the way she moved that made Emma stand quite still for a moment, for though Felicity moved slowly and somehow uncertainly, she moved like Adam, holding her body very erect, her head cocked slightly to the left as if listening to something, the arms swinging to a secret rhythm. So it was Adam coming toward her, Adam's long, gangling body that stopped abruptly in front of her. But that was all his daughter had inherited from him. Her face resembled his in no way. And scanning it as one might scan a landscape for a familiar landmark, Emma thought, I should have asked her for a photograph and I would not be so disappointed now. For Felicity had neither the shape of Adam's face nor any of his features. Hers was a narrow face, freckled like an urchin's. As a little girl it might have been quite attractive. But the eyes were disfigured by heavy-rimmed, much too large, much too old-fashioned glasses, which threw her nose out of proportion. There was a dimple in her chin that looked more like a scar, but above it her teeth, though irregular, were very white in her small, pale mouth. She wore no makeup, not even powder, and her skin glistened as if it had just been scrubbed with soap and water. She wore a kerchief tied so tightly around her head that Emma could not see the color of her hair, only her high, round forehead. She had on a raincoat, a transparent one, which made the blue-and-white checked dress underneath it look worn and a little dirty. Her shoes were those dreadful, clumsy ones special health stores made for people who had to stand a lot. A bag, obviously new, dangled from her right shoulder.

"Felicity?" said Emma. "I'm Emma Fleury. It's wonderful you could come."

"How do you do?" said Felicity, and the quality of her voice was so unexpected, Emma almost started in surprise. It was a deep voice, with just enough hoarseness to make it unusual and haunting. "You are Mrs. Fleury, aren't you?" And when Emma nodded, "I'm afraid I didn't understand anything you said. My ears are so stopped up, I can't hear a thing."

"Too bad," said Emma, raising her voice as much as she could. "But that will pass in a minute. Didn't they give you any chewing gum?"

"I've never flown before in my life," said Felicity Forbes, "and I enjoyed it very much. Thank you again for sending the ticket. May I look for my luggage?" She went past Emma to the baggage cart, and lifted from it one gray suitcase, also new, and a small overnight bag that was terribly worn.

"The porter will bring it. Just give him the slip." Emma

took the luggage slip from Felicity's shoulder bag, where it had been stuck, practically, in the outside pocket, and handed it to the porter, but when the man tried to take the suitcase, Felicity shook her head. "Thank you. It isn't heavy."

Emma went ahead to show the way and Felicity followed, walking like Adam yet not like Adam's daughter at all. She got into the car after holding open the door for Emma, without saying anything more. And there she sat, her hands folded in her lap, with no curiosity as to where she was being taken, without looking about her, docile.

She isn't feeling well, Emma told herself, and started the motor. "It's an hour's drive, if not more. If you feel hungry or want to stop anywhere, don't hesitate to say so."

Felicity nodded, but Emma could not tell if she had understood.

Emma put a blue beret on her head and stepped on the gas, and as the car pulled away, she almost laughed. She needn't have taken a pill to combat her fatigue, Gino might just as well be driving them, for no intimate questions were going to be asked or answered unless she could bring herself to shout everything she had wanted to say to this plane-deaf and, perhaps by inclination, mute girl. Did your father ever mention me? Did he ever tell you that when he was a young man he was in love with me? Did he love your mother? And what was he like? Do you know that I invited you only because I am going to die in a very short while and before I die I have to find out what Adam was like? I didn't invite you because you were his daughter, or because you are an orphan. I invited you because you are the only person in the world who can tell me about him.

She slowed down when she saw that she was speeding, and holding the wheel with her left hand, she searched with her right for the cigarettes lying between them on the seat. She pushed one between her lips, then offered Felicity the package.

"Thank you, Mrs. Fleury, I don't smoke."

"Don't call me Mrs. Fleury. Call me—call me Emma." She had almost said "Emily."

"Thank you," Felicity said again. "You are very kind. But I'd—I'd really feel more comfortable if I could call you Mrs. Fleury, if you don't mind."

"Just as you like," Emma yelled above the noise of the motor and wind, again driving too fast. Felicity said nothing. After a while Emma adjusted the mirror over the dashboard. The girl had closed her eyes. Hard to tell if she was asleep or just resting, exhausted from the strenuous flight from New York to Paris, with only three hours' stop before going on to Cannes. But her kerchief had slipped from her head and Emma saw that her hair was the most amazing color—a fiery red. With her eyes closed, the girl looked younger than her age, resigned and vulnerable at the same time. And once more Emma slowed down and from then on drove carefully, so as not to frighten or jolt Adam's daughter.

It had not been her intention to help Felicity unpack. When she caught the glance, though, with which the butler eyed the one suitcase and little overnight bag, she decided—knowing there were no greater snobs in the world than servants, who could sniff the quality of leather quicker than a dog scents a stranger, tell the price of a garment unfailingly and distinguish at a glance between those who were used to being waited on and those for whom it was a rare treat—that Felicity Forbes had to be protected from being looked upon as "the poor relation." Felicity? Emma swallowed and had to admit to herself that it wasn't the girl's pride but hers that would suffer.

"Thank you," she said to Hannah, who, as usual, had

appeared with that extraordinary sense of timing which at times was as inconvenient as it could be welcome at others. "Miss Forbes will ring if she needs you." And Emma turned to Felicity, who was standing in the middle of the room as if she didn't know why she was there or what to do.

"I hope you will feel comfortable here."

The room was very large. Fleury had used it as an upstairs study, and though it had been done over, it had none of the characteristics of a guest room. The walls were painted pale blue, as if the Mediterranean had washed over them, leaving a tinge of its coloring. A large fireplace with a deep sofa in front of it, a Louis XVI writing desk, a bed built into an alcove whose heavy silk curtains, when closed, made it look like one of the many windows. As always, there were flowers, a silver platter piled high with fruit, chocolates in frail Sèvres bowls, cigarettes in golden boxes and, on the dressing table, a tray with ice water and glasses. The door to the bathroom stood open, revealing blue tiles, the glassed-in tub and a white-padded massage table.

"There's a little terrace out here," said Emma, opening one of the French windows, "where you can sit and sun yourself undisturbed."

"How lovely," said Felicity. "Thank you." Still she did not move but kept looking about her as if she couldn't believe she was to live here. The elderly gentleman who had asked her to come to his office had never conveyed what luxury she would encounter if she accepted Mrs. Fleury's invitation. "An old friend of your father—a distant relative, rather—has asked me to talk to you," he had said. "You won't have the slightest expense if you decide to join Mrs. Fleury for the summer at her house on the Riviera. All you have to do is tell me if you feel like going and, if you do, bring me your passport—you have a pass-

port, don't you? And we'll take care of the rest—visa,
ticket, everything. And if you should need anything special and find yourself short of cash, just let me know the
amount."

This offer she had turned down immediately. To the
proposal of the trip abroad she had said she would have to
think it over and phone him at the end of the week. She
had gone home quite dazed, convinced that she would
not accept the invitation of a woman she had never even
heard of. But she had never been abroad. In fact, she
had never been anywhere. She had grown up in Toledo
and come to New York only half a year ago. She didn't
know if she rated a vacation—probably not, having been
at her new job only four months—and it seemed too
much of a risk to ask. She might lose the job. But she got
all the brochures she could find in a travel bureau and
pored over them at night. The jet would take off from
Idlewild and land in Orly, Paris. Paris. The Riviera. It
was the chance of a lifetime. She was making good
money, but even if she should be fired, she had saved quite
a bit since her mother died. So—she could fall back on
her savings when she got home again, and find a new job
if the worst came to the worst. She was a first-class lab
technician. Only you didn't like to have to get used to people all over again. Mrs. Fleury would also be new. An
elderly woman. A widow, the lawyer had said. "But why
should she ask me?" she had wanted to know, and the
lawyer shrugged. "When they get older, people sometimes
get lonely. Frankly, I don't know. I'm just following instructions." As companion to a wealthy, aging widow?
She hadn't gone through years of study for that, and she
enjoyed her work much too much. But then the letter had
come, and the way it was worded had made her feel not
needed but wanted.

How beautiful everything was, how incredibly beauti-

ful! Felicity stepped out onto the terrace. The smell from
the garden, the dogs playing between the rocks, the wide
beach, the dock, the boat, and the immense space of sky
and water . . . But I don't belong here, thought Felicity.
I don't belong in a house where a butler and a chauffeur
rush up when I arrive, a house with Louis XVI furniture
and a bathroom that has a massage table. I belong in a
small ground-floor apartment that smells of what is being
cooked in its nasty little kitchen with its old-fashioned
equipment, in a room that has a sagging davenport and
worn furniture and hardly any closet space. I wouldn't
know how to behave on a private beach. I'm used to walking in the garden of The Cloisters or on Riverside Drive
when the weather's fine and, when it rains, through museums. And Mrs. Fleury doesn't look at all as if she felt
lonely or needed company. She doesn't even look old. She
must have been truly beautiful once; she still is, with her
silver hair and those fantastic blue eyes. I wish I had her
figure. And she felt ashamed of me. Out at the airport she
felt ashamed of me. The way she looked at me—she
doesn't like me. I'm all wrong. No, I don't belong.

Naturally, thought Emma, the suitcase held exactly
what she had expected—three pairs of panties, three slips,
three bras, two cotton dresses, one flannel suit, two blouses,
one sweater, one cardigan, one silk dress to be worn for
cocktails and kept on for dinner, three pairs of shoes (one
of them sandals), three nightgowns—and all in tissue
paper. But where was the photograph, the leather folding
frame that would hold Adam's picture? Surely Felicity
had taken along a photograph of her parents, if for no
other reason than to show it to her. That much fore-
thought could be expected after she had declared herself
to be a relative of Adam's. Oh, stay out there, thought
Emma, don't come back until I've found it. Let me look
at him undisturbed. And she dug her hands into the little

overnight bag. What did you look like, Adam, before you died?

"Oh, Mrs. Fleury, what are you doing? Oh, please, please . . ."

Felicity had come back into the room and was looking horrified at Emma bent over her open luggage. "You shouldn't have bothered."

To her surprise Emma noticed that Felicity was not only embarrassed but had tears in her eyes. "Anything wrong, child? Do you feel that bad?"

"It isn't that," said Felicity. "My ears are clearing up, thank you. It's just"—and she made a wide, sweeping gesture—"the flowers and candy and your unpacking for me as if—as if—"

It didn't occur to Emma that Adam's daughter had never been made to feel welcome like this before, that she was mistaking the flowers, the fruit, the candy, all the items that were put in every guest room always, as something produced especially for her. She thought Felicity was impressed at last by her surroundings and said briskly, "Wash up, have a little rest, then I'll drive you to Monte Carlo."

After Emma had gone, Felicity sat down on the Louis XVI couch as carefully as if it had been standing roped off in a museum, with a sign saying that visitors were forbidden to touch it. She leaned back and let her hands slide over the heavy yellow-white silk as if she were trying to take over physically the unaccustomed comfort and beauty, and again the feeling that she was hopelessly out of place assailed her. She should never have come. Then she saw the flowers in the fireplace, arranged in an oblong wicker basket with the container invisible and filled to overflowing with the large daisies of the Riviera, and she smiled with delight, as if the flowers alone had made the whole trip worth while. She knelt down in front of them and gently took one away, then, carrying the flower with her, she went into the bathroom and stuck it behind her left ear.

But I don't have the face to go with it, she thought, watching herself in the mirror as she moved her head from side to side. She took off the flower but could not bring herself to part from it, and when she had washed up, she pinned it on the clean cotton dress that was only a little wrinkled. Though Mrs. Fleury had told her she could rest, Felicity felt she should not keep her hostess waiting. She opened the door to the wide, quiet passage and found her way to the top of the stairs. Halfway down to the lower floor she could see Emma sitting in front of the enormous window framed by sea and sky. She looked unreal, like someone painted on a canvas, with a background of different blues, caught in a mood of meditation. Felicity almost turned back so as not to disturb her, but Emma looked up and smiled. "Oh, there you are. Good. Let's go."

"Do you drive?" she asked Felicity.

"No. I never had an opportunity to learn."

And Adam had spent his life constructing cars.

"How's that?"

"We didn't have a car after Father died."

Father. Not Daddy, not Dad, not Papa—Father. And what kind of father had Adam been? But the girl's face was set again, her mouth compressed. Still, Emma could not contain herself. "He died quite suddenly, didn't he?"

"Yes. Very suddenly."

"It must have been a great shock to you."

"Yes."

"I knew him well when he was young, younger than you."

"Yes. You said so in your letter."

"And your mother?" What did she feel when Adam

died, this woman he had married? But Felicity misunderstood.

"My mother was ill for a long time, for years before . . ."

She sighed. She could never tell anyone what it had been like, most certainly not Mrs. Fleury, who couldn't possibly understand what it meant to have to count every penny because everything you had was paying for doctors, nurses, medication, hospitals. And her father missing the renewal of his life insurance by two days, then the plant being taken over by a new management and none of the old directors left who might have done something for Forbes' wife and child. Oh, there had always been enough for rent and food, only never really enough to do things that were pleasant. Felicity sighed again.

"I'm sorry," said Emma. How disturbing that after so many years Felicity should still be reluctant to talk about her parents. From then on Emma avoided personal questions. She pointed out famous landmarks and made small talk until they reached Monte Carlo, where she drove straight to a small, elegant *salon* near the Hôtel de Paris.

"Here we are. Now let's splurge. What is your favorite color?"

And that's why she unpacked for me, thought Felicity. Not because she wanted to make me feel welcome but because she wanted to see what I'd brought with me, and if it was good enough. She blushed crimson, but did not know how to refuse.

"I think the young lady would look wonderful in green," said the salesgirl, bringing out armloads of dresses.

Emma was well aware that Felicity hated to have to come out of the fitting room and turn around like a mannequin, and in the end it was Emma who had to make the choice, for Felicity would not say yes or no to any of the dresses. Only when the salesgirl suggested adding bathing suits and beachwear did Felicity speak up. "My skin won't take the sun," she said. "I don't tan. I just peel and my freckles get bigger and bigger."

When they got in the car again, Felicity turned to Emma. "You're spoiling me," she said.

"That was my intention when I asked you to come."

"But why me?" asked Felicity.

Because you are Adam's daughter, Emma wanted to say, the daughter of the only man I ever loved. And I want you, being Adam's daughter, to look as well as you can. Oh, but why can't you look like him, why is there nothing about you that reminds me of him, of his features, his smile, of his vitality; none of his gaiety or self-assurance, none of his immediate response to everything he saw or heard, and none of his charm?

"Pure selfishness," said Emma. "There are so very few people I can call family. Don't you like being spoiled?"

"I don't know," said Felicity. "It's wonderful but—I'm sure I don't deserve it."

"What terrible things have you done?" Emma smiled to encourage the girl, but Felicity looked grave and far away. "Justice," Emma said, more to herself than Felicity, "Do you really believe in justice?"

"I believe in nothing," said Felicity.

They had just reached the entrance gate to the driveway, but Emma braked sharply and the car came to a halt in the shadow of the widespread wings of the two black marble swans. "Why do you say that, Felicity? A girl of twenty-four, with her whole life ahead of her? You can't mean it."

"But I do."

"How unlike your father you are."

"My father? Please, Mrs. Fleury, I don't want to talk about him, ever."

But you must, Emma wanted to cry out. You must. I

am going to die and I have to find out.

"I hated him," said Felicity. "I still hate him. I always will."

Emma's first impulse was to slap Felicity's face, as she would have slapped a child that had carelessly broken something very valuable, even though it didn't know the significance of price or sentimental attachment. But, used to controlling herself, she merely lighted a cigarette. "But why?"

Either Felicity had not heard or was pretending not to have heard. She was looking up at the swans, a deep frown on her round forehead, as if she were afraid of them.

Adam. How could anybody have hated him? What had he done that his daughter should speak of him with such cold loathing? Emma's mind spun back to the time when she had been young, younger than Felicity. If anyone had asked her then about her father, Jack Starr, Milk-face Starr, what would she have said? "I don't want to talk about him. I despise him. He sacrificed me for his pride. He separated me with a lie from the boy I loved so that I married another man, all because he wanted to revenge himself through me for every slight he had ever suffered." But the Adam she remembered couldn't have made an enemy of his daughter. Jack Starr could not be proved right after all these years, could not finally be justified in having acted as he did.

"Felicity?"

"I really don't want to talk about my father, Mrs. Fleury."

Suddenly Adam's daughter was an adversary and Emma wished she had followed her first reaction to the news of Adam's death and cabled back, "Not interested in getting in touch with Felicity Forbes."

* * *

Scott Warren felt as possessive about Eze as if he had been responsible for building it centuries ago on top of the pyramidal rock, as a stronghold against the barbarians. He insisted, in spite of all arguments, that until he had chosen to live there, people had bypassed it for the better-known panorama of La Turbie. But of course there had always been sightseers walking along the quaint cobble-stoned streets of Eze, marveling at the wrought-iron work of the small balconies and signs, visiting the little museums and the chapel of the Pénitents Blancs, and admiring the magnificent view. It was true, though, that his name attracted thousands of tourists who hoped to see, if not the famous man himself, then at least his house. In this they were usually not disappointed, for during his absence Scott's residence was shown for a small fee. "Good publicity," he had called it when Emma once argued against what she felt was gross immodesty and something that should be reserved for after his death. "Writers can't afford to be introverts nowadays," Scott had said. "They must be showmen or they lose their audience. You know how people are. It takes them only a couple of weeks to forget that they doled out some coins to glance at my dining room and convince them they were invited to dinner." At other times, though, all anyone could see was part of a gray-white wall with a heavy wooden door to which the large, round heads of iron nails and crossbands gave a bluish metallic tinge. Most of the house hung like an eagle's nest directly over the rock. Scott had bought it, a dilapidated ruin, shortly after his first great success, and throughout the years had fixed it up with great passion and doubtful taste.

Emma had telephoned Scott to tell him that she and a young house guest, Miss Forbes, would like to be invited to lunch. "And be nice to her," she had added. "Be gentle.

She's painfully shy, and I think it will give her a lift to meet you."

Felicity lay heavy on Emma's hands; she hardly left her room unless especially asked to join the others. Emma regretted having pointed out the privacy of the little terrace attached to Felicity's room because the girl seemed to have taken it as a suggestion that she stay there. Titus had offered to play tennis with her but Felicity had never held a racket in her life, and Meg had tried to convince her that swimming could be wonderful fun and had offered to teach her. But Felicity would have none of it. If she came down to the beach at all, she appeared fully dressed, bundled up as if for a trip to the Arctic, not an inch of skin showing, wearing Emma's discarded, enormous garden hat, which she had found in one of the greenhouses. Besides, both Titus and Meg were too involved with their own affairs to make any special effort to include a girl who obviously preferred reading and flowers to their company.

Flowers were the only thing about which Felicity showed any enthusiasm. She would talk for hours to the two old gardeners who took care of the grounds, and though she spoke no French except for the simplest phrases, they understood each other perfectly. As bald-headed Auguste put it, *"Ah, Madame, c'est une langue du cœur.* If you love flowers, you know what makes them live or die. And she knows all the Latin names and only has to take a look to see what they need."

A language of the heart. How Emma wished she could establish a language of the heart with the girl, who remained as polite and docile as on the day of her arrival, and just as reluctant to talk about herself, as if she had no plans for the future and could barely cope with the present. To Emma's question how she liked Titus, Felicity replied, "He is very handsome," and asked about Meg, "She is very gay." And Emma knew that Felicity was afraid of Titus's striking looks and stunned by Meg's unconventional and practical attitude toward life. And still there was no key to unlock the secret of Felicity's hatred for Adam.

"Won't I bore Mr. Warren?" Felicity asked now, watching Emma swing the iron knocker against the plate.

"I was just wondering if I wouldn't bore you," Scott's voice said behind them. "An old man like me."

If Scott wanted to, he could be charming, and Emma gave him a quick, grateful smile. Felicity, of course, blushed. "Oh," she stammered, "you're not old. You're not old at all."

He always looked younger than his age, but today, dressed in Bavarian brown leather shorts, barelegged, with only sandals on his feet, his white shirt open at his tanned, powerful throat, a green stocking cap on his head, he looked scarcely more than fifty.

"But do I ever feel my age!" He pointed down the valley. "I've just climbed up from there. Wanted to have a look at the olives. It's a beautiful walk. You must walk down with me one of these days, Listy."

"Listy?" asked Emma.

"Well, Felicity," said Scott. "But if you say it fast, that's what's left on your tongue—Listy. Or do you have a nickname you prefer, Felicity?"

"I have no nickname," said Felicity. She had grown very pale.

"Then from now on you're Listy," and Scott Warren took her hand and led her through the door into an almost square pink brick patio, which lay between wall and house like an antechamber. A fountain splashed in its center, and a pillared colonnade ran along two sides, its narrow, slanting roof covered with tiles in all the colors of the rainbow.

"Now give the old man a chance to wash up, then we'll have lunch."

Old man, my eye, thought Emma, watching Scott showing off like mad, trying to impress the younger generation with his age as if it guaranteed respect. She nodded to him when he lifted a bottle from a tray standing on a table in the shade of the colonnade.

"Yes, I'd like a cassis."

"Nothing for me, thank you," said Felicity. "I don't drink."

"You do in my house," Scott told her with mock sternness. "All anti-alcoholics are thrown down the precipice." And he pointed to one of the open spaces in the wall behind the colonnade, through which could be seen, as through a paneless window, the abyss directly below. "Try it. Your health, Listy."

Who was this girl? It had never been Emma's habit to invite unattached young females as house guests—men, certainly—but this summer she had two living with her, that little sex bomb who couldn't even spell correctly, let alone read, and this gangly one here. I bet she's still a virgin, he decided. Well, maybe since Fleury's death Emma's decided it's in better taste not to surround herself only with men. She always was a stickler where reputation was concerned. As if it still mattered, in this age. But oh, how these young girls must bore her.

"Well, Listy, down the hatch. Come on."

Felicity took one swallow, made a face, drank some more and found the courage to say, "I've read all your books, Mr. Warren. Not once. Often. And I love them all."

"Thank you." Scott bowed gravely, and not even Emma perceived how sincerely he meant it, how deeply im-

portant it was to him to receive affirmation as a writer by
someone almost two generations younger. "I'll be right
with you."

When he came back, he had taken off the stocking cap,
which had made him look like a peasant rather than a
writer, and slicked down his hair, and Emma could see
how surprised Felicity was to find it gray. Scott noticed
it, too, and was childishly cross for a moment, then he remembered her compliments and smiled again and took
them both inside the house.

It consisted mainly of very small rooms, small as the
cells in a monastery, and, like them, the walls were whitewashed. In each of these cubicles stood a couch and a
table, for they were used as spare rooms when the house
was filled with guests. But actually they formed a gallery
that held a quite formidable collection of African art.
There were animal masks, antelope headgear, crossbolts
from Bambara, religious statues from French Guinea, gold
pendants and ancestor statues from the Ivory Coast, masks
from the Belgian Congo—flat-faced, made of antelope
skin or metal plate, with large wooden noses and raffia
beards—and ivory statues depicting action from Bam-
bala, and tribal initiation masks and ceremonial cups.

Emma's taste was too set for her to derive pleasure from
primitive art. She could neither identify herself with its
emotional power nor admire its plastic forms. Like modern art, it made her feel uneasy, an unwelcome witness to
the struggle for individual self-expression, but Felicity, to
her and Scott's surprise, stood transfixed before a symbol
of fecundity, the head of a mother, and Scott, watching
her face, said, "Yes, that's the way I felt the first time I
encountered what are generally regarded as merely ethno-
logical objects—filled with a mixture of anxiety and excitement." And for a moment their eyes met and held,
then Felicity's face was expressionless again and she took

off her glasses as if, with them, she could take off the glance that had met hers.

"They can also make you feel safe," she said, as if security, if it existed at all, could be found only in tribal unity. Then she followed Emma and Scott into an unexpectedly large living room. Here the walls were covered with the trophies Scott had brought home from his hunting expeditions: leopard skins, fish, a lion's head, buffalo and antelope horns, the antlers of deer and rams—all neatly mounted on black ebony plaques, the date of their death inlaid in ivory—the skins of jaguars and snakes, elephant tusks. And why must he hang them up? thought Emma. Does he have to prove his manliness that way? And does he perhaps find a singular satisfaction in being able to look at them any time? And for a strange and horrifying moment she could see her own head mounted between a giraffe's and a zebra's, life-size, like them, her neck severed neatly at the same angle as theirs, her artificial eyes like enormous light-blue aquamarines, and she could imagine Scott, in one of his drunken moods, taking a pair of small horns from the wall somewhere and planting them on her head and telling her she was a doe he had killed. And as her mind lingered on this idiotic thought, she heard Felicity utter a little scream. "But how dreadful! You didn't kill them yourself, Mr. Warren?"

"Of course I did," said Scott, emptying the last of the drink with which he had wandered in from the patio. "And I never had a more thrilling experience than when I—" But Felicity had covered her ears with both hands. "Don't," she said. "Don't tell me. I don't want to hear it," and now the pupils of her eyes narrowed and she looked at Scott Warren with fear and disgust.

"All right," Scott shouted, trying to penetrate the shelter of her hands. "But let me tell you one thing—you're being stupidly sentimental. I understand. Of course I do.

I've been on both sides myself—first wanting to kill, then not being able to. Both are nonsense. One has to achieve a balance in life . . ."

"Let's have something to eat," said Emma, who herself had enjoyed hunting big game and understood Scott, but suddenly felt, like Felicity, that all death was murder, infamous and criminal. She led the way to the terrace, and here, indeed, perfect balance had been achieved, with the sea far below and the sky high above and the terrace built over a deep precipice, seemingly suspended between these two elements.

"I'm sorry," Felicity said suddenly. "You are quite right, Mr. Warren. I was being silly." Balance, she thought. If I could just find my balance, I'd be all right. "I would like to hear about how you stalked and killed them."

Be nice, Emma had said, be gentle. Scott shook his head. "Another time. When you come again and are really prepared to listen." And changing the subject, he asked her if she had ever read a certain novelist. Felicity said yes, and that she didn't like him because he used so many generalizations.

"Don't take such a dim view of generalizations," said Scott, and laughed. "They can be very useful, because often they arouse the curiosity of the young who want to test their validity. And they can help the old to remember and make it possible for the average man to resign himself."

"You think so?" said Felicity, watching Scott lean back in his chair and brace his feet in the elaborate convolutions of the wrought-iron balustrade. But then, before Scott could answer, she cried, "I know whom you remind me of—my father!"

Felicity's unexpected remark startled Emma out of her usual self-control, for this was the first time the girl had mentioned Adam since Emma had stopped the car be-

tween the two marble swans. And Scott caught Emma's
look, one he had never seen in her eyes before—a look
filled with such curiosity, such longing and fear, that
within an instant she became a different person from the
basically distant woman he had known from the time she
was a young girl. I knew it, he told himself. God damn it,
I always knew it. She lied. She deceived even me, damn
her. She didn't love Fleury. She wasn't faithful to him
either. She didn't let me make love to her because she had
a lover, and her lover was the father of this girl.

And fifteen years of living fell from him. He was hitch-
ing a ride whenever he could, and when he couldn't he
was walking for miles—through war-torn country, past
bomb-scarred houses, over bomb-littered ground, past
burnt trees that, with their foliage gone, looked like the
arms of the dead reaching up from their graves in silent
accusation—on his way to Emma, who was a girl no
longer, just as he was no longer the boy he had been when
they had met in the First World War but adult, grown up,
or so he thought. It was raining when he reached his
destination, and many of the trees in the park had been
cut down for firewood. Their stumps had been left in the
ground, like huge mushrooms, cluttering the neglected
park. There were no flowers in bloom and the moat was
dry except for a shiny cover of slime at the bottom from a
recent rain, but a light had been shining in one of the windows of the castle and Emma was there, alone in the vast
house.

And he saw himself as he had lain on the cold floor of
the castle that night, abandoned, moaning with desire
and crying with anger and shame. The fury and frustration came back to him now and shook him.

"Do I?" he said. "Do I really?"

"Yes," said Felicity. "Don't you think so, Mrs. Fleury?"

It can't be, thought Emma. It is impossible that I have

surrounded myself only with men who remind me of Adam. Thiolat because he was young and poor, Titus because his hair is like Adam's, others whom I have liked and helped, but not Scott! And she looked at Scott. Yes. Perhaps. In the way he smiled. No, it wasn't his smile. It was the way he was sitting there with his hands in his pockets, rocking back and forth, his shoulders thrown back.

"Not really," she said. And suddenly she felt very tired, with that recent kind of tiredness that she had to fight so hard to conquer. She glanced at her watch. "Scott, let me have one more cup of coffee, then I'm afraid we must go."

In the car on their way home, Felicity began to cry. The tears ran down her narrow, freckled cheeks from under the heavy rims of her glasses, making her look as if she were offering her face to the gentle rain of a warm spring evening.

Emma asked no questions, made no move that might disturb the girl, and when she finally came to a widened spot on the Corniche where cars could park or turn, she pulled up and turned off the motor. But even then she said nothing, for she sensed that Felicity's tears were not being shed for any particular reason but out of a general feeling of wretchedness. And she slipped down in her seat—making herself as small as possible, so that Felicity could forget that she had a witness—convinced that when the girl had cried herself out, she would wipe her face, smile apologetically and escape back into her usual reserve. She was astonished when Felicity blew her nose prosaically and turned to her. "You know," she said, "my father could have been a man like Scott Warren. Forceful and gentle, but harsh, too. Alive."

Emma's heart began to beat painfully and, Don't stop now, she begged silently. For Felicity had turned from her again and with her head thrown back against the seat, was looking up into the afternoon sky. Go on, go on, speak. . . . But Emma did not utter a word, as though afraid Felicity might react to her voice like a sleepwalker, shocked into sudden consciousness, losing his equilibrium. She was almost certain that Felicity had not been addressing her but was talking to herself, perhaps putting into words for the first time in her life what she had felt and thought all along.

"Did I have another nickname? A nickname I preferred?" Felicity laughed, a small, painful laugh. "I never had a nickname. He hardly ever talked to me. It was almost as if I didn't exist for him, as if I hadn't been there. He didn't talk to Mother, either—I mean, not more than was absolutely necessary. And always politely, as if we were strangers. Whenever I tried to get his attention—oh, I'd bring him a report card or I'd bake a cake—he'd brush me off, the way you brush off a fly that's bothering you. It made me hate him—for not loving me, for making me feel unwanted, for letting me grow up with a father in the house who wasn't a father. Nobody has a right to be that selfish and cruel."

Selfish? Cruel? Whom was Felicity talking about? Emma would have liked to cover her ears, as Felicity had done when Scott had tried to tell her about the thrill of killing. But I wanted to know, she told herself. I wanted to find out before I died what kind of man Adam became.

"I don't know," said Felicity, pushing back a strand of hair that the draft of a passing car had blown into her face. "I don't think I ever really knew him. I don't know what made him the person I knew. I think that perhaps he was quite different when he was young. Maybe it was partly my mother's fault. They met in Copenhagen—he went there on business long before the war—and they had

known each other only a little while when he asked her
to marry him. But not quite a year later he asked her for a
divorce. He said it wasn't her fault, the mistake was his.
He just wasn't the kind of man who should have married, and he should have known it. I think my mother was
too deeply in love with him to believe he meant what he
said. She thought she could win him back and begged
him to give their marriage another chance. At first he
wouldn't hear of it, but she talked him into staying. In the
years before she died she sometimes spoke about it. She
blamed herself for having been stupid enough to try to
keep a man who wanted to be on his own. You see, he
stayed—but he never touched her again. One night he
came home—he had been drinking—and she saw her
chance. And when the three months they had agreed
upon were over and he was going to leave, she told him
she was carrying his child and that she would never consent to a divorce. He went away anyhow, to fight in the
civil war in Spain. Gave up his job and left. I think he was
looking for a chance to be killed, I think he would rather
have died than be tied to a woman and child he didn't
want. And he didn't come back. He stayed in Europe.
But he sent us money regularly. Then one day Mother
found out he was back in the States, at his old job with
Willys-Overland, and she took me to him. She was sure he
would be moved by the sight of his daughter, that something would touch his heart and he would come back to
her. She dressed me prettily and I remember being very
excited that I was to see him at last. She had told me so
many wonderful things about him, and I had prayed for
him every night with her. He was living in a hotel and
he met us in the lobby. I had been told to run up to him
and kiss him and cry, 'Daddy.' She had even rehearsed the
scene with me. And I did exactly as I was told. But when
I grabbed his legs, he paid no attention to me. He looked

over my head and said, 'Take her away.' After that my mother changed. She started being unkind to me. She had set her hopes on me, and I had failed her. Anyway, that's the only explanation I have. And I didn't see my father again for a long time. He volunteered when the war broke out in Europe and joined a Canadian outfit. But I never forgot the expression on his face, the way his voice sounded when he said those three words, 'Take her away.' "

For Emma, it became impossible to recognize the Adam she had known in the picture Felicity was painting. Had he existed only in her imagination—gay, loving, full of life? But he had been full of life and laughter. He had never been cold or bitter, and he had never been mean. And she closed her eyes, appalled. Was this what her father's lie had done?

"I saw him again in 1946," said Felicity. "I was ten. I went to the plant, and I sat in his office for a long time, waiting for him. I hadn't told the secretary I was his daughter, just said I had an important message for him. He looked angry when he saw me sitting on the chair opposite his desk, but before he could say anything I told him that my mother was sick and wanted to see him. He said nothing, just waved me to follow him. We got into his car and he came home with me. From then on he lived with us, because my mother remained an invalid. She had meningitis. I guess you never really quite recover from that. He did everything that had to be done—hospitals, doctors, nurses. Oh, he did his duty, but without love or compassion, like the stranger he had always been. He'd leave the house early but he'd come home almost every evening and just sit there, smoking his pipe and drinking. After a while he began drinking heavily. . . . As I said, we hardly ever talked. None of us." Felicity sighed. "I left notes for him if there was something he ought to know, and he would leave notes and money for me on the kitchen table."

Now Felicity was painting the man Emma had loved as an extreme egoist to whom nothing, not even the feelings of his child, mattered if he wanted his own way. And she wanted to beg Felicity, as she might have begged a thief who was looting her home, not to take everything, to leave her something that could justify having loved Adam. She nearly said, "Let him live a little while longer. Don't kill my illusions all at once. I have lived with him since I was seventeen. I would not know what to do without them."

"One night when he had been drinking," said Felicity, "he came out on the balcony where I was watering the flowers. It was still light enough to see that he was very pale. He sat down and for a long time said nothing. But I could hear him breathing and feel him looking at me, watching me. Suddenly he asked me how old I was. And when I told him fourteen, he said, 'Maybe there's still time for us to get to know each other.' And suddenly he stretched out his hand to me. His hands were beautiful, so alive. I had wanted so often to feel them. But now, when he offered me the chance, I couldn't take it. I don't know why. And he let his hand fall again. He didn't say anything more. After a while I went to bed. But he sat out there on the balcony for a long time and I watched him from my window until I fell asleep, wondering what had made him reach out for me. The next afternoon they called from the plant to say he had collapsed over his desk. He had had a heart attack. After that I told myself he must have felt ill when he came out on the balcony the night before—not drunk but sick, in need of some fresh air—and that he had reached out for me only because he felt all wasn't well with him. So I went on hating him. . . . And then today, when I came into Mr. Warren's living room and saw all those trophies hanging on the wall and he shouted something about wanting to kill and not being able to kill, and that one had to establish a balance in life, I knew suddenly that I had always been—well—lopsided, weighted down by my hatred of my father, and when I realized that—I don't know—I think I stopped hating him."

Felicity sat up straight. "No. Mr. Warren doesn't really look like my father. He just sat there the way my father sat that night, his shoulders thrown back, his hands in his pockets and his feet braced in the wrought iron of the balustrade."

And now for the first time Emma moved, turned and looked at Felicity's pale, freckled face. "I didn't know hatred could be a strength," the girl said, "that it could form one's attitude toward almost everything. And I lived by it. Now I feel lost. What will I be without it?"

Yes, thought Emma. You have lost your hatred, and I an illusion that made life easier. And now she could see Adam clearly, a man who had never possessed the strength to stand up against defeat, a man who had gone through three wars trying to die, trying to escape a life he could not master, a prisoner of disappointment. But she had to accept the fact that there was no time to replace her loss, whereas Felicity— And suddenly it seemed imperative to Emma to give the girl a new strength. And she repeated Felicity's last question. "What will you be? Well, Listy, I think that's something to look forward to, something worth taking every chance for, don't you think?"

It was long past midnight when Meg left the house and, keeping carefully in the shadows, made her way to the garage. The doors were still open, and she slipped between the Mercedes and the station wagon toward the narrow wooden staircase that led upstairs. They should have a pole, she thought crossly as she climbed it. Like in a fire station. Then the picture of Gino slithering down a pole in his elegant white linen uniform made her laugh. One day, though, it might make a nice bit for a publicity column. The gifted young violinist . . . She could see the drawing of Gino hanging onto the slippery post with his feet, his legs twisted into a couple of knots as he fiddled a difficult Scarlatti passage. Then, when she reached the top of the stairs, she could hear the music coming from his room.

Very gently, so as not to interrupt him, she opened the door. He did not stop playing, only his eyes greeted her, and Meg tiptoed across the floor and lay down on the bed. For a while she listened, stretched out on her back, then she turned to watch him.

How different he looked when he was playing! There was no shyness about him now, no awkwardness, only the dignity of knowing what he was doing and that he was doing it well. Even his wide lips had lost their sensuousness. In spite of the deep concentration of his whole body, it gave an impression of subtlety, like a wild animal, thought Meg, poised for a leap. Seen three-quarter face, his chin looked stronger, no longer the chin of a still growing boy, and his fingers were suddenly terribly alive, as if the strength and gentleness with which they manipulated bow and strings were independent of his mind, as if they were acting with their own mysterious knowledge. He seemed far away, another human being, a young man she hardly knew.

Seeing him play always made Meg feel uneasy, and she had to fight down the desire to stop him, to have him change back into the boy she knew. But she realized that she must not give in to this need of hers unless she wanted to make him angry. Funny, to have a violin as a rival. And the way he handled it—as if it were a baby, so carefully, so lovingly. He would even stroke it sometimes, sliding his hand across the belly. "Feel the wood, Margareta. Just feel it. And look at the back." Well, maybe there was something to the shape and wood of an instrument, but she would never understand it, no matter how often he might explain it to her.

He broke off in the middle of a passage, put violin, bow and chinpiece on the table and stood with his back turned to her, motionless.

"That was beautiful," said Meg.

"No," he said. "No good. No good at all. I heard Stern play it this spring in Paris. I cannot catch it. It's in my head"—he hammered a fist against his temple as if he could knock it out of his mind—"but it doesn't sound as it should. It doesn't talk when I play it. What time is it?"

"Almost one o'clock."

He sighed. "Better not try again then. They'll ring any moment now."

Of course. That was why he was still dressed in his uniform. He would have to take some of Mrs. Fleury's dinner guests back to Beaulieu.

"I don't know," said Meg. "They're still playing bridge. Come here, sit by me."

Gino sat down heavily. "I'll never make it."

"But you will, you will," said Meg.

He smiled then. "You sweet. You very sweet."

"But it doesn't mean anything."

"It means that you love me and want to believe in me."

"Your English has improved. A whole sentence without a mistake."

"You teach me a lot," he said, "not only English but how to be good-mannered without servant politeness." And now he gave her his full attention. "New dress?"

"Yes. Aunt Emily gave it to me. Pretty, isn't it?"

"Expensive, too?"

"Terribly expensive."

Gino touched the material almost with awe. "Thin like spider web. Beautiful. Will be long time before I can give my Margareta something really beautiful."

Meg did not answer but looked down the soft light-blue chiffon that flowed to the floor from her waistline in yards and yards of material. The floor was not very clean and she pulled up the hemline, bending down quickly and pulling back immediately, and as she did so, she felt sick. For a moment she sat very still, fighting nausea, then she lay back and lighted a cigarette. "Gino. It didn't come."

"What didn't come?"

"My days."

"Your days?" He still didn't understand, then, suddenly, he grasped what she meant.

"First time?"

"No," said Meg. "I looked at my calendar. I always make a cross. It didn't come in July, and I've always been regular as clockwork. But I thought maybe the different climate, different food, swimming such a lot . . . No. This is the second month."

Gino's face broke into a smile. "A *bambino,*" he said, "Gino's *bambino,*" and he put his hand on her stomach, stroking it gently. As if I were a violin from which he could pluck music, thought Meg, and looked at him in surprise.

"Do you want to have children?"

"I love all children, but Gino's and Margareta's children I love best."

"I mean now," said Meg. "You're not even twenty-two."

"Young parents, happy children," said Gino. *"Oh, amore mio"*—he put his cheek against hers—*"amore mio, amore mio."*

Meg could smell his breath and feel his warmth and almost put her arms around his neck to draw him closer, but instead she drew away. "Let's be practical," she said. "What are we going to do?"

"Marry, of course."

"Marry?" repeated Meg, and the word stood in the room like a stranger she could not identify, a stranger who carried on his shoulders a burden, the burden of responsibility. Marriage meant an engagement party, buying a trousseau, showers, choosing a maid of honor, bridesmaids, ushers, best man, writing invitations, preparing for the great day, fittings for the gown, quarrels about the decorations, where and when and what colors, what flowers, bridal nerves and a wreath of green myrtle and wedding bells and the flinging of the bouquet and a shower of rice like a snow flurry in June—and a honeymoon trip, and years and years of careless happiness. One didn't have children before one was at least twenty-three. A child, thought Meg. I'd be a mother before I've been a bride. And then for the first time she thought of her parents. They were expected on Friday, six days from now. She could just see their reaction. "May I introduce my fiancé?" and in would come Gino in his chauffeur's uniform, holding his cap behind his back. "Aunt Emily's chauffeur, Giovanni Patti. From a place on the Lago di Garda, so small its name can't be found on the map." She could almost feel their silence, as if it were something physical. Her father would look at her mother, his lips compressed, saying nothing, his eyes saying all the louder, "*Your* daughter!" And her mother would return the glance and the accusation, "*Your* daughter, William. Didn't I warn you that you were spoiling her?" And she would cry and work herself into hysterics because that was the only way to make her husband take over when she couldn't cope with a situation, and he would turn to Meg and say, "Margaret, will you please explain what this is all about? You are out of your mind, of course." And

she would say, "Please let me explain. No, don't interrupt." Which they would do, of course, all the time, until
she, too, would start to cry. "He's nobody now, but one
day he'll be better than Stern and Heifetz and Oistrakh,
more famous than Van Cliburn. . . ."

"Marry?" said Meg. "But Gino, I'm not at all sure my
parents will allow me to marry you."

"They will have to," said Gino, "now that there is a
baby."

Meg closed her eyes as if to shut out the truth. Sometimes, as a child, she had put both hands over her eyes,
believing that since she couldn't see anything herself, nobody else could. It didn't work.

"Daddy, Mother, listen—before you say anything nasty
—I'm pregnant."

That would silence them for a while, then her father
would ask, sternly but hopefully, "You're joking, aren't
you?" and when she said no, they would rant and rave
and accuse Gino of having seduced her and got her with
child because he knew she was a rich girl and could be
helpful to his career. And what an expensive career! Years
of study, an accompanist of his own, and even if he was
gifted, didn't it take years and years to break through?
Never, never, whatever she might say to the contrary,
would they believe that their daughter had been the one
who seduced Gino. Girls of her class simply didn't do that.
They were pure and naïve, and loved young men like
Harold. No, of course it was not her fault, poor baby.
There were ways, after all—maybe one could buy the
scoundrel off. And Harold must never know. She could be
sent somewhere where nobody knew her—there were
places for that sort of thing—let her have the little bastard,
and they would assure her that others had given their
illegitimate children away and not suffered an iota from
doing so. After all, she'd never have to see it. And if she

insisted on marrying Gino? Well, if she wanted to be dis-
inherited . . . And it wouldn't be just a threat. Where
money was concerned, her father was adamant, and her
mother would join forces with him because her heart was
set on Harold's goddam Presidential timber and the
chance of becoming the mother-in-law of someone who
was going to amount to something in a world she recognized, not a bohemian one. . . .

"Your parents," said Gino, "they not like me, perhaps,
in the beginning. But they can't do anything to us. They
can't hurt us."

"Oh, yes they can," said Meg. "They'll walk out on us.
You don't know them. They'll not help us, not with a
cent."

"I save almost all my salary," Gino said, trying to speak
slowly now and as correctly as he could, because he saw
that she was frightened. "I spend very little, only on concerts and music and lessons. I have sixty-five hundred and
forty-eight dollars." He jumped up to take his bankbook
out of the drawer in the table. "Here," he said, as if she
wouldn't believe him without proof, and he laid the book
open on her chest. "It say six thousand, five hundred and
forty-eight dollars and thirty-five cents."

"That's not very much," said Meg, and she began to cry
in spite of herself.

"It's more in Italy than here," he told her. "Don't cry,
carissima. Don't cry. We'll make it more. I can work. You,
too. Like Mrs. Webster, perhaps, work that won't tire
you."

"But you saved it so's you could study with that famous
teacher—what's his name?—Villati."

For a second all the blood drained from his face, then
he shook his head. *"Bambino* more important. Is only a
question of time, Margareta, just a question of time. Lots
of artists have been success only after forty. I'm not wor-

ried. I am happy. Very happy."

The telephone rang. Meg and Gino stared at it as if a third person had suddenly entered the room, disturbing them at this most serious point in their relationship. Then Gino jumped from the bed and took the receiver off the hook. The butler's voice came through clearly. "They're just putting on their coats. You'd better hurry."

"You stay here," said Gino. "I be back in half an hour. I bring something to drink. I be back soon as I can."

He smoothed down his hair, reached for the cap she hated, blew a kiss and was gone. For a moment she could hear his steps as he rushed down the stairs, the slamming of a door and the sudden thunder of a motor starting. It reverberated in the floor and made the ash tray on the bedside table rattle. Then for about five minutes everything was quiet until, all of a sudden, he blew the horn so loudly it startled her. But he always did when he drove by the garage and knew she was waiting for him in his room above, like a pilot dipping his wing in greeting.

Now that he was gone, the room seemed unexpectedly small and stuffy. Meg looked longingly at the windows he had closed so as not to disturb anyone with his playing. She didn't dare open them. The servants were still clearing the rooms, somebody might take the dogs out for their last walk. Meg couldn't afford to be seen, now less than ever. She turned the pillow around to where the cover was still cool, and stared up at the ceiling.

Three or four fly-catchers hung from it at strategic points, their sticky brown glue covered with all sorts of gnats, mosquitoes and flies. She had forgotten they were there, and the sight of them made her feel sick again. She turned away to look at something more pleasant. But the flowers that always stood in the stone jar on the floor were wilted. They looked terribly dead. Poor Gino. He had had such a lot of driving to do during the last weeks, with all the preparations for the ball, he hadn't found time to give them water or to ask the gardener for fresh ones. What a sad little room it was. Not even curtains, just shades that gave no privacy because one could see the shape of anything moving behind them. And how cheap the chintz was on the easy chair, such an ordinary, loud design. Heh, listen, my girl, Meg told herself. You'd better not criticize. Don't be so choosy. You've been spoiled by living in Aunt Emily's house and learning to take beauty and taste for granted, but this is how you may have to live —in one room, with a shower instead of a tub and a make-shift kitchen. She sat up and hugged her knees. Yes, this might be how Gino and she would have to live if her parents cut her off. Sixty-five hundred and forty-eight dollars and thirty-five cents. Aunt Emily might help. She might. If Meg went to the old girl and said, "You gave me a chance to find out if my young man is the guy I want, and I want him," she might help. "No family, no back-ground, Aunt Emily—only talent." But did Gino have talent? She couldn't tell. She knew nothing about music, only what Gino had told her. And could she believe him?

Slowly, mechanically, and quite unconscious of what she was doing, Meg pulled one thumbtack after another from the photographs on the wall. The third one gave some trouble and she broke a nail, but finally all the pic-tures were lying in her lap, small snapshots taken with a cheap Brownie, some of them already fading. There was the priest. "He won't drink his poor parishioners' wine or eat their bread." She hadn't known that young priests in Italy earned so little they had to rely for physical nourishment on those for whose souls they were respon-sible. Brought up in a seminary. Because that didn't cost money. And the guide? He didn't look very smart, al-most as if the heavy knapsack and ropes were too heavy for him. Quite old and worn, although he was only twenty-seven. What a profession, to make a living risking one's life in the mountains for other people's pleasure. And the four children that had died during the war—not enough food. Meg could feel her stomach contract. To die of hunger, as if they had lived in China instead of Italy. And those precious chickens. Five all together. If it got cold in winter, they were allowed to live in the kitchen. The bricklayer and his little boy. How common they looked, he in his Sunday best—unmistakably a laborer dressed up to have his picture taken—and the child over-dressed, in long pants when he couldn't be older than four. And the mother . . . "All women run big and fat in my family"—Gino had said it as if he were proud of it. Big and fat. *Mamma mia.* Her relatives. Bricklayer, mountain guide, priest, ah, she had forgotten the little sister, Gabriella. Fat already, too, with blond hair combed all around her plump face like a curtain of curls. Poor child. Somebody should take her to a hairdresser.

And coming from this family, could Gino possibly possess a talent strong enough to lift him above these common people into a sphere of refinement and culture? Lift him above the average young talented musicians who had to make a living playing in coffeehouses or cheap orchestras? It would be a miracle. But then, as Scott Warren had said one day, any real talent is a gift of God, a miracle.

I'm a snob, thought Meg, and began to put the photos back in their places, which was easy, since the paint on the wall showed a darker yellow where it had not been exposed to sun and air. A snob. Titus was right. She began to cry softly. Gino. He was honorable, so goddam honorable. Sixty-five hundred and forty-eight dollars and thirty-five cents. The *bambino* comes first. Honorable and naïve. Not well bred, but that wasn't his fault.

And I love him, she told herself. Yes, I do. I do.

The garage door below closed with a bang. He was back. She dried her tears.

"Sorry I'm late," said Gino, "but they wanted me to drive them to Monte Carlo." He put down three bottles of beer with the triumphant smile of a conqueror. "You know, I never think before—maybe I should try the casino."

"You'll do nothing of the sort," said Meg. "I won't have it. Come, lie next to me. And don't talk about it any more. Just take me in your arms and hold me tight. Hold me tight, Gino. Where is your mouth?"

Only a few days later, Emma was about to lie down for the rest she required every day now when she heard soft, hesitant steps coming along the passage. Since early childhood she had nearly always been able to tell who it was by the way someone walked, without having to see the person. Even now she could recall her father's footfall—quick, light, staccato, like raindrops on a summer morning—while her mother had always walked on tiptoe, as if she were entering a church in which the sermon had already begun—almost noiselessly, audible only because she would stop every so often to cross herself, then the shy, embarrassed tiptoeing would start again. Emma's tutor had tiptoed, too, but for other reasons, and Emma smiled to herself. With him it had been the impulse to surprise that had made him move gently, the hope of catching her doing something he had forbidden, but she always heard him coming because in his eagerness to take her unawares he would lean forward too much, lose his balance and have to put his feet down hard to regain his equilibrium. Scott Warren always sounded like a soldier with full pack on a forty-mile march, and Thiolat had never quite outgrown his habit of pulling up his legs as if he were still walking through the woods of his childhood, expecting to step over a root or a fallen branch. Emma listened again. Titus? No. Titus came down on his heels first, like a skier pressing his full weight down on the slender waxed boards over the icy *piste*. Besides, Titus had left after breakfast, saying he would not be back for dinner. Meg, who was always on the run, had gone to St. Tropez to visit a girl friend who had just arrived from the States, and Felicity—yes, in the house Felicity always walked haltingly and softly, as if she were afraid of disturbing someone. It might be Felicity wanting to talk to her, to knock at her door yet not daring to. . . .

Emma put away the folder in which she kept the list of items needed for the ball—flowers, wine, food, candles, Japanese lanterns, orchestras, presents, extra help, the names of policemen the town would put at her disposal to regulate traffic and guard the gate and beach, the list of guests and in which hotels they would be staying, the names of the dancers from the ballet in Monte Carlo, the tables and chairs needed, the number of rowboats (all illuminated), the platform to be erected at the dock, glasses and dishes and table linen, and the big tent that would be put up to the left of the terrace. But the footsteps that had halted outside her door were moving away. She opened the door.

Instead of Felicity, Emma saw Gino leaning against the wall opposite her room. He had been leaning against a wall like that the first time she had noticed him—his shoulders hugging the stone, but the rest of his body stretched from it so that there had been a wide space behind his legs, and a cat had been slinking back and forth in it. But he had been smoking then and the cigarette had dangled from his lips at an insolent angle, his hands had been dug into his pockets and he had kept his eyes half closed. It had been in a small restaurant in Milan where

people went after dinner to sip some kind of liqueur
called Ambrosia. A cellar. She had asked a waiter who
Gino was. Dressed so shabbily and looking half starved
and savage, he was obviously not a guest and just as obviously not one of the employees, since he never moved,
just stood there leaning against the wall with his feet
crossed in front of him, shifting them once in a while.
"Waiting for the restaurant to close," she had been told.
"Then the man in the orchestra"—there had been a piano
player and a violinist—"lets him have his fiddle to practice
on while he eats his dinner." She had stayed and heard
him play and talked to him, and in the end offered him a
job as a chauffeur because, except for a violin, a car was
the only thing he could handle. The boys in the garage
where he worked had taught him how to drive.

"Gino?"

As far as she knew, he had never come upstairs before.
Whenever she had talked to him about his personal affairs,
it had always been in the library. "What do you want,
Gino?"

His nostrils were quivering as if he had been trying to
find her room by her scent, like a dog. "I know," he said,
"I know I must send butler first to ask if I can see *la
contessa* but I not want him to know I have need to
speak. It is very urgent. Very private."

She knew he would never have been bold enough to
risk her displeasure without a valid reason. "Come in."
And when he had closed the door, "What is it?"

"Margareta. I can't find her anywhere."

"Margareta?" And then she realized whom he meant.
"Miss Meg?"

"Yes," he said. "Meg."

Not Miss Meg, not Miss Brown, but Meg. ("He's nobody, Aunt Emily. Just a young man who wants to make
good. No background, no money—but he's different

from anyone I have ever known. . . .") Somehow Emma
had expected the young man to be somebody from Meg's
own set.

"Meg," she said. "Do you call her Meg, Gino?"

"I call her Margareta. Where is she? I must know where
she is. *Prego.* Please tell me. She gone almost two days.
Always I see her, every night, but last night she doesn't
come. I wait and wait, but she doesn't come. I try to find
her—house, beach, park—no Margareta. No note, either,
little note she always leave in my room every day, saying
all the places she must go, when swimming, when
driving to Nice or Monte Carlo, when eating, everything.
Everything. And no note yesterday, no note all today. . . ."

Meg and Gino. Who would have thought that Meg
would have the courage even to consider if her aunt's
chauffeur was "the right guy"? Emma looked at Gino.
Under his tan he was pale, as if the color of sun and wind
were something artificial he had put on his face. Drops of
perspiration glistened on his upper lip and he was
trembling.

"Miss Meg has gone to visit friends in St. Tropez."

He sighed loudly with relief. He had been almost out
of his mind with worry and had lain awake in the dark,
hot room all night, thinking at one moment that he ought
to be whipped for getting her with child, and at the next
that it was wonderful, a miracle that she should be carrying his son; wondering if he had made it clear to her that
he really didn't mind at all having to delay the pursuit
of his career if they couldn't count on her parents to help
them; then feeling guilty that he had made love to her.
She had fainted the second time. And for over thirty
hours he had been imagining her sick in her room, too
sick to come to him.

"And I so worried, so very worried." He smiled, a happy

smile that showed all his teeth. "So sorry to bother *la contessa,* but Margareta not in her room. She not like that I come to you but even if she not disappear, I come, perhaps today, perhaps tomorrow, to tell you I want to marry Margareta." And now he laughed aloud in triumphant delight, and in that instant Emma no longer saw Gino but Adam—Adam standing in her father's office, a young man with no money, no background, yet so proud to offer the little he had—but she could see her father, too, sitting in his swivel chair behind his desk, swiveling from right to left, from left to right as he looked the young man up and down, this greenhorn who had the audacity to presume he would be good enough for his only daughter. And oh, God, Emma prayed, let me not be a snob now, let me not be prejudiced, let me not think of the difference of our social standing, of class and race.

"Do you love her?"

"With all my heart. From the very first day. I love her because she is beautiful and gay. She laugh about the same things I laugh, and when she is hurt, she cry like a baby. I love her because she is she."

"And does she love you?"

"Of course," said Gino. And he said it without arrogance, as if it were the most natural thing to be loved. "And she knows I will take good care of her."

"But can you?" asked Emma, thinking for the first time of Meg's parents, and thinking for a moment, too, as her father might have thought, He's counting on her parents' position, on their money. He's no fool. He's ambitious, too.

"I believe I can," said Gino with great dignity. "Will be difficult for the first few years, but it say nowhere that we are born only to have it easy. I know Mr. and Mrs. Brown will not like it, because Margareta warn me." He shrugged. "We don't need them. One day they will be proud of me."

"It's not wise for a young artist to tie himself down."

"I know that, too," said Gino. "It is not wise and not practical, and I, too, think it better to wait a few years until I am somebody. And we are young, we could wait."

"Then why don't you? A year at least, or two. You should give all your time to study."

"But the *bambino* won't wait."

"The *bambino?*" Emma repeated, and then she understood. "Meg is pregnant? Why didn't you tell me? Why didn't you tell me right away?"

Gino looked confused. "But I think you understand—that is why I am so worried. I think maybe Margareta not well and needing me and not daring to tell our secret, so you not send for me."

Pregnant. Of course. A boy and a girl in love, meeting on hot, quiet summer nights. Why hadn't she considered the consequences when she gave Meg the chance to find out if she really loved Gino? "How does Meg feel about it?"

"A little sick," said Gino. "Like many women. Dizzy, too. And worried. Not too much, I think, but frightened of parents, naturally, and of you. Is all so new."

Emma could see Meg lying on her bed, as she had lain that morning when she had confessed to being in love with a young man with no money, her legs in their black stockings moving restlessly, the round, sullen face, a child, and now she was to become a mother. Emma's heart began to beat quite rapidly, and for a moment she thought it must be the drugs Jacques Thiolat made her take so regularly. But then she knew that it had nothing to do with her sickness or its treatment—she was as excited as if this child, Gino's and Meg's child, were the child she had yearned for.

Gino, watching her face, saw the frown vanish from her forehead, her stern glance soften, saw her eyes grow suddenly bright, and he grabbed her hand. "I knew—I knew you understand. Please let me know when she come home. Right away, please."

The moment Gino had gone, Emma rang for Hannah. "I can't remember the name of the girl Miss Meg has gone to visit in St. Tropez," she told her. "See if she left the address on her desk, as I asked her to." But Hannah came back to say that, though the desk was unusually tidy, there was no note, nor had Meg jotted down the telephone number where she could be reached on the pad that, as in a well-run hotel, was put in the top drawer of the writing table in every guest room, with stationery, telegram and cable forms and a variety of postcards depicting the Villa du Cygne. It did not occur to Hannah to ask if anything had happened—she had been trained never to ask questions that were not strictly relevant to the services required of her. And though Emma greatly appreciated her reserve, right now she wished it could be broken. She smiled encouragingly.

"How long have you been with me, Hannah?"

Hannah looked slightly startled. "Going into my sixth year, Madame."

Six years, thought Emma. Aren't six years enough to allow a moment of intimacy? Of course it is my fault that she doesn't respond. Besides, she is obviously cross that I didn't reprimand Meg, since Meg has gone right on staying out every night. In spite of this, she asked, "You don't happen to recall the name, Hannah?"

"I wasn't even told that Miss Brown was going away for a visit."

Miss Brown. Emma suppressed a sigh. No, Hannah would be no help. But she could at least show a little con-

cern about her mistress. Or didn't she look upset? Had
the many years of rigid discipline made even the relief of
showing a trace of feeling impossible? Titus might know.
Though it was not very probable that Meg had told him
where she could be reached, he usually managed to find
out what people were doing. But he had gone to meet
Susan. Felicity, perhaps? Only a few days ago she had
seen the two girls sitting in the Mercedes, Meg explaining to Felicity, who was taking driving lessons, the work-
ings of a foreign car. Gently she knocked on the door of
the girl's room, and the low, hoarse voice, which seemed
to belong to another person, called out, "Just a moment,
please. Who is it?"

"Emma."

"Oh."

The wood of the door was too heavy to allow Emma to
hear the steps approaching, but she heard the key being
turned in the lock. Really! Why did Felicity still think it
necessary to lock herself in?

The girl was in the process of dressing. She had thrown
a robe around herself and while opening the door was
struggling into a sleeve of her cheap little kimono. How
unlike Meg, thought Emma, who liked to parade her
lovely young body as naked as possible, who knew no
embarrassment, and to whom the idea that she might embarrass others was unimaginable.

"I'm sorry," said Felicity. "My room looks so messy.
I'm going to tidy it, of course, before I go out."

She looked at Emma apologetically, as if she expected a
scolding. Then she smiled. "I've never had so much to
choose from," and she pointed at the dresses spread out on
her bed and on the chairs.

"Going out?" asked Emma and, with the extreme
politeness that always startled the young generation, "May
I sit down?"

"Oh, I'm so sorry." Felicity blushed crimson, the blood shooting up through her face to be stopped at the high cheekbones, as if they were a natural barrier. From there it ebbed back slowly to color her long, thin neck. I must try to teach her not to blush, thought Emma. Delightful as it is to find young girls still can blush, it betrays too much. She sat down in the chair Felicity had cleared. "Where are you going, if I may ask?"

"To St. Tropez—that is, if Mr. Warren really comes."

Face to face again with the deeply ingrained pessimism of so young a girl, Emma put all thoughts of Meg aside for a moment. "Why shouldn't he come if he said he would? He's picked you up before."

Felicity shrugged. "I don't know. People promise things in a moment of kindness, then forget about them. And he said it so offhandedly—Monday, three o'clock."

"I wouldn't call that offhand. I'd call that very precise."

"You would? You would really?"

Emma saw the flicker of a smile brighten Felicity's face and shuddered at the thought that the girl, unsure whether the plans of the day would be carried out, was still dressing for the occasion. She nodded emphatically. "Of course, Listy, of course."

And now, assured, Felicity began to speak rapidly. "Scott said he might take his boat, just cruise for a while, and then have dinner in St. Tropez—I forget the name of the restaurant—and we might stop in Cannes on our way back. There's a gala night at the casino, and he wants me to see it. That's why I find it so difficult to dress. I don't know . . . I'm not sure . . . I don't want to be over-dressed and yet"—she blushed again—"I do so want to look right on the boat, in the restaurant, at the casino."

"Naturally," said Emma, just as though she, too, had once had trouble deciding what would be right for an occasion. "Why don't you put on that dark-green linen dress to start out with, and the heavy yellow cardigan? I think that would look charming, and you might pack the flowered chiffon in a bag, with another pair of shoes and an evening wrap. Then if you find you *are* going to Cannes, you can change on board. The boat has two cabins, you know."

"I was going to save it for the ball."

Emma nearly told her of the surprise she had in store for her. You will have a white lace dress, she almost said. I ordered it from Berthe the other day—white lace over a white satin petticoat, and a short white silk coat. The coat will be embroidered with hundreds of little white rhinestones, but the dress will be quite plain—plain and full. I'd like you to wear white orchids. I told the florist to make them up like a tiara to wear in your hair. It's really your outstanding feature and should be shown off. You'll wear it open, your silky red hair that couldn't possibly be dyed—long and open like a flaming mantilla. But I'm going to insist on makeup even if you fight me tooth and nail. You'll use powder and rouge properly for once. And you won't have to wear glasses. The contact lenses will be ready. Of course they'll hurt a little at first. I wish we could have got them before, but the occulist had to send to Paris for them. But you'll have a couple of days to get used to them. Without glasses you still won't look beautiful—you never will, my darling—but you can and will look attractive. In a piquant sort of way, certainly not like any other woman, with your freckled skin and your freckled eyes. . . .

"You really think I should take it? The dress?"

"Of course," said Emma. "Don't ever save things for special occasions. By the way, have you any idea where Meg can be reached?"

Felicity shook her head. "Somewhere around St. Tropez. Curly's people have rented a house, she said, but she didn't exactly know herself where it was."

"What's Curly's name?"

"I don't know."

"If you happen to run into Meg, would you please tell her to come home?"

"Is anything wrong?"

"No," said Emma. "What could be wrong?"

"I don't know," said Felicity. "I'm always afraid something or other might be wrong. I don't mean anything by it."

There it was again, the timidity, the innate fear Emma had been trying to combat these past weeks—it colored the girl's whole outlook on life. "But you mustn't always be afraid."

"I know," said Felicity again. "You know, Aunt Em, I think I was born afraid. My mother had a bad time with me. They had to use forceps. I lay all wrong. Maybe that has something to do with it. I try to fight it, honestly I do. But just when I start believing everything will be all right, something goes wrong. Father seemed to be perfectly healthy that morning he died, the job I wanted so much was mine, then in two months the firm folded, and the boy I was going with fell in love with my best girl friend. Oh, but I've told you all that. You know, I still don't quite believe I'm here in Europe, in this beautiful house with you," and she smiled at Emma with confidence.

And I, too, will leave you, thought Emma. Whatever I may have begun to mean to you, you will lose it. All I can do is give you some affection for a little while, and a glimpse of a different way of life. But when I'm gone, you won't have to skimp any longer. That may be a consolation to you, and then again it may not. It is easier, though, to cry in comfort. But there isn't much more I can do for you. From then on you'll be on your own.

"If I were you, Listy, I'd believe in the law of averages.

You've had a bad time." She put her hand over the girl's. "One shouldn't take oneself too seriously. Nobody is just one person but many. I mean, you don't have to regard yourself only as a girl who has been disappointed over and over again. Put that girl away. You can be another girl, too, and another. And you alone can bring them to life. And different things can happen to every one of them."

If only someone had told her that at Felicity's age. Would she have believed it? Quite possibly, if it had been said by her father or Fleury, somebody whose authority and experience she trusted. But nothing had been farther from their minds.

"Perhaps. I'll try."

And Emma saw Felicity glance covertly at the clock on her bedside table, and knew she should go now and leave Felicity to finish dressing. But she felt a certain dread of being alone, with nothing to divert her thoughts from Meg—Meg, who might have fainted over the steering wheel or driven too fast to outrace the problems that must be on her mind. There was, of course, a chance that Meg was having one of those heart-to-heart talks with Curly, and that Emma was worrying for nothing. She lighted a cigarette. "Don't mind me," she said. "Go right ahead and make yourself pretty. Or am I disturbing you?"

"No, no," said Felicity. "But—I wear falsies." Once more her face was dipped in blood. Then, determined not to let her embarrassment make her late for Scott Warren, she let the kimono slip from her shoulders. Now, except for her panties, she was naked, and Emma realized suddenly why Felicity had refused to wear a bathing suit on the beach, that all her explanations, which had sounded so logical and were certainly valid—that her skin could not take any sun, that ever since she could remember she had had to avoid strong light—had also been a subterfuge. She had not wanted to let anyone see her undressed. That was why, at Madame Berthe's, she had managed to keep out of sight until, in the privacy of the small fitting room, she had slipped alone into the dress that was to be tried on. That Felicity was painfully thin nobody had been able to overlook, but now Emma was shocked by the frailty of the girl's body. Like a young colt, like a boy. What the girl apparently had no idea of was that in the meagerness of her body there lay a certain charm . . . a *pixie's*.

"What's wrong with falsies?" Emma asked. "Meg wears them sometimes."

"Does she really?" Felicity's eyes opened wide in disbelief. "Maybe I'm just stupid, but it always seems—well, like cheating to put on things . . . to pretend."

"But that's silly," Emma said. "Why do you think falsies and girdles and eyelashes and powder and rouge and lipstick were invented in the first place?" Oh, the sincerity of this child, who would rather not enchant than fake a figure or coloring that was not her own. "Come here and sit down at your dressing table and let me make you up."

But the girl had nothing, just a lipstick, one, and some powder, a hairbrush and comb, some cold cream—a standard brand—and toilet water. Emma went into her room and came back with her makeup kit. Astringent, a lotion to smooth the skin and cover some of the freckles, green and pink cream, mascara, lipsticks, rouge, perfume. "No —don't look yet. Oh, Listy, we must get some pounds on you. Tell me, have you ever been sick?"

"Just the usual things—appendicitis, measles, colds . . ."

"Some vitamins and liver injections would— There you are."

Felicity sat speechless. For a moment her lips parted,

revealing the small, irregular teeth, which should have been fixed years ago but which now no longer looked disturbing but beautifully white against her makeup, rather amusing little teeth suddenly, like pearls that hadn't been properly assorted for size.

"Didn't you ever try to make up your face? Not even in school?"

"I thought it was hopeless."

"Nothing is hopeless," cried Emma. "Nothing." And, "Nothing?" her voice echoed back to her. "Don't you know better?" Hers was a hopeless case. Leukemia was hopeless. There was no hope for people stricken with leukemia. But nothing should be hopeless for Felicity.

"But tomorrow morning, or whenever I take it off," said Felicity, still staring at herself in the mirror, "I'll— I'll be horribly shocked. My real face will disappoint me and I won't be able to bear—"

For a second then, Emma's assurance faltered. Oh, yes, she thought, I know what you mean. There are nights now when I want to sleep with my makeup on, so that I might wake up and not have to face the pallor of my skin in the morning, the deepening lines. Then she forced herself to smile. "But Listy, darling, cosmetics are the magic wand of our times. We don't need fairies any longer to transform us. How do you think I look when I wake up in the morning? But I also know that with just a little care I can change my face in no time, as you can yours. Because it's all there—the good lines, the shape of eyes and lips. Hurry up now or Scott will think you're not coming."

She walked over to the window and lifted the curtain. A boat was cutting through the water at high speed, the angry white foam in its wake looking like the spray a skier creates when he violates the virgin snow of a mountain. How pleasant to know that Scott could be kind, thought Emma, watching his custom-built boat turn in the direction of the dock. "There he is now."

"I'm almost ready."

Emma turned away from the window to look at Felicity once more, trying to see her not with compassionate eyes but objectively, as Scott, as others would see her. And though she herself had worked like an expert beautician on Felicity's plain face, she was startled now at the change she had wrought. It was as if the girl's face had been something inanimate, like a table someone had decided to paint over to hide the worn places, the rims glasses had left, the scars of cigarette burns, and that now, shining with a new color, was unrecognizable.

"Take a look at yourself," she said, reaching for the bottle of perfume and pressing the rubber ball of the atomizer, directing the fine stream of scent at Felicity's head, neck and chest. "See how pretty you can be when you spend a little time on yourself. And don't forget it. Don't forget that anyone would be proud to be seen with you as you look now." She certainly wasn't the same girl Emma had introduced to Scott a few weeks ago.

She walked downstairs with the girl and out onto the terrace, and watched her run down to the beach along the water's edge and up to the dock. There the dogs came racing to meet her, chasing each other, barking and yelping, their ears flapping, and Felicity stopped to pat them. Then she turned and swung her suitcase in the air like a flag. Emma waved back. She remained standing above the wall of blue hydrangeas until she saw Scott hold out a hand to help Felicity jump into the boat. And it sped away . . . away . . . away . . . leaving her alone. Like life speeding from her, leaving her to be obliterated. Eight weeks since Thiolat had told her she had at most six months to live. Eight weeks. Eight weeks out of six months.

As if suddenly exhausted by her race with time, she sat down in the shade of one of the umbrellas fastened to the deck chairs and looked up at the noble front of the pink house. And it seemed to her that she would be giving in to death before it had reached her if she gave in to the tiredness she had felt all day. Only one more week and she would have arrived at the main base of her journey, the ball, and when she had passed it, she would go away. And she would no longer see the sun kiss the walls of the Villa du Cygne, the blue of the hydrangeas against the deeper blue of the sea; see nothing of what she had loved so much, not the serpentine line of the shore, not the different greens of tree and bush, not the changing colors of the rocks, almost black, shiny like the coats of seals when the water wet them, reddish brown when they were dried by the wind, and almost white, like the up-turned bellies of fish, in the bright light of noon. She would never again cut the fat camellia blossoms or run with the dogs or listen to the birds calling to each other. In other centuries, thought Emma, when people still believed in gods, the things they had treasured most were sometimes buried with them, together with toys to play with and food to eat on their long, long journey. And suddenly the sand below changed into the sand of a not too faraway desert, and she was crossing a river in the dawn of an already hot morning, mounting a white mule and riding alongside the water until she had to turn off where a dusty road led into the Valley of the Kings—a white, hot, dusty road that seemed to go on forever. She saw a pyre burning and everyone dressed in white, the red necks of vultures and a woman jumping into an inferno of flames, screaming once in protest and terror but obeying the custom of her country; the body of a dying child sewn into some kind of cloth and put into a small boat that was set afloat down a wide stream; an

old man waiting on the side of the road, too tired to return the greeting of all those who walked past him in
reverential silence, following the reindeer to new pastures
he would never see. But she, she would not cross into a
valley of death or throw herself into a fire or sail down a
river or sit waiting by the roadside. She would give a ball,
and dance, and nobody would know that it was her
inauguration into death.

She heard steps and looked up. Titus was coming out
of the library carrying a drink. He looked disheveled and
dejected, and he stood there not seeing her, not seeing
anything, just staring down into his glass. Emma would
not have called his name had it not seemed negligent to
miss any chance of finding out the address of Meg's friend
in St. Tropez. He started, nearly dropped his glass, then
covered the distance to her chair with two long strides
and sat down on his haunches, rocking back and forth.

"What are you doing out here at this hour of the day?"

"You make it sound as if four o'clock in the afternoon
were a highly indecent hour for me to be sitting on my
terrace."

"It spoils the picture I have of you," he said. "I imagined you napping on the couch in your dressing room under the flimsiest of coverlets, a beatific smile on your lips,
dreaming of the ball." He took her right hand and
kissed it.

"And I thought you were with Sue," said Emma, and
lighted a cigarette.

"We have been banished," said Titus, speaking lightly
and mockingly, as he had not spoken for a long time now.
"A cable came today, in the morning. Night letter, of
course—he's the saving type—giving the glad tidings
that Mr. Webster would arrive in time to grace the ball
with his presence."

"But you knew he was expected sometime or other."

"But unexpected is that the lady, instead of making the best of the days left us, decides she has to be by herself— all by her pretty self, which is not so pretty if you'd seen her just now, her eyes swollen, her nose red. Why do women have to cry? I am sure you never did, or if you did, you had the good grace not to let anybody see you at this vulgar occupation."

Emma drew back. "Titus—are you making fun of Sue?"

"Of course I am." Titus rocked back and forth in ever-quicker motion. "What else is there left for an ardent lover who finds himself unexpectedly exiled? But what I don't know is, Is she crying because she still loves him and is afraid of losing me or because she loves me and is afraid of breaking with him?"

No, she had not cried, but oh, the torture of that night when she had refused Scott, knowing that he was right, that she could have found oblivion with him. Why hadn't she?

"Perhaps she doesn't know herself," said Emma. "Be gentle, Titus. Be patient. Don't rush her. Don't threaten her. Don't ask her to make up her mind just like that." She snapped her fingers, and the gesture startled her. It didn't go with her, not at all. It was a gesture Meg made. Where was Meg?

"Patient?" repeated Titus, and he smiled his broken, arrogant smile. "For almost eight weeks we have been together, night after night. If she still doesn't know— And I'm bored. Man, how I am bored, bored, bored!"

He rose from his crouching position, gulped down his drink and flung the glass against the wall of the house. It sailed through the air, catching the sunlight in its flight, changed for a moment into something alive, a huge iridescent butterfly, then it broke with a high-pitched crack. At once Titus said, "I'm sorry. I'm terribly sorry," and went to pick up the shards. She watched him kneel down, his back bent in humility, his long hands moving quickly and, careless of cutting himself, trying to gather together the broken pieces. Maybe in talking to Susan she had thought too much of Susan and what she might be missing, and not enough of Titus.

"Titus."

He stood leaning against the house wall now, between two of the high French windows, holding one hand stretched out as if he were offering the world the remnants of the broken glass, holding the other, the right one, to his mouth, sucking the blood from the palm he had cut. A bleeding young Greek god, unsure of his power.

"Titus!"

"It's nothing. But I had forgotten how sweet blood tastes and how appalling it looks."

He turned on his heels and was gone, disappearing inside before she could call him to her in a more commanding voice.

After a while Emma rose and went into the house, lingering for a few minutes in the living room for no reason except that she loved it—the elegant furniture, the two fireplaces opposite each other, both exactly alike, only the one mantel was genuine Louis XV, the other reconstructed to match it. Then she crossed the hall and went slowly upstairs.

She had already passed Meg's room when it came to her that she had just seen something small and pink on the floor move in the slight draft from the open window. She retraced her steps and there, in front of Meg's room, lay a handkerchief—a tissue, rather, the kind Meg used.

Emma did not pick it up. Many years of protocol had taught her not to bend down impulsively for anything that had fallen to the floor. Instead she laid her hand gently on the doorknob. It gave. Unlike Felicity, Meg was not afraid to have anyone enter her room. She was lying in bed but not asleep, her head turned sideways on the pillow, facing a miniature radio that was playing softly. She was apparently so absorbed in whatever she was listening to that she did not hear Emma enter. It made Emma feel like an intruder when Meg turned suddenly and sat bolt upright.

"Aunt Emily!"

"I guess you didn't hear me knock," Emma lied. "Hannah told me you were back and I just wondered if you'd care to have tea with me." Over a cup of tea in the privacy of the library, Meg could surely be eased into talking about her problem. Then the fact that Meg was in bed but not asleep brought back all her anxiety about the girl. "Feeling all right?"

"Fine. Just terribly tired." Meg yawned loudly. "I don't think we got an hour's sleep, Curly and I, I mean. We were up all night dancing and . . ." She yawned again. "Excuse me, Aunt Emily, but if you don't mind I'll skip tea, maybe dinner, too, and just stay in bed and rest."

It was quite obvious that Meg had no intention of revealing anything yet, and Emma, with her innate respect for privacy, immediately decided not to force the girl's confidence. "Of course," she said, and turned to leave. She had almost closed the door when she remembered her promise to Gino. There was no question in her mind but that Meg had sneaked into the house without having seen her lover, for Gino would have told her about his conversation with Emma and in that case Meg would not be keeping up this pretense. Even if she were to send word to him that Meg was back, safe and sound, Meg would know as soon as she saw Gino that her aunt was fully aware of the entire situation. Then Emma's having kept silent might be misconstrued and embarrass Meg, and in the end make it more difficult for both of them to talk frankly. So she opened the door again and said, "Have you seen Gino?"

"Gino? No."

"He was worried about you."

"Gino? Why should Gino be worried about me?"

Emma came into the room again, closed the door gently and sat down on Meg's bed. She could see Meg frown and noticed that the girl didn't move to make more space but lay motionless, avoiding Emma's eyes. "You don't have to pretend any longer. Gino told me."

"Told you what?"

"Everything."

"Everything?" repeated Meg, and Emma smiled to herself because Meg was being cagey, determined not to say a word until she knew just how much Gino had told.

"Yes, everything. About you and him, that you fell in love and that you are pregnant."

Meg didn't answer but fumbled with the radio, turning its knob until it blared, then shut it off. "Aren't you shocked?"

"If I am or not, what difference does it make? It's your life, Meg, and nobody is going to cry or laugh for you. But it was wrong of you to worry the boy. I can imagine that it was a shock for you to find you were expecting a child, but you should have told him you were going to visit a friend instead of running off without leaving word for him."

"Maybe," said Meg.

"After all, consideration is what matters most in any relationship, consideration and respect for the other person. And in your case you're going to have to be doubly tactful."

"I couldn't tell him," said Meg. "He wouldn't have let me go."

"Of course Gino would have let you go. He would have understood that there are situations when a girl likes to talk things over with another girl."

"It isn't that," said Meg. "You misunderstood, Aunt Emily. I mean Gino would never have allowed it. Oh, never. I know him well enough for that. Never, never."

"Would not have allowed what?"

"To abort his child."

"Abort his child?" whispered Emma. "Abort his child? Meg, what are you saying?"

"That's what it's called, isn't it?—when you have it scraped out? Abortion." And she began to cry. Emma could only stare at her. She could not say a soothing word or take Meg's hand or help the girl dry her tears. "Don't look at me as if I were a monster. . . ."

Life, Emma thought. Life . . . and you killed.

More than anything in the world she had wanted a child, not because it would be Henri's or because it was important that an heir be born to the proud name of Fleury but because giving life was an act of creation, her fulfillment as a woman, the only fulfillment she could hope for. She had been pregnant once, after ten years of marriage, but the child, a boy, had been born dead. And it seemed to her that Meg, in killing her unborn baby, had in some strange and incomprehensible way killed Emma's child, which should have lived even if she, Emma, had died—lived to bear children that would carry her blood, carry on her life, link after link, in a never-ending chain.

"How could you, Meg?"

"What else could I do? You tell me. You know my parents. They would never, never have given their consent—I mean, helped us."

"I would have helped you. Why didn't you come to me?"

"I thought it over," said Meg. "I thought it over for a

long time, for a whole night. If I had really wanted to marry Gino, I would have come to you, Aunt Emily."

"But why don't you want to marry him when he is so willing? Even ready to sacrifice years of his career just so—"

"Do you think he'll make it?"

Emma could not be merciful now, or keep the scorn out of her voice. "Yes, I do. I certainly do. He's enormously gifted. Why didn't you ask me before if that's what you were afraid of?"

"Because," said Meg, "I don't love him enough to accept any sacrifices from him. I know myself, Aunt Emily. I am moved, touched, call it whatever you like, when anybody is that good—noble is the better word for it, I guess—but I know that after a while I'd have begun to hate him. Because I could never sacrifice anything that really mattered to me, and I don't want to be under any obligation."

"You wanted a chance to find out if he was the right . . . guy."

"Well, he isn't, he isn't. Don't you see? I'm honest. At least I'm trying to be honest. He's better than I, more decent, honorable, sweet. But I'm honest. I know our marriage would end up a mess. Oh, stop looking at me like that, stop looking at me, Aunt Emily! No, I'm not prepared to learn to adjust and to have his family for relatives. I'm only eighteen and I just can't face it. And I don't want to see Gino again. I couldn't bear it. I couldn't. You tell him. And fire him. Please, please fire him!"

"You'll have to talk to Gino yourself," said Emma. And after you have talked to him, she thought, I will beg him to leave and I will try to make it up to him. But you must tell him what you have done so that he will never think I am lying or trying to buy him off.

"I can't," said Meg. "I won't."

"You'll have to," said Emma. "If you had the strength to go through with an abortion, you have the strength to tell him." She rose, not looking at the girl, who was whimpering now, and crossed the room to the door. "You'd better take a sedative," she said, "and stay in bed." And then her sense of responsibility returned. The girl might be in need of more than a sedative. She probably should have proper medical care. Where had she gone to murder her child? Where did eighteen-year-old girls find a doctor for that sort of thing in a foreign country when they hardly spoke the language? And here in France, where the penalty . . .

"I think I'll call Doctor Thiolat to have a look at you."

"That's not necessary," said Meg. "He saw me about an hour ago. He says I'm perfectly all right. If he had let me go yesterday I'd have come home right away, but he insisted that I stay put for a full twenty-four hours."

"Thiolat?"

"Oh, Lord!" Meg clamped a hand over her mouth. "And I promised never to mention his name. Don't tell him I told you. And don't tell my parents. Please, Aunt Emily. It's all water over the dam now. And nothing would be changed."

"No," said Emma. "I won't tell anyone."

Three days before the ball, Jacques Thiolat came into the consultation room, where Denise was straightening up. "I won't need you this afternoon," he said. "I'm going now, and won't be back today."

"Thank you," said Denise, "and if I may ask—" But the door had already closed on him. For a moment she stood looking at the closed door as if it had been slammed in her face, then she turned and walked to the window. She could see Thiolat cross the street quickly and get into his car, which he had parked opposite the house in the shade of some trees, and drive away. Alone, she went back to her work, took some instruments out of the sterilizer and put them into a glass cabinet. She emptied the wastepaper basket, scrubbed the basin, pulled a fresh length of paper over the examination table, lowered the shades against the sun and turned off the air-conditioner before she went up to the third floor of the villa, where she and Jeanne lived. Each of them had a bedroom to herself and a living room that they shared. Jeanne had already taken off her uniform and was lying on the worn, comfortable couch, reading a magazine. "Gone?" she asked, without looking up.

"Yes," said Denise, and sat down in a chair.

"Not much of a practice, have we?"

"It's the end of the season," said Denise.

Jeanne let the magazine fall to the floor. "I'm glad I'm going to Paris for my vacation," she said. "Two months from now, at the most. Who is Mrs. Harrison?"

Denise shrugged. "I think she's that daffy blonde who used to come in here almost every day last year. Or is it two years ago? Why?"

"Well, he's seeing her, isn't he?" said Denise. "On the days he doesn't come back to the office. At least that's where he said he could be reached in case of emergency. At the Hôtel de Paris, in Monte."

"So it is," said Denise.

The telephone rang, and since it was standing on the floor next to the couch, Jeanne picked it up. "If Dr. Thiolat ordered blood, of course he'll want it," she said. "Be sure and hold it for him." She banged down the receiver. "Stupid," she said, answering Denise's questioning glance. "They say they're short and wondered if he still needed it. He hasn't come by for it yet. Now why doesn't he have it sent? Do you suppose there's an accident somewhere? Or maybe he needs it for Mrs. Harrison?"

"How would I know?"

Jeanne rubbed a bite on her left leg. "You're worried about him, aren't you?"

Denise didn't answer.

"I don't blame you," said Jeanne. "I'm worried myself. I've never seen him look so bad or behave so peculiarly. He hardly goes out, just sits there reading. Not novels, either. Heavy stuff—philosophy, history, even the Bible. Maybe he's ill."

Denise started, then saw Jeanne yawn without trying to cover her open mouth in which the gold inlays glittered like costume jewelry, and she realized that Jeanne was bored and had only wanted to upset her for a little excitement.

"Or maybe he and Madame la Comtesse have quarreled?"

"He wouldn't quarrel with her."

"Oh, I don't know," said Jeanne. "A couple of days ago when I picked up the phone, she was on the line and I heard her say impatiently, 'Not today, Jacques. I'm too busy.'"

"And she is," said Denise, defending Emma because she had to defy Jeanne. "The preparations for the ball take all her time. That's going to be some do." But back into her memory swept a week many years ago. Emma Starr Fleury had lost her child. Against her wishes the doctors had saved her and she had been quite sick afterward. At the time, Denise had nursed Emma—that was still in the period when she adored the woman who had recommended her to Jacques Thiolat, picking her out from a group of young nurses at a hospital that was one of her charities. After that, and for quite a long time, Emma had refused to see Thiolat, as if he were personally to blame for the fact that she had not had a successful delivery, and Thiolat had sighed whenever Denise reported to him. "If only she would realize that there was no other way."

"The ball . . . *merde,*" said Jeanne. "Are you really going?"

They had been invited to join the spectacle after the dinner was over. "What a masochist you are, punishing yourself." She shook her head. "He'll dance with her, he'll hold her in his arms—"

"Oh, stop it!" said Denise.

"He won't get around to dancing with you, if that's what you're hoping for."

"I've danced with him," said Denise, and she smiled— the smile of a young girl. "When we were out in the country or when she invited us to the castle for the harvest festival or a hunt. He's a marvelous dancer."

"That was when you were young," said Jeanne, and reached for the box of candy. "By the way, I've made a date for this afternoon and I don't want you along. Sorry. But why don't you go and make a fortune tonight? You usually win when you're worried."

"A good idea," said Denise, and rose.

During the many years she had spent on the Riviera, she had learned to enjoy gambling on her days off and on lonely nights when Jeanne irritated her, or Thiolat dined at the Villa du Cygne or was out with patients or friends. But she always played with very small sums. After having studied various systems assiduously and found none successful, she had invented one for herself that seemed to work very well as long as she didn't risk more than a week's wages, though it let her down when she invested bigger sums.

It was pleasant to ride along the shore toward Monte Carlo, and she wondered lazily if she would ever have enough money to afford a car of her own. Then her thoughts wandered back to Jacques Thiolat. Jeanne had been right—he not only looked ill but he didn't act like himself. Something had happened to him and she had tried without any success to find out what it could be. He had always been a moody man but never short-tempered. For weeks now he had been flaring up at the slightest provocation, and he had lost his smile. Even when he had been working hard, which wasn't the case now, he frequently asked her to join him for a nightcap or a late cup of tea, but lately he seemed to have no need for company, not even hers. There had been nights when she had heard him wandering around the house until the small hours of the morning, and twice she had tiptoed downstairs to listen at his door and heard him moan. But he couldn't have quarreled with Emma Starr Fleury or she would not be coming to his office as regularly as ever, even more often.

Denise got out at the stop in front of the cinema and walked down to the casino. She loved to walk under the high, proud palms. It made her feel as if she were on a South Sea island. She looked at her watch. It was early, not yet two. But the café to the left of the casino was crowded. She glanced at the terrace of the Hôtel de Paris. So there was a difference in price—so what?

A waiter found a table for her away from the balustrade, and Denise ordered lunch. She reached for her purse and took her compact from it. As she powdered her nose, she could see in its square mirror a white Mercedes come to a stop in front of the stairs leading up to the terrace, and a bellboy shooting out to open the door, as if catapulted from a sling. Emma Starr Fleury, all in white, in the simplest of white linen dresses, a bunch of daisies stuck in her belt—flowers never seemed to wilt on her—a white cardigan slung over her shoulders, carrying a large-brimmed white straw hat in her hand, her only jewelry a pearl choker around her slim neck. How slim she was, almost too thin—she must have lost a lot of weight. Money, thought Denise, it's money that keeps you trim and young. But once, when she had been very young and voiced her envy of money to Emma, Emma had looked at her and shaken her head. "You're wrong, Denise. To be self-sufficient is the greatest good fortune." And Emma had both, thought Denise—good fortune and she was sufficient unto herself. She had everything.

She watched Emma tip the boy, come up the stairs and disappear inside. But the way Denise sat, she could also see into the great hall of the hotel, and she saw Emma go up to the desk at its far end. And suddenly she knew who Mrs. Harrison was—an old friend of Emma's, an American whom she had introduced to Thiolat. Mrs. Jonathan Harrison, the oil millionairess from Houston, Texas.

As Denise turned to the food the waiter had put on her table, she could see herself, as if in a mirror, in the pane of the French window that stood open, folded back against the wall—a middle-aged woman with middle-aged spread. I need a new girdle, she thought. Maybe I shouldn't gamble but spend the money on clothes. A new hairdo might help, too. She put her hand up to her hair. Years of dyeing it had robbed it of all softness. It felt dead. Suddenly the food on her plate no longer looked tempting, the fun of watching people seemed shallow and the anticipation of gambling, and perhaps winning, had lost its charm. Denise waved to the waiter to pay her bill, and as she bent forward slightly to catch his eye, she saw Jacques Thiolat mounting the steps, carrying a quite large case in one hand and an oblong object carefully wrapped in the other, neither of which he relinquished to the bellboy. His transfusion kit. Denise watched him cross the hall. Unlike Emma, he did not stop at the desk but went straight to the elevator.

There was nothing strange about the fact that Emma

Starr Fleury should want to keep an old friend company while she was having a blood transfusion, except that Jeanne had asked who Mrs. Harrison was and speculated if the blood could have been ordered for her. And that puzzled Denise. Because Jeanne kept the files and should have known.

Denise forgot about paying the waiter, sat back in her chair and couldn't get the thing out of her mind. When she finally left, she took a cab back to Nice. The house was empty. Jeanne had gone and the servants, a couple, had left a note on the hall table saying they would be back at five. Denise sat at Jeanne's desk for a long time, staring at the fireproof file case in the corner before she dared open it. *A, B, C, D, E, F, G, H*—there was no card for Mrs. Jonathan Harrison from Houston, Texas. Only a card for a Mrs. Alan Harris. She must have got them mixed up. Harris, Harrison—yes, Mrs. Harris had been the daffy blonde who had used thousands of little complaints as an excuse to see Jacques Thiolat. Mrs. Harrison was a tall, dark-haired, dignified woman.

Denise went through the alphabet again, this time spreading out all the *H*'s on the floor to avoid any oversight. Then she put all of them back again. Then she called the Hôtel de Paris and asked for Mrs. Jonathan Harrison. "Mrs. Harrison is still in London," she was told.

Denise put down the receiver and her hands were cold. Why had Jacques Thiolat gone with a blood-transfusion kit to a woman who wasn't there? Who was still in London? And what was Emma Starr Fleury doing there? Unless . . . Blood, of course, blood was given for various reasons; it did not necessarily have to be anything serious. But then why the secrecy? Why not in a hospital? Or here at the office? Or at the Villa du Cygne? For a moment Denise hesitated. She could feel her heart beating in her ears. Then she shrugged, the little shrug with which she acknowledged the hopelessness of any situation, and went quickly into Jacques Thiolat's bedroom. It was a small, almost austere room, quite unlike the rest of the house, which was almost showy. A narrow bed, a bookstand, a desk, a chair—a completely different facet of the elegant man who dressed with such immaculate, luxurious taste, fussed over his food and seemed so much in his element among the members of the international set. But which was real and which a pose, Denise did not know, nor had she ever really pondered the contrast.

The desk was not locked, and stuck away under other folders was one marked "Personal." An ordinary file card lay on top. It gave no name, just the letter *E*. And a date: "June 26th, 1960. Lab report: Lymphoblastic leukemia. Characteristic number of mononuclear non-granular cells." And a question mark: "Four months?" And another question mark, then: "July 10th, first blood transfusion . . ."

Denise did not read on. She put the card back where she had found it, and the folder below the others and closed the desk. She went upstairs to the third floor, murmuring as though she couldn't believe it, "Leukemia . . ." In her room she threw herself on the bed and stared up at the ceiling, her eyes dry and hot. If she had believed in prayer, she would have prayed. "Lord, don't let her die . . . don't let her die. Sick, yes—then he's got something to live for, to keep him alive. Then at least he'll be happy taking care of her, and in the evenings he'll still need me. But don't let her die. If she dies, he'll die, too. If she dies, I'll have nothing. He'll live on only for her memory and not allow anyone to profane it. No one. God in heaven, let her live."

After a while Denise got up, unlocked a drawer of her

chest and took from it a bottle of ether. She sprinkled a few drops on a wad of cotton, went back to bed and held it under her nose. It was the quickest way she knew of to fall asleep.

"No," Emma had said when Thiolat had first told her that blood transfusions were imperative. "I won't go to a hospital. I'm too well known around here. There would be talk. And I won't come and have it done in your office. I don't trust Denise or Jeanne. They have been with you too long not to regard everything you do as their personal affair. And I don't want their pity. And at home"—she had shaken her head—"that would never do. But I know where. Ann Harrison offered me the use of her suite at the Hôtel de Paris while she is away, in case I ever wanted to stay overnight or change for some occasion. There I can come and go as I like. She won't be back from England for some time. Then we'll see."

And it had been a good place for it. For the room had none of the cold efficiency of a hospital nor the intimacy her own room would have held, but was filled with the personality of another woman. There were still quite a few of Ann Harrison's things around—photographs in silver frames on the dressing table, a silly little felt lamb on a chair, a typewriter in its case, a heavy golf bag with a few clubs that had not been needed. Here Emma could almost believe it wasn't she lying in bed but another person, somebody she didn't know very well. But this was the last time she could use it. Ann would be back the day after tomorrow, for the ball.

Four more days.

"Well, I made it," she said softly, but she was saying it to herself, not to Thiolat, who was sitting in a chair he had moved up to the window opposite her bed. Of course he heard her. He nodded but made no comment. Since that day in early summer, when he had told her the reason why she was feeling so unusually tired and weak, and she had asked him not to remind her that she was going to die, he had kept the promise he made to himself to treat her as if there were no reason for concern, and had forced back all questions that were not absolutely necessary. Yet she must be tired. If she was, though, her face did not betray it. She was probably using more makeup than usual, and she never allowed him to see her without it any more. Possibly she used atropine to make her eyes as shiny and large as they were right now. He could rely only on the tests he had made, all of which showed that the treatment of drugs and blood transfusions had been beneficial. The hemorrhagic tendency had disappeared, the enlarged nodes were under control and the change in the peripheral blood and bone marrow was favorable. Her illness had entered into what could be called a subacute state. He had not dared hope for this but had not been surprised, given Emma's mentality, which seemed to be just as potent as Aminopterin.

"Comfortable?" he asked.

"It's all right."

"You want me to read to you? I brought along some poetry."

"No, thank you," said Emma. "I just want to lie quietly."

This was the first time she had seen him since Meg had told her about the abortion, and she found it hard to look at him, to have to listen to his voice. And when, a little while before, he had touched her, inserting the needle into her vein and fixing it so that she could even move her arm a little, a feeling of such physical antipathy had assailed her that she had almost got up and told him she could not take it today. Reason had made her erase from her mind that morning on the beach when she had seen him as death personified and had tried to outswim him, but now again she could identify him only with death. I should have cut all ties with him that night when he killed my child, she thought. And she could see herself lying in her room in the castle on the Loire, her body racked with pain, her fear of death miraculously dispelled. Nothing had mattered but that the child should live. Thiolat was bending over her. "We can't save you and the child, Emma. We can save only one."

"The child, then, the child. Under all circumstances, the child." And she had tried to convey her demand to the obstetrician standing at the window, but he had not seen her fluttering hand or heard her weak voice. "The child, Jacques." But he had saved her.

I should never have seen him again after that. Why did I?

She stared up at the glass container above her. Like raspberry juice, she thought, dark-red raspberry juice. Who had given this blood? A man? A woman? A girl or a boy? She wished she knew. It was strange that, drop by drop, the blood of some unknown person should be flowing into her veins to fight the anemia in her body. She should be grateful, but she was not, not really. She was merely accepting the help of a stranger to maintain the necessary percentage of hemoglobin.

Drip, drip, drip.

But the sight of the slowly diminishing liquid took on a language of its own, translating the thoughts in her mind. "Mur—der—er . . . mur—der—er . . . For Jacques had murdered again. Meg's child.

Drip, drip, drip.

And there was no justification for it this time, healthy and young as Meg was. It had been done for convenience, to help make Meg's life easier. Gino had cried that morning—had it been only a week ago that he had come to say goodbye? They had not talked about it. It had not been necessary. Poor Gino. But he was an artist. For him it would not be so hard to get over this terrible first rejection. He would channel his grief—the helplessness of having to face what he could not understand, his self-doubt and fury—into his work. But by what right could Jacques possibly defend such a criminal act? If she were to ask him, he would answer, "Because I love you. Because if I hadn't done it, Meg would have gone to one of those men or women who make a profession of it, and more often than not the consequences are disastrous. Nor could I allow a scandal to upset you. These last few weeks or months of your life should be as pleasant and serene as possible. I tried my best to convince her of its wrongness, but she was determined. And for your sake I forsook my principles and risked my neck. . . ." But Emma did not ask. She had promised Meg not to mention that she knew about it and she had never gone back on her word. So she lay there, watching the blood dripping into her veins, asking herself how, when she knew he made decisions as if he were God, she could possibly have endured his self-righteousness all these years.

Drip, drip, drip.

Because you mattered to him, she told herself. From the moment he first saw you in that dingy little general store, you mattered to him. He never asked for anything but to be allowed to love you. And you needed his love because he was a flame at which you could warm your hands without catching fire. The one person who made no demands on you.

Drip, drip, drip.

And it was a shock to discover that instead of having been the one to give, she had been the one to receive.

Thiolat was watching her, trying not to let her notice that his eyes were searching her face like searchlights that flash into the night at regular intervals, hoping for the answering signal of a lighthouse—which would be her smile of recognition. In these last weeks he had suffered deeply under the deterioration of their relationship and though he was well aware of the strange sympathies and antipathies anyone facing death developed, he blamed himself quite irrationally for her attitude toward him. It made him feel as if he had somehow failed her, done something to offend or annoy her, and in the night, when he could not sleep, he kept reiterating every word they had exchanged since that day at the end of June, when he had had to tell her she was fatally ill. That he could find nothing in which he had been remiss was torture, worse than if he could have thought of a reason. Then at least there would have been a chance to remedy whatever it was. She had not even mentioned again that she would leave the Riviera in September. It was his only hope now, once the ball was over, that in the time left, their old relationship would be re-established, perhaps even develop into a new closeness only he and she could share.

"Emma, you told me two months ago that after the ball you would go away. Have you made up your mind where you want to go?"

His voice startled her, his words shocked her back suddenly to the reality of her state of health.

Drip, drip, drip.

And now it was not the blood dripping into her veins but dripping from her, all life dripping away. And she wanted to cry out, "No! It can't be true!" And knew that she had not really believed she had to die, in spite of what he had told her and all the books she had read about the disease.

"There are spontaneous remissions!" Emma cried.

"Yes."

"I know they're very rare."

He remained silent.

Drip, drip, drip.

And a fear assailed her such as she had never known before. It came in waves. The first seemed to paralyze her legs, the second to reach her hips, the third gripped her chest, the fourth took her breath away. She had hoped for a miracle. Unconsciously she had believed the woman in the small restaurant who had followed her to the washroom to bring her a towel. "One must never give up hope. . . ." The ball had been like a shield she had carried to ward off death. But now death was no longer coming toward her, death was enveloping her. Turn as she might, she could not defend herself.

"And what is there after death? What do you believe?"

"As a doctor?" He shook his head.

"Forget about science."

"Believe? In logic."

"Then logic is God for you?"

"You might call it that."

Drip, drip, drip.

If I had had my child, thought Emma, then there would be a link, a beautiful link, between past and future. Then something of me would be left, be alive.

"You should have let me die that night and saved my child. You knew that was what I wanted most in the world."

"I knew," he said. He had never forgotten that night, when the obstetrician, turning his back on them and watching the great swans in the moat swimming majestically in the moonlight, had left the decision to him. "And I went to Fleury with your request to save the child, even if it might cost your life. He wouldn't hear of it."

"But that was a mere gesture on your part, wasn't it?" she said. "You went in the hope of affirmation, but you would have defied Fleury if he had said yes."

She was right, of course. But this Thiolat could not admit. If Fleury had said yes, save the child, he would still have let the boy die.

"I did what was best."

"For yourself," said Emma. "Not for me. You couldn't face losing me. Without me, your life would have had no meaning, so mine had to be meaningless, too."

"Emma—"

But Emma had averted her head. For, having saved her then, he was delivering her to death now. And nothing would be left of her. Nothing.

Emma spotted Susan Webster after she had left the Hôtel de Paris and crossed the palm-studded avenue to the café on the other side. There, close to the entrance, under a huge and, at this time of the season, slightly faded umbrella, Susan sat alone at a table for two. In front of her, untouched, lay a pack of postcards, held together by a rubber band, a pen and a menu. Emma had wanted to talk to her ever since Titus had flung the glass against the wall and disappeared inside the house with his hand bleeding. Two or three drops of his blood had trickled onto the sun-baked stones of the terrace, and immediately a fly, lured by the smell, had settled on them. And somehow the sight of those drops had haunted Emma. But she had not liked to press the girl when it had been obvious that Susan wasn't ready to talk about it yet. But now Susan was smiling at her, her grave little face alight with surprise and pleasure at seeing Emma, and Emma sat down, motioned to a waiter, and ordered some iced tea. He had hardly gone when Susan said, without any attempt at small talk, "Jim arrived yesterday." She nodded toward the casino's impressive façade. "He's in there now. He's never been anyplace where one could gamble, and he wanted to try his luck."

Vaguely Emma remembered Titus telling her that Susan thought gambling highly immoral, but apparently the man she had married did not, nor did Susan seem to resent this. "But he wasn't supposed to come until tomorrow, was he?"

"No," said Susan. "He took me completely by surprise. He didn't even wire the change in his plans nor the time when his plane would land. He didn't phone from the airport. He simply walked in. I was asleep in the garden and when I heard steps coming up the path, I thought it was Titus. But it was Jim."

And what if Titus had been there? What if Jim Webster, in involuntary imitation of such classical situations, had come home to find his wife in the arms of a lover?

"You know," said Susan, "at that moment, at that first moment, he looked like a stranger to me—a man I knew, of course, but with whom I had never shared any intimacy. I wonder if men feel the same way when they see their wives after a period of separation—as if you had to learn to know each other all over again."

She lighted a cigarette, inhaling deeply, and Emma wondered suddenly if Fleury, as a man, had not in that sense always been a stranger to her, a man who had never, in all the many years of their marriage, taken it for granted that he could enter her bedroom at any time, but had knocked at her door, almost as if by appointment, immaculate in his blue silk dressing gown, his white ascot folded around his neck, his blue suède slippers— they had never looked worn or even comfortable but, rather, as if they were replaced automatically before they got to that stage—smelling no longer of his cigar but discreetly of Eau de Cologne, and always, always freshly shaved. Somehow she had never been able to connect Fleury the man, with whom she had shared her life, with

Fleury the male, who at regular intervals had shared her bed.

"I had planned," said Susan, "to pretend I wasn't feeling well when Jim finally got here—a headache or a sore throat, anything to gain a little time. But it didn't work out that way. I had forgotten that he was never really considerate or at all sensitive to my moods. He had come thousands of miles, I was his wife—we went straight to bed."

She stretched out her hand across the marble top of the table, as someone drowning reaches for something to cling to. Emma put hers gently over the trembling fingers.

"I lay there," said Susan. "I don't know what I'd expected. I was so sure he would notice I was different, that he would feel I was no longer the same, but he didn't notice a thing. He didn't notice a thing, Mrs. Fleury."

She took her hand away from under Emma's and made it into a fist, trembling for a moment in her disappointment and confusion. "There was a moment when I wanted to get up and say, 'Jim, don't touch me. You mustn't touch me before I've talked to you.' Something like that, something honest and straightforward, but I couldn't move. And you know why I couldn't move? You know what kept me in his arms? The realization of how terribly easy it is to fool a man."

"Man or woman," said Emma, "anyone who trusts you can be cheated."

"Because they trust you. I know that now. And I guess when one is decent, one respects that trust and doesn't violate it. But I did. And when I woke up this morning, I felt awful. Unclean. But still I didn't want to tell him."

Had she ever felt unclean, unclean in mind and body? Emma stared across the café into the green of the garden that surrounded the casino. And for a moment she could remember only what it had been like when she first came to Monte Carlo with Fleury, as a young wife—the glamour of uniforms and magnificent evening gowns, the liveried chauffeurs and footmen flinging open the doors of fancy new automobiles and old-fashioned equipages, the sound of music through the open window, the red-plush-carpeted steps of the grand staircase leading to the Cercle Privé, where the sky was the limit and fortunes were lost overnight—in the days when gentlemen had not yet learned to earn their own living and one committed suicide when one's money was gone. Or for love. Now all was changed. Girls and boys in blue jeans walked through the lovely gardens overlooking the harbor, and the stakes in the casino were low enough for anyone to try his luck. Buses brought tourists by the carload, and when you looked up, you hardly ever saw people you knew.

Unclean? Yes—when she had gone back to London from France fifteen years ago, with Scott's lips and hands imprinted on her flesh like a brand on the hide of an animal, the memory of his weight still pressing on her body and mind. She told Fleury that Scott Warren had turned up unexpectedly in the empty castle, and he had nodded. "He telephoned and I told him where you were." And that had been all, although Henri had always known Scott was in love with her.

"But Susan," said Emma, "won't you have to decide what you want?"

Susan avoided Emma's eyes and put both hands around the glass of iced tea, to cool them. "Titus or Jim? I thought so, too, but I'm not sure if I think so any longer."

"I don't know what you mean."

"Whom do I love more?" Susan said, and she shook her head. "I wonder if that's really the question. Why do I have to make the decision on the basis of love?" And suddenly she looked like a child who has discovered a monster in the nursery, but also like a child who, having overcome its initial fear, doesn't know whether it shouldn't take advantage of the situation.

"Then don't call it love. With whom would you be happier?"

"I don't know," said Susan. "There was a moment during the night, when Jim fell asleep with his head on my shoulder, when—when he seemed everything I had ever wanted of life, and I hated myself for ever having given in to Titus. But it taught me something about myself. There are men who can't be content with one woman and I'm afraid I belong to the women for whom one man isn't enough. And perhaps deep inside me I've always known it and been faithful only because I was afraid to face what I was."

No, no, Emma thought. Cowardice played no part in my decision to remain faithful to Henri. There are obligations one acknowledges without a selfish motive, concepts one cannot violate without violating one's innermost self. She frowned sharply. "Aren't you exaggerating? Look, my dear, at this moment you—"

"But it's a question of need, too!" cried Susan. "Jim needs me. Oh, yes, he does. There's nothing in the world for him but me. I know that and I've always known it. And I need him. But I need Titus, too. Only I thought it wasn't possible until last night. Last night I found out how easy it was to cheat, I found out I could like sleeping with them both, and I began to see things quite differently. Jim would never know unless I told him."

For Emma, physical fulfillment had been a drug, appeasing the need for satisfaction but not quenching the desire for a specific man. There had been a time when she thought of Adam while Fleury was kissing her. But that Susan could even remotely consider the possibility of being a woman for two men at the same time . . . The spot in her vein where the needle had gone in began to hurt, and Emma put her left hand over the elbow of her right arm as if she could grasp the pain and still it.

"Susie, you can't live a lie. You'll be split in two. You'll lose your self-respect."

"I have already," said Susan, "last night, when Jim came and I couldn't make up my mind and didn't warn him."

"But you'll lose your respect for him, too. With every time, there'll be a little more contempt."

"I don't owe him anything after yesterday," said Susan.

"Yet you agreed that only those who trust can be deceived."

"But where does he get the right to trust me?" cried Susan. "Just because you don't steal or kill, has anyone the right to take it for granted that he can trust you and make no further effort to find out what's going on inside you, or if you've changed? That's too simple."

Definitely, there was now fury in the girl's eyes. "You're hurt and angry," Emma said. "You feel humiliated and insulted. But revenge, Susan . . . Titus loves you. He wants to marry you. You can't use him as an instrument of revenge." In her mind she could hear his broken, arrogant laughter, his voice, the voice of a boy mocking grief. *We have been banished. . . .* "Doesn't he mean anything to you?"

"That's just it. He does."

"But he would never be satisfied with an affair with you."

"I know," said Susan. "He told me the very first evening. But he's coming to New York. He's going to be a customers' man with quite a big firm, I understand. From October first. And he's going to do illustrating on the side."

Emma frowned sharply. ("Be patient, don't rush her," she had told him.)

"Don't hurt him, Susan."

"I'll try not to." Susan got up. Suddenly she looked tired. "I'm afraid I have to go."

When the bus reached Eze-sur-Mer, the driver turned around to tell Felicity she had reached her destination. But the girl who in Beaulieu had asked him to be sure to call her, and please not to forget that she had to get out at Eze, did not look up. She sat so deeply absorbed in her thoughts, he had to whistle to rouse her. Then she shot up from her seat as if it were on fire, and without thanking him jumped down to the street.

"I tell you what," Scott had said. "If you really want to go for a walk, then let's take the path from the sea up to my mountain. With every step you take, the landscape changes, so you can imagine you're in countries far from the Côte d'Azur. We'll meet halfway. I'll walk down and you walk up—fair enough, since you're younger. And after a little rest we'll climb back up together."

As she took the footpath above the railroad tracks, she found that he had not exaggerated. For the first few moments she could still see the rooftops of the village; then only the beach, like a white pearl left there by a southern sea; then suddenly there was no longer the smell of hot cement, gasoline, flowering shrubs and water, but only the aroma of pine, and as she looked up, the mountain seemed to have lost its formation and become a dense, mysterious mass, like a rain forest in Brazil, closing in on her and stretching endlessly below and above her. Only a few minutes later, it was torn by a ravine that transported you to the Alps, a brutal, frightening abyss. Then, just as unexpectedly, the rocky path led past a gentle plantation of olive trees, as on a poster advertising a vacation in Italy. And it was here that Scott had said he would meet her, among the yellow green of the low, gnarled trees. But he was nowhere to be seen.

Felicity sat down on the sparse grass that grew between the trees, leaned her head against the bark of a trunk and glanced up through the willowy leaves into a sky that was like the blue cup of an enormous bell. Today there was no fear in her that Scott might have forgotten his promise to meet her. The afternoon on the boat, the dinner at St. Tropez, the hour in the casino at Cannes had convinced her that he had taken her along not because he was doing Emma a favor but because he liked being with her. They had been alone, and this fact had surprised her at first, even frightened her a little—for how could she assume that her company would suffice such a famous man?—and she had said something to the effect that if he wanted to meet friends in St. Tropez or Cannes, she certainly wouldn't mind.

"I feel comfortable with you," he had replied, "almost as if I were alone." And she had understood that he meant it as a compliment. As it would have been a compliment if her father had ever allowed her to stay in the same room where he was working, paying no attention to her, just looking up once in a while and giving her a fleeting smile. Scott had even let her steer the boat, trusting her to follow his directions, while he had fixed their two fishing rods and put them over the side. He had caught nothing, and his disappointment, too, had been something he let her share. Later, in the harbor of St. Tropez, among hundreds of boats of all types, he had brought a tray with ice and drinks from the galley, and they had sat, like all the other boatowners, leaning back in comfortable chairs, drinking and watching the life going on around them on the quay. And though it had been like sitting on a silver platter being offered up to the people strolling by, who ogled them shamelessly, Felicity had not been embarrassed by the remarks of strangers about the color of her hair. Then Scott had taken her hand, and because there had been no other way, the harbor being so crowded, they had jumped in and out of boats together until they reached one from which they could step onto the pier. In the restaurant they had been given the best table and the full attention of the waiters, and he had chosen every dish for her as though she were a child who couldn't read. She had never felt so cared for in her life. "But I thought you had house guests," she had said at one point when it had seemed incredible that it was really she sitting there with a world-famous writer, and he nodded. "So I have. But why should I be bored with them? They have good food, good wine and each other."

Now and then, people had stopped at their table and glanced curiously at her, and each time Scott had risen from his chair and introduced her with French politeness as "Madame Forbes," but made it obvious that he preferred not to have his privacy interrupted. On the way back to Cannes, they had changed and emerged from the cabins at the same time, he in a white tuxedo, she in the flowery evening gown she was then so glad not to have saved for the ball, and they had bowed ceremoniously to each other. In the casino he got someone to make room for her at a crowded table and stood behind her, explaining the rules of roulette as a father might explain a game to his young daughter, and he had left her on her own while he had gone to play at another table. She had been lucky. The chips had piled up in front of her—round green ones, red ones, oblong white ones—and people had started to comment about it. Some had even waited to place their bets until she had pushed her chips across the table or called out the numbers she wanted to the croupier. And then suddenly Scott had been at her elbow and said in a whisper that he was all out, and could he borrow from her? Just like a father asking his daughter to help him out. She had never known such happiness, even though the evening hadn't ended quite as she had expected. For Scott, when she had met him later at the bar, was very drunk, so drunk that it had been hard to lead him outside. He was singing at the top of his lungs —"Give My Regards to Broadway"; "Over There, Over There"; "Lily Marlene"; "Tipperary"—and cursing the French and the Americans, the rich and the poor, weaving like a sailboat in a heavy storm and leaning heavily on her. But she hadn't minded Scott's drunkenness, hadn't minded it at all. She was reminded of her father and the many nights when he couldn't find the way to his bedroom and had bumped into the furniture, cursing wildly.

When they had reached the boat, Scott had suddenly sobered up. "Listy," he said, "I think I'd better put you in a cab and curl up in my cabin," and she had come home alone in a taxi. The next morning he had called, not to apologize, of course, but to say that he would like to see her again. "He makes me feel wanted," she had told Emma, and Emma smiled and nodded. It took a man of Scott's dynamic personality to slash away at the barriers of inferiority.

Now, before she could actually see him on the rocky path, Felicity could feel him coming, as one feels electricity gathering before a storm. His vitality seemed to stir the leaves in the trees, to loosen bits of stone from the rocky path and make the sun dance before her eyes. He was singing again. But there also came through the air a hollow sound, the hollow sound two cupped hands produce if you clap them together. She couldn't imagine what it was until he came in sight. He was leading a little gray donkey; every now and then it refused to budge, and he would slap its rump.

"See what I just bought? Always wanted one to lug up

the wood. And I've christened him Isaac, because he looks
as if he were laughing at me, at anybody stupid enough
to buy a donkey. Did you know 'Isaac' means 'laughter'?"
And as if on cue, the donkey rolled back his leathery lips,
bared his teeth and made a noise that sounded like a
greeting.

Scott tied the animal to a tree. He was wearing the
Bavarian shorts again and the white shirt and green stocking cap in which Felicity had first seen him. But now the
shirt was wide open, baring his strong chest, and Felicity
saw the drops of sweat glistening on his skin. He was
probing the blade of the ax he had brought along, and
he now laid it on the ground, apparently satisfied with
its keenness. "There's one over there," he said, pointing
to a dying olive tree, "I might cut down later. I always
like to have enough olivewood in the house. Or didn't I
tell you I carve? Whenever I get stuck, I try to express
myself in another medium. How's my little girl? Exhausted from the climb?"

"Only hot," said Felicity.

"And thirsty, I hope," Scott said. He went over to the
donkey and took from the basket on its left flank two
bottles of red wine, a sausage and a piece of cheese. All
this he brought to Felicity to hold while he tore out several handfuls of grass to make a little pile to set it on.
Then he uncorked the bottle, took a deep swallow, wiped
the mouth with his elbow and said, "Drink, Listy—that's
my girl. We can't be out of step, can we? You stone-sober
and I . . ."

"Couldn't you work this morning?" asked Felicity,
who knew by now that Scott got up at five, and on just
a cup of coffee would work through until noon, then have
done with writing for the day.

"No," and he said it angrily. "Damn it all!"

He wasn't quite sure why he was stymied, why his

thoughts wouldn't let themselves be phrased but whirred in his brain like hummingbirds. He could see them—there they were right in front of him, sucking honey from long-stemmed blue-and-white delphiniums, but the moment he tried to catch them they were gone, flown away, disappeared, and his nerve endings shivered like the blossoms and his ears could still hear the sound of their wings. He wasn't used to being unproductive, and it frightened him because he knew writers could dry up. He had been pondering it for weeks now, restless and frustrated. Perhaps it had something to do with his blurting out to Emma about the dead soldier's diary. Maybe he was trying unconsciously to write in a different way, just to prove to himself what until then he had taken for granted but never dared put to the test—that he hadn't needed to use another man's style to express himself. And now Emma had brought this goddam little creature into his life to disturb him further, to make him suspect Emma had made a fool of him. Scott took another swallow.

Ever since he had been a young man he had adored her, desired her—never mind whom he had loved, whom he had been married to and with whom he had wenched. He hadn't left out anything—why should he have? But never mind all that, it had nothing to do with it. In the back of his mind there had always been Emma. She put him in motion whenever she as much as looked at him with those strange blue eyes. How much more could he have achieved if she hadn't refused to move with him?

He drank again, and when he took the bottle from his lips, some of the red wine trickled out of the corners of his mouth down his chin and onto his chest. He didn't really hate her for having refused him. There were women who had to remain unattainable. And he had found a certain amount of consolation and peace in this knowledge, and had brought her the books he had written, the fruits of his labor, as a pilgrim sacrifices at the altar of his god. And now, to have to think that she had led him by the nose, had denied herself, not for Henri, virtue, ethics, a moral code, call it what you like, but because there was somebody else, always had been—to realize now that what she had given him was a nod compared to what she had given this other man, the father of this girl.

"You should have a bite to eat," said Felicity, trying to slice the hard sausage with his pocketknife. Scott watched her. Whenever he tried to sound her out about her father, she clammed up. Even on the boat, when he had talked to her at length about himself—telling her about Chicago, where he had been born, about his father, who had run the big boats across the lake for a steel company—she hadn't volunteered any information about her own childhood. He opened the second bottle.

"Please don't drink so much."

"Why not? Doesn't your father drink?"

"My father?"

"Well, you said the first time we met that I remind you of him."

Felicity smiled. "Yes, you do," she said, and didn't correct his assumption that Adam Forbes was still alive. And strangely enough he was—in a way, now more than ever. Now that she didn't hate her father any longer, he had been reborn for her in the person of Scott Warren as a man who could have been like Scott. But though she was unwilling to part with this image, she was also dimly aware of the fact that for her own good she ought to separate the two. It was easier, therefore, to pretend that her father was still alive.

"Does he look like me?"

"Not at all," said Felicity. "He is very tall and his hair is like gold."

Yes, that had been the strange thing. In spite of three wars, hard work and heavy drinking, he did not have one gray hair. "His eyes are blue, blue like the sea, and they seem to change like the sea. They grow deeper and lighter, sometimes gray, sometimes green. And I've never seen him bad-tempered. He was born with a smile."

For Scott there arose from her description the handsomest of men. And he had never been handsome. He had always resented his size, his stockiness, the roughness of his features, his unimpressive eyes. "Artist?" he asked, for Emma had always had a weakness for creative people, people who were not what she called "pedestrian."

"In a way," said Felicity, and that, too, was true. And pride, pride of her father, was a pleasure she had never been able to indulge in before. "Doesn't his name mean anything to you? Forbes—Adam Forbes. He's very well known. He invented many things—all automotive. He helped develop the Jeep."

"Oh, yes," said Scott, though of course he had never heard of the man. "Now I remember him. You certainly love him."

"Everybody does," said Felicity, and now she took another swallow from the bottle. "Everybody loves him. Everybody. There isn't a person who meets him who isn't bewitched," and she stretched her arms wide, then let herself fall back on the grass, crossing her hands behind her head.

Adam—Adam Forbes. Tall, blond, blue-eyed, with a smile that had been born on his face, as other people were born with clefts or warts. A man famed for his inventiveness. A man who didn't have to borrow any ideas.

"But in what way then do I resemble him?"

"You don't really," said Felicity, and she looked at Scott, looked at him for a long time, taking in all of him —the play of muscles in his forearm, the wine that had left a red spot on his chest, his strong throat—and said with great finality, "It's because you are both *men*. That's why. You have the same approach to life. Perhaps your experiences—I mean the ones that matter, that leave an impression—have been the same. He was in both wars, too, and then. . . ."

And the memory of the dugout came to Scott, the hole in the side of the mountain that he had pulled Emma into, away from death, and her screams as he tried to make love to her. How often he had admired her for her decision to go up to the front that morning! Now it occurred to him suddenly that she hadn't gone up to the front that morning because she was interested in the welfare of hospitalized American soldiers but because she was hoping to find her lover. Possibly, too, she had never cared what happened to her friends in France in '45, or about the castle, but had left Fleury in London to meet Adam Forbes. He could feel it again, how she had slipped out from under him after almost— No woman could be so cold, so cruel except a woman who was deeply, sensually in love with another man.

"Mrs. Fleury," said Felicity, putting a blade of grass between her teeth, "thinks I'm right."

But he had forgotten what had last been said. "Right about what?"

"About the two of you resembling each other."

The wine tasted bitter on his tongue. It couldn't be that Emma had been attracted to him only because he reminded her of Adam Forbes, that for her he had never been a man in his own right but a man with no identity of his own—not in his work, not as a lover.

He stared at Felicity. Her hair was spread around her head on the dusty green grass, forming a half circle, so that her face seemed like the white blossom of a water lily. And then he knew what had changed it. "No glasses. You've taken off your glasses. Can you see all right without them?"

Felicity had thought he would notice it right away, because when she had looked at herself in the mirror this morning, the change had been unbelievable to her. But it had been too egoistic, perhaps, to expect him to notice when there must be so many things of much greater importance on his mind. But now she smiled happily and tapped the pocket of her dress in which she was carrying her spectacles.

"No more," she said. "Mrs. Fleury had contact lenses made for me. Oh, she's wonderful to me, as if I were her daughter." And she took the blade of grass from between her lips, which remained parted a little as she suddenly realized fully how much Emma had done for her: First the invitation, then fetching her from the airport herself when she could so easily have sent Gino, buying her a new wardrobe, introducing her to beauty, to luxury, explaining with inexhaustible patience thousands of little things Felicity had never known, the talks in the morning when she was allowed to have breakfast with Emma—which more than anything else made her feel as if she belonged—going out with her, being introduced to her friends as if Emma took it for granted that people would like her, making it possible that she could lie here in an enchanting olive grove with Scott Warren sitting at her side, both of them suspended between the sea and a blue sky.

"I wish she had been my mother," said Felicity, and a thought went through her mind and poured across her lips. "And she could have been. She's known my father since she was seventeen." ("Be nice," Emma had said, "be gentle.") The memory of her voice infuriated Scott, and suddenly Felicity, lying on the grass next to him, was no longer Felicity—she wasn't even the daughter of the man Emma had loved, she was Emma herself. He rose and flung the bottle into space and pulled off his shirt.

"Hot?" asked Felicity.

He fell upon her like a tree, crushing her under his terrible weight. Felicity did not scream, she fought him as Emma had, only moaning softly. "Oh, no, please, no. Scott, please—Mr. Warren—Mr. Warren," as if the absurd calling of his surname and all it meant might bring him to his senses. But he didn't hear. Holding her to the ground, he unbuttoned her dress and she lay under him finally, white and frail and unable to move. And her frailness, her youth, her fear, her horrified amazement struggling in disbelief with her dying trust, all the factors that should have moved him only aroused his rage and it surged to the surface, as something deeply buried and suddenly released knows no limitations but has to erupt and spend itself. And the scent of her terror filling his nostrils only added to his excitement.

"I'll teach you to taunt a man."

His breath was a cloud of alcoholic fury. "You goddam little bitch, you. You hear me? I'll teach you, I said. So you'll never forget, so you'll remember it every day of your goddam life."

Not Emma any longer but every woman who had ever taunted a man. Not his frustration alone but the frustration of all men searching for compensation, everybody's helpless anger when face to face with his limitations, the hurt pride of everyone humiliated and the terrible need of all human beings to leave an imprint. And the sweetness of revenge carried him into her body. "I'll make love to you until you faint, and then never again. Never. And if you want it, I'll laugh at you until you fall on your knees and beg me, yes, beg me. I'll teach you, I'll teach you."

Twilight had set in when Felicity regained full consciousness. Though she had opened her eyes two or three times before, she never found enough strength to sit up, to look about her, to think, and had remained lying on the ground. She had not even grown aware of her nakedness. That her skin felt chilled had merely seemed an outward radiation of a burning inner cold, but now as the evening wind touched her, she shivered, looked down at herself and discovered that she was naked. She reached for her dress, which lay crumpled and dirty next to her, two buttons missing at the front, and for the next few minutes it became imperative that she find those buttons, as though if they could be found and sewn on again, everything would not be completely lost. But when she finally held them in her hand, she knew she might just as well not have found them, and let them drop to the ground again. She put on her panties, which were torn, and scrambled into her dress wrong side front, then changed it around. Fleetingly it occurred to her that it was strange nobody should have come by and seen her and helped her, or notified the police that there was a naked girl lying in the olive grove. Then it didn't seem strange any longer, for she remembered that the spot where Scott and she had met lay some distance from the footpath, which was rarely used anyway. Besides, the olive grove was private property—most of the mountain belonged to Scott.

When she started to move, she had to sit down again. Her back felt as if it had been broken. Her whole body hurt with a dull, heavy pain, as if she had been buried under the rubble of a house that had caved in. Her eyes were hurting and she removed the contact lenses and

reached into the pocket of her dress for her glasses. One
lens was crushed, but the left one was whole. She put
them on, blinking into the evening. Then, hugging her
knees, she rested her head on them and tried to recall
exactly what had happened and how it had come to pass,
but could find no explanation. Scott had been drunk, he
had been furious—perhaps in her ambiguous state of
mind she had flirted with him a little, feeling so safe with
him, as if he had been her father—*a* father—and feeling
so wonderfully unsafe because she no longer wanted him
to be a father or to be regarded by him as—what did he
call her?—a "little girl."

"I'll teach you to taunt a man."

But she hadn't taunted him. Where was he? He must
be around somewhere. It was impossible to imagine that
he would abandon her, lying naked where he had thrown
her, and she lifted her head, calling softly, "Scott . . .
Scott . . ." But however often she called—in the end
quite loudly—there was no answer.

Felicity forced herself to get up again and began to
search for him under the trees. Somewhere, surely, she
would find him, asleep perhaps, for it must never, never be
that he wasn't there to explain, to at least try to make her
understand what had happened between them. But Scott
was nowhere. Still she went on searching for him, whis-
pering his name because she could not believe in such
depths of humiliation. Then she saw the little donkey—
still tethered to the tree, forgotten—and realized that she,
too, had been forgotten, left behind, discarded because
she had no further value.

She wanted to cry then, but she found she had no tears.
Instead she thought, I must call the house and tell somebody that the donkey is still here. She almost slipped on
some of the olives that had fallen to the ground, green and
hard as fresh nuts, before she reached the path. Walking

downhill, she didn't lift her head once to look at the changing panorama. For the rest of her life, she knew, she would see only the olive grove from which there was no escape. When she came to the ravine, its contours now blurred by the dusk, seeming a valley of shadows, she stopped. She stood for a long time, trembling on the brink of decision. But to be found at the bottom would indicate suicide, and her death must not burden anyone.

Half an hour later she reached the stop where at lunchtime she had jumped from the bus. The way she looked, she didn't dare use a public vehicle. In front of a shopwindow, using it as a mirror, she combed her hair, then stood at the curb holding out her hand. A car coming from Monte Carlo stopped, a jalopy full of young people. Felicity sat on the top, which had been folded back, between two young girls, who asked her where she had her hair dyed and wouldn't believe her when she said the color was real, so to avoid more questions she finally named the hairdresser Emma used. When they reached Villefranche, she thanked them and from there walked back to the Cap. At the Villa du Cygne she would not have been missed, since Emma knew she had gone off to spend the day with Scott. And nobody noticed her entering the house; everybody was far too busy with the final preparations for the ball.

In her room the bedside lamp was burning, for Emma had a phobia about darkness and a light was turned on in every room, always, as soon as night fell. Felicity didn't have to be afraid that a light in her room would betray the fact that she had returned.

Spread out across the sofa in front of the fireplace lay a beautiful white gown; on a chair a coat embroidered with hundreds of rhinestones; on the table, on top of a shoebox that held new evening slippers, was curled, in a bed of blue velvet, a string of small, even pearls of the most exquisite color. There was a note in Emma's neat, clear handwriting: "For Listy, hoping you will have a good time."

Felicity looked at the dress, the coat, the slippers, the necklace, and the note, all proof of Emma's love—the only person who had ever cared for her deeply. Why? But the question she had asked herself so often during the last weeks had lost its importance. Slowly she shook her head as if in answer to the demands of these new presents; tears began to prick her lids, and she wished Emma had not given her all these beautiful things, for that made it impossible for her to kill herself before the ball. It forced her to live through this night and another day and into another night with the mortification of her mind and body.

She went into the bathroom and closed the door tightly so that the noise of running water would not attract attention to her room. When the tub was full, she got into it and the warm water closed around her aching body like a soft caress. Like magic it blotted out all her thoughts, and her body relaxed as the warmth of the water penetrated her blood. For a while she sat there not thinking, merely responding physically to the unexpected relief. Then she put back her head, not caring that her hair was getting wet, and stared up at the ceiling, trying to remember how she had imagined it would be the first time with a man she loved and who loved her. But she found it impossible. Because all she could feel suddenly was Scott's enormous weight forcing her into the ground, burying her. And everything that had been dim and blurred in her memory when she awoke in the grove came back to her—the violence of his mouth, his brutal hands, the power of his legs, the mad rage with which he had raped her. And the words he had spoken screamed at her from the tiled walls as if they had been caught there in an echo, then diminished in force until they were a soft whis-

per that was no longer addressed to her. And suddenly
Felicity knew that what had happened had nothing to do
with her, nothing whatsoever, except that her body had
been used.

She sat up abruptly and reached for the soap and brush
and began to scrub herself as if she could wash off Scott
Warren. When she felt clean, she pulled out the plug
and let the water run out while she sat on the rim of the
tub watching it flow down the drain. It was unbelievable
but true. And since it was not she to whom he had made
love, it had also not been she who had been rejected. She
turned on the shower full and strong and stood under it.
Scott's fury, his threats—they had had no connection with
her. They had been addressed to somebody else, and that
was why he had gone away. He hadn't left her—she had
never existed for him, and that was all there was to it. It
was an accident, like falling and breaking a leg, a break
that would heal again. It was no reason to kill oneself. It
had happened to other women and they had survived.

When she came back into her room again, the first
thing she saw was the dress, and this time she went up to
the sofa and touched it, then she touched the coat and
held up the pearls to her neck. As she turned around she
caught a glimpse of herself in the mirror, clean and white.
And she put on the pearls.

Yes, she thought, tomorrow I'll wear them. Then she
took them off, put on slacks and a pullover and left her
room to look for Emma and thank her, but she could not
find her. Hannah told her that Mrs. Fleury had already
retired.

Felicity did not go back to her room. Now she was too
excited to sleep or be alone. Everything in her was in
motion—so many thoughts were running through her
mind, she had to put them in order. And she wandered
through the rooms that had already been set up for the

festivities of the next day, with extra chairs and tables, and flowers in profusion everywhere. Then she went out on the terrace and saw the great white tent to the left, its flap open and electricians in blue smocks putting up the wires. Titus spotted her and came out, wiping his forehead with one of the large red peasant handkerchiefs he was so fond of wearing.

"Be an angel and get me a beer."

But the kitchen was filled with the caterer's people, boxes, dishes and great serving urns, and nobody would let her go near the iceboxes, which were already crammed with food. So Felicity went to the bar in the library and mixed a highball. She mixed herself a drink. While she was gulping it down, Meg came in.

"Lucky girl! You haven't got parents arriving for the ball," she said carelessly, thoughtlessly. "Mine are a holy bore. But I finally got them to bed. *I* need my beauty rest. Or is there anything I should be doing? Your hair's wet."

"I just washed it," said Felicity. "For tomorrow."

"Well, if I had hair like yours, I'd wear it open and plain." Meg had never paid her a compliment before, and Felicity smiled in surprise, said good night and carried the highball to Titus.

"Have you seen the platform yet?" he asked, pointing to the big square float in front of the dock. "That's where we're going to put the orchestra, and the dancers will perform while we eat."

"I'll have a look at it," Felicity told him.

She went down the path between the rocks, and as she walked, the great lights went on above the tent—they were testing them—so it was brilliantly lit and there were no shadows. The sand was still warm from the sun, and Felicity took off her shoes and carried them. A gangway had been put down from the dock to the platform, and on the platform itself a stage had been erected. Felicity

went up the few steps, came down at the other end and
walked to the edge of the platform. There several ladders
hung into the water, to reach the rowboats. They were
painted in rainbow colors and Japanese lanterns had been
fastened to the wires that supported the canvas shelter.
It was peaceful here. No sound from the house penetrated
the night, only the whisper of the water lapping the shore,
and as Felicity sat down on the highest rung of one of
the ladders, even the light fell away and she could see
only the Mediterranean, with a rising moon silvering it
as if in promise.

For a long time Felicity just sat there, letting the quiet-
ness of the night calm her. But tomorrow, she thought
then, tomorrow Scott will be here and I will have to face
him. And like a cloud the fury of his sex went through
her mind. But she shook her head. This she had to forget.
She had to think of him as she had before, and she would
—an elderly man who reminded her of her father. Her
father? No. She didn't want to think of him again either.
"I don't hate my father any more," she had said to Emma
after she met Scott for the first time. But had she really
hated her father?

Startled, Felicity moved so violently she almost fell,
but as she gripped the sides of the ladder another revela-
tion came to her. She had loved her father. And only
because she had loved him, and he had not acknowledged
her, had she hated him. And she had built her life around
him, her dreams, her hopes, and when he died she had
still looked for him, looked for him in every man. And
now—Felicity held her breath—now, suddenly, there was
no need any longer to transfer the love she had felt unconsciously for her father to any other man. Because of
what had happened between her and Scott, the need had
died. Scott had killed it.

The platform rocked gently with the tide—like a ship,

Felicity thought. She had never been on a ship, but now it seemed to her that she was on a boat, going somewhere. She did not know where nor did she care. She was free. She had found her balance. Abruptly she let go of the sides of the ladder. Free, she thought, and wrapped her arms around herself as if she had to touch this new person she had become. She looked up into the sky at the moon high above her, and in its cold, white light she could feel her past leaving her. So she sat there for a long time until a great, wonderful tiredness filled her entire being. Then she leaned forward and rested her head on her knees. Dimly she was aware that she ought to get up and go back into the house. This was no place to fall asleep. But it was so beautiful out here, with the moon and the stars and the knowledge that she was heading toward a miraculous new life. Tomorrow, she thought . . . tomorrow . . . But she was too sleepy to plan what she would do tomorrow or the next day or the next . . .

She felt her eyes close again. With great effort she pulled herself together, rose, and teetering on the brink of exhaustion, yet filled with the elation of hope, she turned to climb back onto the platform. But in the uncertain light of the moon she mistook the width of the ladder's rungs, which were slippery where the sea had washed over them, and lost her foothold. Nobody heard her desperate screams for help. In the Villa du Cygne all the lights had been extinguished. Everybody was asleep.

The telephone call came early in the morning, and it came from the little police station of the village of Saint-Jean-Cap-Ferrat. Hannah, on her way up to Emma's bedroom with tea on a small silver tray, took the call, hunching her shoulder nearly up to her cheek to make a cradle for the receiver because packages had been piled high on the telephone table, leaving no room to put the tray down.

She thought that the call had something to do with the men the village was providing to guard the road, the entrance and the beach for the night of the ball. At first she didn't understand what she was being asked, and when she did it made no sense, but when she finally grasped the meaning of the question, she forgot that the table was crowded and set the tray down to take better hold of the receiver. It toppled, the pot broke and the tea spilled all over the floor. Then the receiver fell from her hand, and she let it dangle and turn crazily on its cord while she flew upstairs. But having reached the top, she stopped, suddenly not knowing what to do, where to turn; though for a moment she was tempted to burst into her mistress's room to unburden herself, as well as to witness how the news would affect Mrs. Fleury, she fought down her desire for sensation and knocked instead on Titus's door.

He was still fast asleep and, as was his habit, sleeping in the nude. Hannah pulled the sheet, which had slipped three-quarters to the floor, over him before she called his name; then, when he did not answer, she grabbed him by the shoulder and shook him.

"Police?" he murmured. "Accident? What the devil—" Then, suddenly fully awake, he sat bolt upright. "Look in her room!"

Hannah came back to say that Felicity's room was empty, her bed hadn't been touched, and now, white and trembling, she stammered, "I don't believe it. It can't be true."

"See if she's in the garden," Titus ordered as both of them rushed down the stairs. "Or in one of the greenhouses. She often—" He picked up the dangling receiver, said "Yes," listened. "Thank you. I'll be right over." But he remained standing, automatically trying to disentangle the cord of the phone. Then he gave up and went outside and into the garage and started his car, not even waiting for Hannah to return. "A tall girl," the policeman had said. "Tall and slim. We thought we recognized her by her red hair as one of Madame la Comtesse's house guests."

Not quite five minutes later, he was ushered into a back room of the police station and a man removed a white sheet from a body that had been placed on a table. Titus needed to take only one look to nod in confirmation. Only last night Felicity had mixed him a drink, had carried it out to him, to the tent, and he had pointed out the platform where they were to dance tonight. He stared at the drops of water still dripping from her hair to the bare wooden floor as if she were still alive, as if she had just come back from a swim. Dead.

As if in a nightmare, he heard someone tell him how, about an hour ago, Felicity's body had been discovered on the other side of the Cap. It had been carried around the point and washed up on the shore. A doctor Lefèvre from the hospital had pronounced her dead, saying she must have drowned about eight hours ago and been in the water a little longer than that. Face, belly and legs were already swollen. They were going to move the body to the morgue when Pierre here had recognized her as the young girl who so often accompanied Madame la Comtesse. And what a shame it was—just today, the day of the ball. Maybe an investigation would not be necessary, but of course there was the question, Had it been an accident or suicide?

"Suicide?" said Titus, and shook his head. Never. He had seen her at about ten o'clock last night and she had been in excellent spirits. So he was asked to come to the office, where a clerk took down everything he knew about Felicity and about the last time he had seen her. Titus realized then that he knew as good as nothing about the girl who had been under the same roof with him for more than six weeks, and he nearly cried because it struck him as tragic and unfair that he should know so few facts, but they seemed enough for the police. He was being thanked for having come, for agreeing to answer more questions if necessary, and was allowed to leave.

For a while Titus drove around aimlessly, passing without seeing them the huge statue of the virgin, the little cemetery where soldiers from the First World War who had died in the hospital here lay buried, the Grand Hôtel, where Emma had taken two floors for her guests. Then he found himself quite unexpectedly on the driveway leading up to the Villa du Cygne. He stopped the car and lighted a cigarette. There was no way of sparing Emma, not even for a day. Sooner or later she would discover that Felicity was missing, and no lie would convince her that the girl, on this day of all days, had gone off by herself for reasons of her own. Besides, the police might call again. Though Titus had never bothered his head about Emma's relationship to the girl, having been too much involved in his own affairs, he knew that Emma had been especially fond of Felicity from the beginning, and the idea of how much she would be hurt made him cringe.

"Madame is having her coffee," Hannah, who had apparently been waiting at the foot of the staircase, told him as soon as she saw him on the landing. "She asked me to call Miss Listy. They usually had coffee together. But I said she was still asleep and that maybe it was better to let her sleep because of tonight." Her eyes searched his face and Titus nodded. Then he added, and was surprised at the unintentional sharpness of his voice, "I hope you haven't mentioned anything. Nobody must know. Not today."

He had not known that Emma had formed the habit of having breakfast with Felicity. He had always thought of this particular hour as a very private one, which Emma needed to herself to get ready to face the demands of the day, and before knocking at her door, he went into his room, where he kept some Scotch stuck behind the hats in his closet. He didn't bother about a glass, just drank from the bottle, wiped it, took another gulp and put it back again.

Emma was in the room that, on the bell board in the servants' quarters, was marked "Morning Room." Titus had never been in it before. In a way it wasn't a room at all but rather like a terrace that had been glassed in; except for a huge fireplace, it gave one the feeling of entering a greenhouse, for there were flowers everywhere and exotic vines climbed the whitewashed walls, some even trailing from the ceiling. In several cages, hidden behind plants, parrots chattered.

"Why, Titus," said Emma. "Up so early?"

She was dressed all in white—her favorite color, as Titus knew, but also, he thought, the color of grief in far-away lands. Under the white terry-cloth bathrobe she wore white silk pajamas, and she had tied a white kerchief around her head. It revealed the lovely bone structure of her forehead and temples, otherwise almost hidden by her hair.

"I understand everything is in order and that you did a splendid job of supervising last night." She pointed to a chair. "Sit down and have a cup of coffee. Or have you breakfasted already?"

"No, thank you," Titus said, and sat down and watched Emma lift the heavy silver pot to fill the cup that had been meant for Felicity.

"Is there anything you want to talk to me about?" Emma smiled, trying to be helpful. "Susan?"

"She can't seem to come to a decision," he said. "Anyway, not yet. I took your advice. I've decided to give her all the time she needs. I'm going to New York in the fall. I'm going to try my hand as a customers' man."

Emma stretched out a hand, and seemingly from nowhere a parakeet shot through the air, folded his wings and landed on her finger. Should she warn Titus? Should she, very carefully—?

"Emma"—Titus cut into her reflections—"Emma," and he sounded so unlike himself that Emma looked at him questioningly. "There has been an accident." And now Titus spoke so quickly that Emma had trouble understanding him. She frowned.

"An accident? Don't speak so fast, Titus." She moved her hand abruptly and the bird took flight.

"A fatal accident," said Titus. "I'm afraid—I'm afraid there is nothing we can do. Felicity—Listy—"

His mother had looked like that, so white, so still, the morning they had found her in bed with an empty bottle of sleeping pills on the bedside table. And suddenly Titus knew why he had felt happier at the Villa du Cygne than anywhere else in the world. Not because of its beauty or the luxury it offered but because Emma somehow reminded him of his mother. They didn't look alike— or perhaps they did, since all true beauty has essentials in common, so that it didn't matter that his mother had been tall and dark and green-eyed, while Emma was small and silver-haired and her eyes were blue—but both of them had carried a spirit of gallantry like a noble mask. Like Emma, his mother had been an aesthete—never mind what she had done. The only difference was that the one had been able to live without having to humiliate herself, and the other had had to crucify herself to meet her obligations.

Emma listened without saying a word while he told her all he knew. And she didn't move, nor did she look at him even when he was through.

"Say something," whispered Titus, as he had whispered that morning kneeling at his mother's bedside, not believing she was dead. "Say something." But Emma did not seem to hear him. Titus tried again to break the silence, to make her respond, and in his despair he began to repeat all he had already told her—about the call, the police station—then he murmured, "And of course when they asked me what I thought, I said it couldn't possibly have been suicide."

He must have forgotten to mention the policeman's routine question, for Emma faced him suddenly, her eyes open wide. "Suicide?"

"No, no." Titus shook his head. "I saw her last night. She was all excited. I've never seen her quite so alive. She was looking forward to the ball like a child to its first party. And the moment I mentioned that the platform had been put up, she said she'd take a look at it. Oh, God," he groaned suddenly as it occurred to him that it might have happened there, that Felicity might have stumbled in the uncertain light and fallen from the platform into the sea. "If only I hadn't mentioned it. If only I'd gone with her. I saw her walk down to the beach. We'd just turned on the lights to test them," and he stopped, trying to remember what the policeman had said about a Doctor Lefèvre—that Felicity had been dead a little more than eight hours.

"Yes, it must have happened down there," he cried. "It was about ten when I asked her to get me a beer, but she couldn't find any and brought me a highball instead. Yes, that was around ten, and the call came at seven."

"She couldn't swim," said Emma.

"If only I'd remembered that," said Titus, "I'd never have let her go down alone. But I forgot. There was such a lot to do and I was tired." He looked at Emma as if he hoped she would absolve him, but she only made a listless gesture with her hand and left him between the vines and the flowers, closing the door behind her.

She didn't ring for Hannah to help her dress. She dressed herself, slowly and with great care, as if it mattered to her that she look immaculate. Don't think, she told herself, don't think. You have invited five hundred people who expect you to be a gay and amusing hostess. There will be time to think later. But you have to notify —whom? Felicity has no parents to grieve for her, no boy who will be desperate at losing her. She is a stranger to her few relations.

She crossed the corridor and went into Felicity's room. The bed was untouched, as Titus had said. And Emma sat down on it, remembering the afternoon when Gino had told her about Meg's pregnancy, and she had come in here waiting for Meg to return, and had watched Felicity dress. Her eyes fell on the evening gown and coat, spread over sofa and chair, and the box on the table with the new slippers, and she saw that they had been touched, and that the chain of pearls had been moved from the jeweler's case and was lying next to her on the bedside table. Tomorrow, Emma said to herself, tomorrow I shall make all the arrangements. But a moment later she asked herself in despair, Where would Felicity have liked to be buried? She didn't know. The gardeners might. Old Auguste, who knew her favorite spots, the flowers she had liked best. Which ones? The graceful anemones? She had said they looked like dancers with little green skirts. Or the fat white roses one could mistake for masterpieces in marble if their scent hadn't betrayed them? She had loved all flowers, but which one would she have chosen?

Emma rose slowly, and as she rose from the bed, something slipped from it to the ground. A pair of glasses, one of the lenses crushed. Emma picked them up and stared down at them and could hear Felicity's voice—"I'm going to wear the contact lenses for practice"—and could see Felicity standing in front of her. "If you're sure there's nothing I can do for you—Scott Warren has invited me for the day. He wants to show me his mountain." Emma had said the butler or somebody else could drive her up to Eze, but Felicity had shaken her head. "Thanks, I'll take the bus. Really, I'd rather. Anyway, I want to walk half the way up."

Suddenly it seemed imperative to find out what those last hours of Felicity's life had been like. Emma glanced at her watch: ten o'clock. Scott would be at home now. He always worked in the morning.

He was in his study, one of the small rooms that reminded her of a monk's cell. There was nothing in it but a narrow cot, a bookshelf that held paper and clips, and a small desk with a typewriter on it. It did not face the superb view over the coast but had only one window, almost under the ceiling, for Scott claimed the beauty outside would make it impossible for him to create beauty on paper. He couldn't write against such competition.

"Tell Mr. Warren I must see him," Emma said to the manservant who opened the door, and she went past the little rooms that held the African sculptures Felicity had found so attractive, into the living room, with the trophies on the wall. She was staring at them, thinking how appalled Felicity had been the first time she had seen them and wondering if Scott had ever got around to telling her of his hunting experiences, when he came into the room.

He never dressed when he was working, just put on a dressing gown if someone came. The one he had on now was old and faded and held together by a worn leather belt. His hair stood wildly around his head and he was wearing no shoes. Emma could see his big, bare feet and part of his strong legs, which the dressing gown did not cover. And suddenly the tears came—tears that couldn't be cried alone because then they would flow endlessly, nor cried in the presence of a young man who was not yet a man, but that could, strangely enough, be wept here, with Scott. But Scott had never seen Emma cry and he stood helpless.

"Em! For God's sake, what's the matter? What's the matter, old girl? Come, come. Who would ever have believed you're human? Come on, tell me—what's wrong?"

When she could finally speak again she said, "Felicity is dead."

"Felicity?" Scott repeated as if he had never heard the name before, as if he couldn't place a person called Felicity in his mind.

"Listy," said Emma, "and she spent her last hours with you."

"Listy?" said Scott. "What did you say? Did you say—" and he sat down next to her in one of those chairs that were all wrong on the Riviera, that belonged in some hunting lodge because they were covered with the pelts of zebras.

"She's dead," said Emma. "Dead." And she held her hand to her mouth to stifle a sob.

"Dead?" said Scott as though he couldn't believe it. "Dead?"

He had forgotten about the girl. He had come home last night at about eight, according to the housekeeper, maybe earlier. He hadn't wanted any dinner but just sat there drinking for a solid hour, then he had gone to bed and slept straight through until five. He had had a cup of coffee and immediately started to work, the words pouring from his fingertips effortlessly. Now memory awoke in him, slowly, almost tangibly. He could see a man walking down the rocky pass of a mountain, dragging a little donkey behind him. The man was wearing leather pants and a white shirt and a green stocking cap and was thinking, Why the hell do I put on such a getup, like an actor dressing for a part? Whom am I trying to fool? The man had been drinking for quite some time before he left his house, and he slipped once, scraping his knee on the stones. At first he cursed, then he began to sing as if the song pouring from his chest were a third arm or leg that could help him keep his balance.

"She drowned," said Emma. "Did she ever tell you she couldn't swim?"

The man walking down the path was desperate. He hadn't been able to create for weeks. He was frustrated, angry, and the sun was hot. Why in the world did he have to walk at this time of day? Mad dogs and Englishmen—and he whistled the tune. But it didn't wipe out the fury in him, which was rising in his throat like vomit.

"You'd better have a drink," said Scott.

He got up and poured two glasses full from a bottle of Calvados.

"I didn't see her when she came home," Emma went on after she had taken a swallow. "I went to bed early last night," and she almost added, as Titus might have done, If only I'd stayed up. If only I'd left word for her to come in and see me, no matter how late, to say good night.

"But Titus saw her. Titus pointed out the platform on the dock and Listy went down to look at it."

Scott poured himself a second glass. The Calvados was aged and it warmed his insides. Again he could hear the man cursing the donkey and cursing himself for having bought the damn animal, then laughing because he had found a name for it. Isaac. And getting furious again. And looking at the ax he had taken with him. Once he got the blade to bite into the yellow flesh of a tree, maybe his fury would pass.

"The doctor fixed the time of her death around ten last night."

There had been a girl in the olive grove waiting for the man, a girl in a white-and-green-striped linen dress. A girl with red hair. A girl who compared him to her father as if he had no identity of his own. The father was a beautiful specimen of a man, or so the red-haired girl had said.

"She must have missed her footing somehow in the dark, mistaken the sea for a part of the platform—we don't know."

All of a sudden the man was terribly close. He was standing directly in front of Scott. Scott rose to go over to the bar where he had put down the Calvados. But the man followed him, and when Scott reached out his hand for the bottle, the man lifted his hand, too. And the hands were the same.

"How did she feel when she left here? Or did you see her home?"

"No," said Scott.

"I'm sure it was an accident, but the police wonder if by any chance it could have been suicide."

"I made love to her," said Scott.

"You—what?"

"You heard me," said Scott. "I made love to her. I was drunk and I made love to her."

The hole in the ground. He had not been drunk then, just elated because he had escaped death, but even now Emma could feel the brutal power of his arms throwing her onto the straw pallet that was there for soldiers too sick to stand. The room in the castle—again he had been sober, yet she could feel his weight pinning her down. To think of him drunk . . .

"Suicide," said Scott. "As if fornication— Damn it! What a fool!"

Emma stared up at the wall. Several weeks ago, when she had first brought Felicity here to meet Scott, she had thought of one of the little does on the wall as herself. But Felicity had been that doe, that innocent, virginal little doe.

"Damn it!" said Scott again.

Emma took her eyes from the wall. She looked at Scott. "Damn you!" she said.

He was so surprised he stared at her, then he roared with helpless laughter. The great lady, the great lady out of character, sitting there with her eyes blazing, cursing him in a loud, clear voice. He hadn't known that her voice could have such volume.

"She didn't mean anything to me," he said. "That's what I meant. The stupid kid—taking it personally when I really wasn't making love to her at all. When I was really making love—" He looked at Emma, his eyes forcing hers to meet his. "All these years," he said, "yearning, wanting, and you—she was the daughter of the man you love, wasn't she? Wasn't she? The daughter of Adam Forbes, because of whom you denied me."

"Suicide," said Emma. "So it was not an accident but suicide."

He was shaking, trembling like a tree before it falls. "Forgive me," he said. "Em, I was drunk, I didn't know what I was doing. Em, for once in your life hear me out!"

But Emma rose. "I never want to see you again," she said, walking past him out of the room.

PART
THREE

AND now the Japanese lanterns were being lit, the white ones hanging like little moons in the trees bordering the driveway; then the pink ones below the terrace, which threw back their soft light against the stone of the house, making it look as if the last rays of a setting sun were still caressing it; then the blue ones along the beach, coloring the rim of the sea; then hundreds and hundreds in the rose garden, all shapes and colors, shedding life on the sleeping flowers; and finally those strung around the platform, all of them yellow, while the ones in the row-boats, swinging with the tide, were matched to the colors of their boats.

Emma leaned at the open window of her bedroom staring out at the night being prepared to receive her guests, five hundred people who expected her to be a gay and amusing hostess, and she shivered. Don't think, she told herself. Concentrate on them. You must concentrate on them. She heard the orchestra on the terrace tuning up, notes fluttering like little moths to where she stood, and she turned and left the room.

Titus was waiting for her in front of the huge window on the landing. "I thought you might like a drink," he said, pointing to a tray with two glasses and a bottle of champagne on a small table next to the wide couch. Emma nodded gratefully.

"How splendid you look," he said, raising his glass to hers.

Her dress seemed to be made of spun silver, and she was wearing her famous black pearls—no other jewelry,

225

just the round, matched pearls and the earrings that went with them. But white orchids were fastened to her gown, and they swayed gently with every move she made, as if they were still blossoming. Titus was scanning her face. Impossible to tell what she was thinking. Abruptly, almost rudely, he began to talk about his own affairs.

"I'd hoped Susan wouldn't come. But Mr. Webster apparently insisted on seeing a really grand affair, so they'll be here," and he smiled his broken, arrogant smile.

He would have gone on if Meg hadn't appeared at the top of the staircase, all innocence in a cloud of pink tulle. "Where's Felicity, Aunt Emily? She promised to fix the flowers in my hair." She held out a bunch of red sweetheart roses.

"Felicity is in the hospital," Titus said quickly, then added more slowly, "Looks like appendicitis. We don't know yet."

"Gosh," Meg said. "Poor baby. What a shame. She was looking forward to tonight. Are they going to operate? I had mine out when I was nine. Titus, can you fix my flowers?"

"You'll look damn silly with flowers in your hair," said Titus. "Fasten them to your belt or shoulder or something. And don't you dare drink out of my glass."

The slamming of a car door echoed from the courtyard, and Emma pushed Titus's sleeve up to his wrist. It was only a quarter to ten.

"I'll bet that's my parents," said Meg. "They're always afraid they're going to miss something."

"We'd better go," said Emma.

Of course it was the Browns, Helen and William Brown, in the pink of health and full of joviality, looking so much like an advertisement in a women's magazine, they seemed to have stepped out of the pages for the occasion.

"You certainly needed new tails," Meg told her father.

"Did you buy this outfit, Mom, or did you borrow it from Mrs. Banding?" Her parents chose not to hear her remarks.

"Well, Emma, long time no see!" said Mr. Brown, rubbing his hands. "I say, this is quite a house."

"We're so grateful Meg could spend the summer with you," said Mrs. Brown. "You should read her letters. Just raves. What a wonderful place this is! Photos never really give a true picture, do they?"

"Would you like to see the other rooms?" asked Emma, but of course the Browns had come early because they wanted to remain in the hall to form a reception line with her, and she waved to a waiter to serve them drinks.

The next one to arrive was Princess Steffany, who lived in a small villa on the side of Cap Ferrat facing the bay of Villefranche. She, too, liked to be on time, but for a different reason. She hated champagne and wanted to make sure there was a small *flacon* of brandy reserved for her. This she would tuck into her huge old-fashioned embroidered bag and help herself every now and then, pretending it was medicine whenever she wanted to take a nip. She was quite old, over eighty. If the turban she always wore had been removed, it would have revealed the fact that she was bald. Emma kissed Steffany and nodded to Hannah.

The Princess was followed by Jacques Thiolat, elegant as usual, but without his famous winning smile. Emma held out her hand. "So glad to see you, Jacques," and Thiolat bent and kissed it gravely.

"Dad," cried Meg, "this is the most marvelous doctor in the world! He should check your liver, and I'm sure you wouldn't have to take any more of those nasty pills." She put one arm around her father and took Thiolat's hand, drawing them both inside.

The Smiths from Washington arrived, and Sandy

asked immediately, "What about those rumors, Emma?
I mean, that you're going to be offered an ambassadorship?"

"And don't you dare turn it down. You'd be just marvelous for it," admonished his wife.

"I'd love it," said Emma.

Suddenly there was a whole group of people compli-
menting her and walking past her into the *grand salon.*
A little while later, Susan and her husband came in all by
themselves. Emma would have recognized Jim Webster
anywhere from the photo she had seen in Susan's room.
He looked younger than his age; the crew cut made his
sober, intelligent face seem more like a student's than a
full-grown man's. He bowed ceremoniously and made a
trite little speech about how glad he was that his wife
had pleased Mrs. Fleury, as if Susan were a little girl and
he an older brother, proud of her accomplishments.

Another group. And another. French, Italian, American and English friends. Ann Harrison, in whose room
Emma had lain pretending it was not she who was re-
ceiving a blood transfusion. "Almost missed the plane.
I'd have sued the airline!"

"*Comtesse . . .*"

"Emily, darling . . ."

"*Contessa . . .*"

"*Sehr verehrte Gräfin . . .*"

"Your Excellency . . ."

"Emma, this is a very great pleasure indeed. . . ."

"How sweet of you to think of us. . . ."

"You know, we had planned to go to Russia, but of
course. . . ."

"Hi, Em."

Scott's voice. Emma drew back, then turned to stare
after him. Had he not understood what she had told him
this morning—that she never wanted to see him again?

Rage and disgust made her tremble. But her guests were still streaming in; she composed herself.

Two young princes from Siam. A well-known astrologer from England. A Chinese poet who had escaped the Iron Curtain's fall. Several young Swedes, all healthy and blond. Her Japanese painter friend. A Belgian princess with a famous architect. A French playwright with his mistress, the only one who had dared bring someone who was not invited—or had she overlooked a note asking permission? Ortalo, the great brain from Italy, whom people compared to Fermi. A bearded maharaja, his wife in a glittering sari. The Dutch ambassador to the United States. Three half-baked millionaires who—you could tell by the dust on their shoes—had decided to walk rather than drive from the hotel; their wives, all three of them, dressed by Dior, stylistically one jump ahead of the season. The witty, sarcastic cartoonist who had once depicted her riding one of the wild black swans at the entrance gate. Late, of course, was the star from Hollywood, an exciting and beautiful woman who had conquered audiences all over the world when she had been only twenty and had understood, with intelligence and one or two face-lifting jobs, how to retain her attraction. Even later, to assure himself a full house, was the famous Shakespearean actor. But then male actors were the vainest of all human beings.

More and more people. And suddenly the hall was empty, the front door was closed from outside by the servant checking the list. Everybody she had invited had come. Everybody was there except Felicity.

In the huge tent, the tables had been arranged in the shape of a horseshoe, leaving an open oval space for those who wanted to dance between courses. The first was therefore the smallest, while the others were graded above each other on individual platforms, in ever-increasing size, giving an effect of low, wide steps. They were covered with lace laid over pink satin. Thousands of tiny roses had been pinned to the lace and wound in garlands around the wires that supported the tent, filling it with their sweet, strong scent. Silver candlesticks stood in front of every plate, each of them set on a round mirror so that their reflected, trembling light created movement and shadow. Tree roses in lacquered white vats stood at each end of the tables and at the sides of the entrances. All the tables had a perfect view of the float, brilliantly lit for the performance of the *corps de ballet* from Monte Carlo. And the dancers seemed to float from the background of the night sky like gossamer clouds: *Les Mirlitons,* the *pas de deux* from *Swan Lake,* the dance of the Willis from *Giselle*—ballets that had always cried out for a nocturnal setting. And the sweet, melodious music hung like an invisible curtain of sound over sea, beach and garden. When the musicians, placed in boats around the float, stopped playing, the band hidden behind a screen of roses on the terrace started up with modern dance music. There was a waiter to every three persons, since Emma detested slow service or insufficient attention. She sat at the table farthest from the entrance, between the French Ambassador to the United States and the American Ambassador to France. She sat very erect, as she always did on great occasions, eating leisurely and very little, drinking sparsely, an animated smile pulling at the corners of her mouth, listening attentively, or so it seemed, to what was being said at her left or right. Titus, glancing at her whenever he could no longer stand the sight of Susan sitting in the tier below him, thought, What a truly great lady she is. Just like my mother. Smiling and listening as if what they're saying really interested her. And though he was convinced that she would not see it, he lifted his glass and drank to her in silent admiration.

It's unbelievable, Thiolat marveled as he watched Emma out of the corner of his eye. There she sits, looking more beautiful than any woman her age. And so alive. She even seems to have put on some weight. Nobody would ever suspect. . . . He tried to recall the afternoon when he had last injected the needle into the frail whiteness of her arm, the faraway expression in her eyes, her question about what he believed in. Instead of a few days ago, it seemed long since past that he had sat next to her in the hotel room of a stranger, almost as if the person needing the blood transfusion had not been Emma. Her self-control was— He searched his mind for a word that would describe it, a word that had eluded him all these last weeks but that came to him now: Frightening, thought Thiolat, and having found the word, he was terrified, for it made him realize suddenly that Emma might not need him at the end, might not allow him to see her weak and afraid.

How can you sit there and smile, Scott wondered, aware of every move she made, the gracious way she leaned her head to one side in a gesture of listening, the gentle movements of her hands, the rapid change of expression in her face. How can you behave as if nothing mattered but that your goddam ball come off exactly as you planned it? And what am I doing here? Why did I come?

In spite of his sober appearance, he was quite drunk, with a drunkenness that held him outwardly immobile, as if he had rammed himself into a coat of armor that left him no room to move and played the damnedest tricks with his mind, lighting it up every now and then as if firecrackers were going off in his head, illuminating it with bright flashes of light, fountains of light—but they didn't last long enough for him to find what he was trying to find.

He plunked down both elbows on the table, staking out forbidden territory, and ignoring those seated next to him, leaned his chin into the cup of his hands. I came here, he thought, because you told me you would never see me again. You always mean what you say. And I must talk to you. Why did I do it? I don't know. I still don't know. But I've got a feeling you do. And you'd better tell me.

Another firecracker exploded behind his eyes, and he could see her standing in his living room, damning him. No, he said, almost aloud. It wasn't revenge. I've had so many women, I didn't have to have you. Sure, there was a time when I— I don't mean that bitch of a cave. Then I just wanted to feel alive all the way. But fifteen years ago, yes, then I was curious, then I wanted to see what you were like when you— Hell, no. You're wrong if you think I couldn't forget being rejected by you. Everybody gets rejected over and over again. Come to think of it, though, I didn't. Let's say I was cautious enough most of the time to make goddam sure I was wanted before I took a chance. Maybe that little girl had something I needed. She respected me. But you wouldn't know what that means to a man who's lost his self-respect. No, that isn't it, either.

He lifted his head and looked at Emma. Christ, how he hated her!

Hate, and he rolled the word on his tongue as if tasting something new. But it was true. He had carried hate with him ever since that day in Nice when he had found her sitting in the little café and had told her about the theft he had committed on a dead man, blurted out the secret of his fame, babbled like someone insane in his great need to relieve himself, in his loneliness and frustration and self-doubt, confessing his crime to her as if she were a priest who could absolve him. And she hadn't even been shocked; she'd merely said sanctimoniously, "But you could have made it on your own."

Suddenly the woman in the magnificent evening gown, with the black pearls around her frail, long throat, disappeared before his eyes and he could see Emma only as she had looked that day in the cave, dirt and straw clinging to her hair and dress from the long crawl through the tunnel, her mouth open wide in a scream. If she hadn't hollered holy murder in that stinking hole when he'd wanted nothing but the reassurance that he had truly escaped death, he'd never have gone out and sat at the mouth of the dugout and found the dead soldier and his diary. That was when his hatred had started. Then—when he began to read and know that he'd never turn in the diary.

The funny thing was that he had been aware of this hatred all these years, but to admit it would have made it a reality he could not face. As far as Emma was concerned, he had forgotten it. As for his fraud—well, for a long time he'd been able to put it aside. And on those days when he'd felt memory stirring in him, he got drunk, and made damn sure he'd hidden the key of his room, even from himself, so nobody could enter or he get out until he was sober enough to control his tongue. But that day in the café it had suddenly surged up from some unknown depths, surged to the surface without warning. But he had been conscious of what he had done only when it was too late, after Emma left him and disappeared inside the restaurant. He had made it a fact. Something he couldn't forget any longer, or deny, or push back into oblivion. It was alive. Vitally. Vividly. Because now someone else shared his knowledge. And he had fled the café, unable to stand the sight of Emma—the sight of a witness. For that was what she had become. Ever since then he had wished her out of existence, and his animosity had grown every day.

"Get me a whiskey," Scott said to the waiter. Champagne always made him sick. "A double." And with the whiskey warming his insides, another realization flashed through him. Even then, even at that point he had not allowed himself to hate Emma for the honest reason. He had had to invent something that was less uncomfortable than the truth. Yes. I made myself remember things—a legitimate reason, a man's hurt pride. Or maybe I was really hurt. Once. But why did I take it all out on the girl? Was it because I couldn't stand anything so decent, so innocent, so trusting? Trusting me, of all people—a thief, a clown, a fake. Or did I see her in my drunkenness as Emma? And because I couldn't blot her out, did I have to take her? Make her a part of me, a part of my fraud? Or did some dreadful need to liberate myself . . . It's all so mixed up—the dead soldier and Felicity; the diary; the cold night in the castle. Part of it's true and part of it isn't. But which part is?

He didn't know.

He looked at Emma again.

Emma was oblivious of the many glances in her direction, or, rather, she was so used to having people watch her that she paid no attention to anyone except to the men sitting on her right and left, and not very much to them, either. Nothing of importance was ever said at so large a dinner. A few phrases of pretended interest or something amusing usually sufficed to keep a conversation going, and these dropped quite automatically from her lips whenever they were needed. When dessert was being served, somebody got up, clinked his glass, cleared his throat. The music stopped abruptly and the chatter died

down. Emma sighed. She had not expected a speech tonight, at a ball. But apparently there was always someone
who wanted to hear his own voice. There was nothing
she could do but smile, lean back in her chair and affect
the right mixture of pleasure and modesty as the expected
words in honor of the hostess were being spoken. She had
had to sit through so many of these speeches, and they
were always the same. Normally she didn't even listen.
But tonight certain phrases caught her ear—not the ones
praising her beauty, her charm, the pleasure of her company, her generosity, her capacity for friendship, her
loyalty, but those explaining her success as a woman, a
hostess, a personality by the fact that it could have been
achieved only by someone who had led "a rich and full
life."

A rich and full life, thought Emma as she danced her
first dance with the American Ambassador to France,
and the past came to life. The early-morning rides with
Henri, breakfast interrupted by telephone calls that had to
be taken, the hours spent with the social secretary, with
the chef, with the gardener, reading newspapers and
bulletins and mail to keep up with the news, the boring
luncheons, the tiring fittings, the meetings with charity
organizations, the horrible teas, the endless cocktail parties, the openings of shows that had to be attended, the
exhibitions at museums and galleries, so few of them re-
warding, agricultural fairs, strenuous dinners, the nightly
walks with Henri and the dogs, the planning, the tension
and sheer hard work of making a new home in a foreign
country, perfecting oneself in a strange language, getting
accustomed to alien mentalities, customs, climate, food.
The long trips, the hundreds of minor ailments that could
never be permitted to interfere with one's appearance
somewhere. If she had succeeded in anything—in being a
wife who could be trusted, a charming hostess, winning

friends for France and establishing useful contacts for her
native land—it had been possible only because she had
in every circumstance fulfilled her obligations. Nothing of
any value could ever be achieved unless one did one's
duty, no matter how small or large the issue.

And she went on dancing—with the handsome young
prince from Siam and Sir Archibald from the British
Foreign Office, and the tall, good-looking Russian who
spoke eleven languages and avoided mentioning politics,
about which the French Minister talked on and on, as if
he were delivering a speech at the Quai d'Orsay.

But duty, thought Emma as the strain of the evening,
the cacophony of voices and music, the warmth and the
smell of hundreds of scents made her feel faint, duty was
apparently a concept that had become rare as a way of
life. Hadn't it been Thiolat's duty to refuse Meg an abortion and call her the moment the girl had turned up in
his office, or whatever place they had met, so that she
could have talked to the child and prevented the crime?
And how abominably Meg had behaved. Instead of feeling the slightest regret . . . And Susan, shamelessly taking her time to make up her mind, respecting neither
Jim's feelings nor Titus's, her mind on nothing but her
own satisfaction. What a fool she had been to believe in
their innate decency, to try and help them to find the
courage to live.

Emma stopped short. Courage? Did it take courage to
expose one's own vulnerability? Not to care about defeat
but to act, knowing that the chances were you would be
defeated, yet acting just the same, in spite of the fact that
the odds were against you. Instinctively she had known
this all along, that she was missing a vital part of her
existence, yet she had evaded asking herself why. Now,
suddenly, she could no longer blind herself against the
truth. She had been content to conduct her life the way

she had because she had always been afraid. Out of fear.
Yes—fear. Not because she was, as she had sometimes
told herself, passive by nature. Her passivity had only
been one of the consequences of her deep dread of suffering, and she had used all her strength to detach herself,
to stay aloof from any personal relationship.

When had it started, this fear that had rendered her
inactive and rigid?

When her mother had asked her to pray for a little
brother? Or later, in school, when she had found out she
was not being invited to the party the whole class had
been talking about for weeks? Or when she believed
Adam had deceived her, or when Henri had told her why
he had married her?

But then I was caught, she thought, caught in a marriage I could not break. But in the same moment she
knew that if her desire to experience life on her own
terms *had been stronger than her fear,* she would have
found a way. Meg, Susan, even Felicity had had the
courage to participate, while her courage had merely been
the courage demanded of a woman in her position—killing a snake without showing fear, walking erectly across
a market place when a sharpshooter, hidden on one of
the rooftops, had sworn to shoot any white person who
dared set a foot outside. Adam, thought Emma. Did I go
on loving you because I didn't dare risk losing the security
of a love that never had to face reality? Was I loyal to
you, Henri, only because I was hiding behind principles,
being faithful to a code I had chosen because it would
protect me?

And everything she had been proud of all her life fell
like a statue from its pedestal, and shattered into a thousand pieces. Her unwavering adherence to her principles,
her faithfulness to Henri, her pride, her feeling of superi-
ority, her sense of honor, her self-control, her dignity, her

standards. There they lay, a worthless heap because they had been subterfuge, used to evade any issue that was threatening, void of everything that might give them meaning, because she had never used them as weapons against temptation but, like jewelry, had guarded them against robbery instead of letting them guard her.

She stared at the lanterns swinging outside on the terrace in the night wind. Japanese lanterns. They, too, were a hangover from childhood, from the parties to which she had not been invited. Only once had she tried to break away from her terror of becoming involved emotionally, had tried to extend herself—when she had told Henri that she wanted a child. And suddenly she knew that the death of her child had in a sense been the end of her. And it was what she had held against Thiolat subconsciously, blaming him so that she would not have to face her own cowardice.

She turned her head looking for Thiolat, and at once, as if he had been waiting for a sign from her, he caught her glance and made his way to where she was sitting. "Emma, I haven't had the pleasure of dancing with you yet."

Emma rose and followed him out to the terrace.

"Don't dance if you feel too tired," he said. "I asked you only to rescue you so that you could relax a little and sit quietly with me somewhere."

But Emma shook her head.

"You know," she said, moving in his arms to the rhythm of the music, "I can see things quite clearly now. What I've done is try to fit life into my *salon*. I mean, I took from life only what would not disturb me, what could not interrupt the security and harmony of my house. And life seemed satisfactory because I could choose what I wanted. Personal involvement was out of place for me. It didn't fit in. Beauty and harmony, it seemed to me, should be the goals of a civilized person."

Thiolat felt the dreadful depression that had settled over him earlier in the evening leave him. At last she was explaining why, throughout the years they had known each other, she had behaved as if she were unaware of what he felt for her.

"I understand. I do, Emma. And if anybody achieved it, you—"

But Emma interrupted him. "I thought of people who let their desires or needs run away with them as somehow contemptible. I overlooked the fact that beauty comes to life fully only in contrast to ugliness."

"In order to master life, you have to keep reality locked out."

"Yes," said Emma, "I know that now. But if you wrap yourself in the security of a dream, if you keep aloof from any action you might dislike in yourself or in others, if you risk nothing because you don't want to be hurt, would you call that living?"

He stared at her in surprise. Was she—could she be reproaching his passivity? Hadn't she said the exact reverse of what she was saying now only a little more than two months ago, when she thanked him for never having mentioned what he felt for her?

"To surrender without a struggle is to commit murder of oneself," Emma said, "against all the chances inherent in life, against one's own capabilities, one's opportunities, against one's identity. And that's what I've done. But I didn't know it. Did you?" What was she talking about? It failed to make sense. And anyhow what did it have to do with their situation? Perhaps she had had more to drink than he was aware of. Thiolat watched her beautiful eyes close.

"Emma, you're tired. There's no reason why you shouldn't withdraw. It's way past one o'clock."

"I'm wide-awake," said Emma. "I've rarely been so . . ." and she lifted her head and smiled at Thiolat, and the brightness of her smile brought back the apprehension he had felt at the beginning of the dinner, when, watching her, he had been frightened by her self-control. Suddenly exhausted by his own tension, which had been building up in him for weeks now, he could no longer control himself. "Emma," and his voice was almost harsh, "let me come with you."

"Let you come where?"

"Wherever you have decided to go." And when she still looked at him uncomprehendingly, he added, "You planned to go away after the ball. Or have you changed your mind?"

The ball.

And within an instant, awareness broke over her like a tidal wave. She looked at Thiolat. Again she saw him as Death. Death—tall, slender and elegant, with graying hair, dressed in tails, with the little red ribbon of the Légion d'Honneur threaded in his right lapel, reminding her in a harsh, impatient voice that she had reached the point of no return—the ball.

When she had stood at the window of her room watching the lanterns being lit, when she had stood in the hall to receive her guests, she had not remembered the reason why she had invited all these people, or that the ball would terminate forever the part she had chosen to play in life. For a moment it seemed incredible to Emma that she should have spent two months occupying herself with all the minute details of its preparation only to have its significance escape her when it finally came. And then she realized that it was Felicity's death that had erased all consciousness of the closeness of her own. And as she grasped the power of her grief, she understood that for the first time since that evening in Florence when Henri had revealed what their marriage was based upon, she had permitted herself to love.

In the face of death she had lost her fear of life and reached out for it. Through Meg. Through Susan and Felicity. And now it was assailing her with brutal reality, making her doubt her motives, flinging accusations at her, making her responsible for everything that had happened during the last nine weeks—abortion, adultery, suicide. Neither Meg nor Susan nor Felicity might ever have acted as they had without her influence. They had been too young to know that illusions are granted only the shortest life. All they had been prepared to do was risk their dreams. It had been her influence that had encouraged their innate desires and needs. No matter how selflessly she had tried to help, she was answerable, now and forever, for the consequences of their separate actions.

Emma swung in the circle of Thiolat's arms and looked around her at the festive, dancing crowd that held her imprisoned, looked for Meg and Susan and for a frail redheaded girl. "Whatever I have done," she wanted to cry, "it is commitment alone that justifies living." But even as she phrased the words in her mind, she was filled with the ambiguity of her emotions, feeling guilty and exhilarated at the same time. The music stopped and she stood very still, trembling with the impact of life itself. But Thiolat mistook her trembling for terror, and he said —hating himself for bringing it up at a moment like this, when she had apparently been able to forget the cardinal point of the ball, but unable to curb his panic—"You will need care. I can't—I won't let you go off alone. Where do you plan to go?"

Suddenly Emma could look at him with pity and understanding. "I really haven't given it a thought," she said softly.

She saw him frown, saw an expression of disbelief enter his eyes, and she forced herself to smile. "Let's not talk about it now—perhaps tomorrow, or the day after tomorrow. Good night, dear Jacques."

All at once she felt very tired. Just for a moment, she thought as she went into the house, I'll stretch out just for a moment.

It was only when she had reached the first landing that she saw Scott sitting on the couch in front of the window. He sat like a hunter in his blind, resigned to wait as long as necessary, yet alert to the slightest sound. Now, when there was no longer a chance for her to avoid a confrontation, he rose.

"Emma, listen. You must—I—" and he grabbed her arm as though, if she tried to escape him, he would force her to stay. But she made no move. She did not even seem aware of his hand on her arm. Neither rage nor horror, not even annoyance or impatience, showed in her face. She was looking at him quietly, her eyes narrowing slightly, as if for the first time since she had known him she knew who he was.

All words failed him. Whatever he had thought before —however he had phrased in his mind what he wanted to say, to tell her, to confess, to explain—he could no longer recall. His lips opened and closed in a voiceless cry for help.

Emma sighed. "Poor Scott," she said and gently brushed his hand off her arm. "Poor Scott"—and she turned and walked up the stairs and along the wide corridor to her room. There she lay down on her bed.

For a while she lay motionless, not thinking, hardly aware of the music drifting up through the open windows on a gentle wind. Then gradually she remembered the morning she had awakened with the knowledge that the span of her life was limited, and how she had decided to use the time left her to explore her surroundings, as she had explored the foreign countries she knew she was about to leave—pretending that she had only just arrived, so that everything familiar might once more be strangely beautiful and impressive—until, on her journey to death, she would have reached the ball.

And here it was. Going on below her. People dancing and laughing—hundreds of people—people who meant nothing to her. But it was true, even though Thiolat had not believed her—she had made no plans for what she would do once the ball was over. Somehow she had thought about it only quite vaguely. About going away somewhere—where? Wherever she went, she would have to witness her own helplessness and dependence, the wasting away of her body and mind.

Hopeless, Thiolat had said.

There was nothing she could do but wait—here . . . there . . . anywhere—wait passively, patiently, day after day, powerless against death. But was she powerless? Life itself offered weapons against such senseless, demoralizing surrender.

Elation swept through Emma. The decision was hers. Not her father's, not Henri's, but hers. And then Emma knew why she had not thought about what she would do after the ball, why she had not been able to contemplate any action on her part for facing death. She had never accepted death as a part of life. But since it was, it offered a choice—a way of dying and a time for dying.

She knew exactly where the pills were that Thiolat had prescribed for Henri when he could no longer sleep well. And as she let the tablets dissolve in a glass, then swallowed them, she remembered the drawing that had once annoyed Henri, the cartoon depicting her riding a wild black swan. Now she had chosen to ride a wild black swan, no matter where it would take her.

Outside on the terrace the lanterns swayed in a sudden gust of wind, then steadied again to throw their soft pink light into the dark.

Music, dancing, laughter. The ball, like all Emma's parties, was a huge success.

CHRISTINE LAMBERT
is the pseudonym of
a well-known European writer.

97748

Lambert, Christine
The Ball

mrs m redmas
Kelly